TALES OF THE GHOST SWORD

HIDEYUKI KIKUCHI

Translated by Ian MacDonald

THAMES RIVER PRESS

Shadow Wife

ON HIS WAY BACK from the castle, Obori Shinnosuke dropped in at the home of his former colleague, Sakakibara Hisama.

Hisama was well known around the fief for his skill in the Hoki style of sword fighting. But his genius had proved his undoing. Having lost his job with the clan's Criminal Investigation Division, he now made his living teaching swordsmanship and calligraphy to neighborhood children. His former colleagues, fearful lest his prodigious talent should go to waste, repeatedly appealed to their superiors, and they in turn to the clan higher-ups, to have him reinstated. But to no avail. His offence—giving his lordship's son a sound thrashing when he showed up at the dojo looking for a sparring partner—was simply too grave.

To make matters worse, Hisama, at the tender age of twenty-four, was as prickly as an old geezer.

"Be patient, your time will come," consoled one of his former colleagues.

"Spare me your clichés," retorted Hisama, showing him the door. "I wait for no man!"

His former boss, Inspector Shoji Bannai, conspired with the department accountant to secretly pay Hisama a monthly retainer of ten *ryo*. But when the Inspector sent one of his men over to Hisama's house with the first installment, the former detective shouted: "I accept your concern, but after the way I've been treated I'll be damned if I'll accept the clan's money—now get out!"

"Well, if that's the way you feel..." replied the man, biting his tongue.

2

No sooner had he spoken than Hisama, reaching for his sword, yelled, "I don't need your or anyone else's pity!"

In the end, everyone agreed they should just leave him alone for a while.

The fact that it was "a while" and not "forever" testified to the young man's enduring popularity with his former colleagues. Once the furor had died down, they again began discussing ways of helping him out.

Popularity with his colleagues was one thing, marriage was another. Hisama was a confirmed bachelor. What's more, it was well known he wasn't particularly fastidious about either his appearance or his housekeeping.

The man who had gone to Hisama's house in Toyacho to try to deliver the money related how, while standing in the doorway, the stench of sweat had assaulted his nostrils. When Hisama finally emerged he looked as though he hadn't shaved or changed his kimono for days and his face and clothes were smeared with grime. He showed the man through to his room, where the bedding had not been put away and dusty piles of books were strewn across the floor. The man said that in his rush to leave he'd practically had to claw his way out of the room.

And yet Hisama could easily have married if he'd wanted. Tall, fair-skinned, ruggedly handsome, and much admired for his skill as a swordsman, Hisama at one time had had no shortage of marriage proposals, some of them extremely attractive. Sae, the daughter of Sugisawa Mondo, his lordship's chief adviser, for one, was so pretty she could turn heads all over town. But Hisama had rejected the proposal saying he couldn't afford to keep such a beauty.

Then there was his colleague Sahashi Kyosuke's younger sister, who could not only read Chinese but had been running the household ever since their mother's death. But Hisama had rejected the offer in an extraordinary manner, telling Kyosuke, who was exceedingly handsome himself: "Surely you don't expect me to marry a woman whose brother is better looking than I am? From morning to night it'll be 'But Brother says this' and 'Brother says that' echoing like a damned mantra in my ears!"

If anything, such churlishness seemed to endear Hisama to his colleagues all the more.

"We've *got* to find Sakakibara a wife," one of them would say, arms folded in thought, to his comrades.

"Yes, but…"

Another of them would invariably remind the others of the previous two attempts to marry off Hisama, and that would put an end to the discussion.

Actually, Hisama *had* been married once (as anyone would have guessed from the fact that he no longer lived at home with his parents). Exactly what sort of woman could pass muster with so notorious a crank was for a time a subject of much speculation throughout the clan.

As it turned out, she'd been quite ordinary, neither beautiful nor highly educated. Nonetheless, the couple had spent three happy years together before she was carried off by an illness.

"No doubt it's because Hisama was so fond of her that he's refused to marry again," his friends concluded, nodding silently to themselves.

Then about two weeks ago someone had broken the news:

"There's a woman living at Sakakibara's house!"

In those two weeks, the rumor had spread like wildfire among Hisama's former colleagues.

But when people asked what *sort* of woman, the reply was either:

"Err, well… from what I've heard, she's a merchant's daughter, seventeen or eighteen, with cheeks as rosy as cherry blossoms."

Or else:

"Rumor has it she's a woman of a certain age… a widow cast aside by another man."

In short, it was as good as anyone's guess.

Obori Shinnosuke's purpose in visiting Hisama today was to get to the bottom of these rumors.

To Obori's surprise, Hisama appeared at the door immediately.

"Oh, it's you," he said, making no attempt to hide his annoyance.

Obori was undeterred. On the contrary, seeing Hisama actually put him in a good mood. Though his face had become gaunt, Hisama's general expression was cheerful. He'd clearly shaved and washed his hair recently.

"Quickly state your business and leave."

4

"Come, that's no way to greet an old friend," said Obori, stepping inside. "I've been out drinking and my throat is parched. Since I was in the neighborhood, I just thought I'd stop in for some water. I won't be a minute."

This approach disarmed even the likes of Hisama. It wasn't for nothing that his colleagues had said that if *anyone* could handle Sakakibara Hisama it was Obori.

Observing that Obori had already taken off his swords, Hisama seemed to give in to the inevitable. "Damn drunkard!" he muttered, cursing his visitor as he showed him through to an inner room.

So it's true! Obori marveled quietly to himself as he glanced around the room. Never in his life had he known a bachelor pad to look so tidy. The bedding was folded and all of Hisama's books were stacked neatly in one corner. There wasn't as much as a speck of dust on the tatami.

He wanted to ask, *did* you *do this*, but he quickly stopped himself. He felt he might go insane if Hisama answered "yes."

"Wait here," commanded Hisama. "I'll bring you some water. Drink it quickly and go."

As he watched Hisama disappear toward the kitchen, Obori reflected on the situation:

There was a woman living in the house—that much was certain. She seemed to be out at the moment, but one could infer her existence from the order that prevailed everywhere one looked. True, Hisama's annoyance was a bit odd, but given his personality, if he *had* suddenly gone and gotten married again, he would prefer having his fingernails pulled out to introducing his new bride to a former colleague.

My business here is done, thought Obori. *I'll just drink the water and go.*

Hisama returned with a ladle of water.

Obori took the ladle and downed the water in one gulp. "Boy is that good!" he said, handing the ladle back to Hisama. "My stomach feels like new again."

"What's so funny?" demanded Hisama, frowning.

"There's more to you than meets the eye, isn't there, lover boy?" said Obori, a big grin on his face.

"Whose eye? I won't have you making slanderous accusations. Now go."

"I *know* what I saw," said Obori confidently, in no mood to back down.

"And *what* exactly did you see?"

"A woman walking along the corridor; she disappeared into the kitchen—just before you returned with the water. I only caught a glimpse of her profile, but she's obviously a beauty—a merchant's daughter, judging from her clothes. C'mon, why don't you introduce me to her?"

"There's no one," asserted Hisama, "in this house but me."

"There you go again. Unfortunately, I *saw* her."

"Whatever you *think* you saw, it must have been a hallucination. Now get out. If you don't I'll…"

Hisama turned toward the stand in a corner of the room upon which his swords rested.

"All right, all right—I'm going. But if you've taken up with a woman, it's best you introduce her to us sooner rather than later."

"How dare you!" Hisama lunged his long body toward the sword stand.

Obori bolted for the front door, stopping only to slip into his straw sandals before racing out of the house.

Hisama stood inside the front door listening to the sound of his friend's footsteps receding down the street. After stepping outside to make sure Obori was gone, he returned to the room and opened the shoji he'd shut earlier.

"Sayo," he called out toward the kitchen.

"Yes?"

The voice came from behind him.

He turned. Standing in a corner of the room was a young woman with an unusually pale complexion.

Hisama thought she'd probably be pleased to know that Obori had adjudged her a beauty based solely on a glimpse of her slender aquiline nose. But *when* had this beauty of his returned?

"Our unwanted guest has gone."

"Thank goodness," the young woman answered.

Her manner of speech was that of a merchant's daughter, but her voice was solemn. There wasn't the least hint of a smile on her face.

6

"People have started to notice. You'll have to disappear."
"I *have been* during the day. That's why your friend didn't see me."
"He said he did."
"Apparently that happens sometimes."
"I can't afford for it to happen *at all*. Once people start to talk, one never knows how far it will go. It'd be most inconvenient if the Chief Inspector should come to hear of it."

The brilliant swordsman folded his arms and looked at the girl whom he called Sayo. Her pallid, lifeless face turned a shade paler.

"Please don't worry," she said. "Until you have helped my soul attain nirvana, I promise I won't get in anybody's way."

Her voice was like ice water running down Hisama's back.

Despite his first impulse, Obori himself saw to it that word of Hisama's new wife went no further.

The next day, when he reported for work, Obori overheard one of his colleagues, a man by the name of Tamura, say something that gave him pause:

"Hey, you know that rumor about a spirit who haunts the riverbank?" said Tamura. "No one's seen her lately."

A spirit, huh? Obori thought. *Maybe...*

Though the job of the detectives in the Criminal Investigation Division was to root out malfeasance among their fellow samurai, the nature of their work required Obori and his colleagues to keep abreast of what was going on in the world outside the castle, amidst the merchants and other members of the lower classes. Tamura first brought back news of a ghost down by the Okawa River. Half of his colleagues had gotten a good laugh out of it; the other half had dismissed it as nonsense. Obori himself had been in the latter camp, but the rumor seemed to be true after all.

One of Tamura and Obori's colleagues — a man by the name of Hachiya Magokuro —an expert in the Raijin Shinkyo style of sword fighting, had set off for the riverbank where the sightings had occurred. This had taken place two months ago. Obori did not know what had transpired there, but the following day Hachiya had not reported for duty and had stayed away from work for ten days.

On the eleventh day, when he finally appeared, he looked a different man. Seeing his wasted appearance, the other detectives on duty jumped to their feet in surprise.

At the time, no one dared ask Hachiya about the cause of his transformation. As it turned out, they didn't have to. That night Obori had gone out drinking with his colleagues, Hachiya among them. In the bar that night there was a great lush by the name of Yasumoto attached to the Minor Works Corps. Emboldened by liquor, Yasumoto questioned Hachiya about what had happened down by the river. Everyone held their breath and pricked up their ears.

"I *saw* her," said Hachiya.

A hush fell over the bar.

It was an entire month before Hachiya—apparently through the miraculous power of prayer—was his normal self again.

Then, four days after Obori visited Hisama's house, Hachiya stopped showing up for work again. Given what had taken place before, this time Hachiya's boss personally went to look in on the truant detective.

This is what Hachiya, looking pale, told him:

"S-s-she's… at S-S-Sakakibara's house."

His teeth wouldn't stop clattering.

Inspector Shoji ordered Obori to go around to Hisama's house to investigate.

"I can't help feeling this strange business is all just nonsense," Obori's boss had said. "But since it concerns one of our own, we'd better get to the bottom of it."

Hachiya apparently had an acquaintance who lived in the same neighborhood as Hisama. It had been while on his way home after visiting this friend that he'd seen the woman standing in the garden as he passed Hisama's house.

"Hachiya had gone to see this friend to announce his recovery and to thank him for looking after him," continued Inspector Shoji. "Now he's back where he started—ironic, isn't it?"

Obori bowed his head silently.

8

OBORI DECIDED to stake out Hisama's house.

For six days he saw no sign of the woman. That itself seemed odd—to Obori anyway. He thought of Hisama's tidy room and well-groomed appearance. No, there *had* to be a woman living in the house.

During the day, children would come to Hisama's house for tutoring in calligraphy or swordsmanship. Obori would see them in the garden brandishing bamboo swords or wooden sticks. In between lessons Hisama would occasionally leave the house to run errands. Twice while Hisama was out, Obori snuck inside and had a look around.

Not a soul...

Hisama used the eight-mat room at the back of the house for giving calligraphy lessons. The children had recently gone home; the room was a mess. Obori waited about ten minutes. Still, there was not a sound inside the house. Perhaps the woman had gone home to visit her parents.

After watching the house for about ten days, with no sign of the woman having returned, Obori snuck into the house again. Some children had come for their lessons the previous day. But apart from Hisama's bedding, which still lay on the floor in disarray, the rest of the house attested to the invisible hand of his phantom housekeeper. There was only one possible conclusion: the woman was there but Obori could not see her, and she only appeared after dark.

Late one night, two days later, Obori paid Hisama another visit. This time, the moment Hisama saw his friend standing at the door, the annoyed look on his face changed to resignation. To Obori, it had, *so the cat's out of the bag, is it,* written all over it.

Once they were seated face-to-face in Hisama's room, Obori announced triumphantly: "I just saw her."

From his tone it was clear he would not brook any more evasiveness on Hisama's part. At last he'd spotted the woman standing in the garden by the side of the house. He immediately barged in and confronted Hisama.

"Oh, yeah?" grunted Hisama sullenly.

"She's a looker—no doubt about it. But her beauty's not of this world. Her skin is like marble. Is she a... spirit?"

"Why don't you ask her yourself?"

"I intend to. Where is she?"

"Right behind you."

Obori whirled around. A pale white face hovered before his eyes. He cried out and reached for his sword on the floor by his right knee.

"Stop! It's useless," shouted Hisama, but quickly added, "On second thought, go ahead and try. That'll save me wasting my breath—you'll find out soon enough whether she's a ghost or not."

It was all Obori could do to keep his teeth from rattling in his mouth. "Easier said than done…"

The woman's beautiful countenance was tilted down at the floor. Her eyes turned upward in their sockets to stare at him. It was a look his wife often gave him when she was especially annoyed. Only *this* was a thousand times scarier.

"Do you know her?" he finally managed to ask Hisama.

Obori's hand remained clasped to his sword; he couldn't have let go even if he'd wanted to.

"No."

"Then why has she come? Don't tell me you—"

"Don't be absurd!" Hisama snapped. "*I* haven't killed anyone." The color had drained from his face—and for good reason.

Two years ago there had been a spate of random murders in the castle town. Before it was over about seven people were dead, cut down in the street by an unknown assailant. As one of the victims had been a police constable skilled in the art of self-defense, people had come to suspect that the serial killer was not only a samurai but an expert swordsman, perhaps someone bored with the practice ground who had yearned to try his hand on a live subject. Or maybe he just wanted to test the efficacy of a new blade. An unprecedented manhunt was launched but the culprit was never found, which led to rumors that he might be someone high up in the clan hierarchy.

"Okay," Obori conceded. "But then why has she come to *your* house? Did she pine to death for you?"

"So what if she did?"

"Really?"

"I'm just kidding—don't be an imbecile." Hisama reserved this kind of verbal abuse for his oldest and closest friends—no one else would have tolerated it.

Suddenly, his face assumed a weary look, as though he was about to unburden his heart. "But you *are* right about one thing," he went on. "She *was* one of the serial killer's victims."

"Is that so?"

Just then the woman introduced herself. "My name is Sayo," she said, her eyes fixed on the floor.

"Ah, I remember now!" exclaimed Obori, striking his knee with his hand. "The daughter of a textile merchant in Sogacho—you were the fifth victim."

"That's correct."

Obori felt his hand relax its grip on his sword.

"Then tell me this—are you a spirit?"

"Yes." Sayo nodded.

Her voice did have a ghostly quality. Not that it *couldn't* have passed for human, but as the sound waves struck his eardrum, Obori felt a chill spread over his body.

"So this man—Sakakibara Hisama—has wronged you; that's why your soul can't attain nirvana—is that it?"

"No, I bear him no grudge."

"So why are you here? Don't tell me you have an attachment to this house?"

"Obori," interrupted Hisama angrily. "Are you going to snitch to the Chief Inspector?"

"I'm not going to *snitch*, as you put it. I'm going to report the findings of my investigation to my superiors."

"But you intend to talk?"

"First tell me what's going on. Then I'll decide. In principle, I'm obliged to make a full report, omitting nothing. After all, I can't march into the Chief Inspector's office and announce, 'Former detective Sakakibara has shacked up with a ghost,' and expect him to say, 'Right, got it.'"

"Sir—" broke in Sayo. "What will the Chief Inspector do if this gentleman tells him about me?"

"Good question," said Hisama. "One thing he *can't* do is barge in here with his men and cut you down; a sword would be useless against you. I suppose he'll call in a priest. Apparently, the abbot of Tenrin Temple knows a sutra that's very effective in exorcising spirits."

"My goodness! What shall I do?" exclaimed Sayo, looking as though she might swoon. She placed a hand on the tatami to steady herself, a gesture Obori always found attractive in women. Strangely, it seemed even *more* seductive to him because she was a ghost.

Obori's reverie was short-lived. As he felt Sayo glaring at him the hairs on the back of his neck stood up.

"Are you determined to report me to your superiors?" she asked. Her eyes exuded a ghoulish glow.

The color drained from Obori's face. *She really is a ghost*, he thought.

Sayo suddenly rose. He realized that—contrary to popular belief—ghosts indeed had legs.

"If you insist on doing so, I will have to defend myself. You leave me no choice but to possess you. Are you prepared to die?"

"You're in no position to make threats against the living, ghost."

Obori's shifted his long sword to his left hand and gripped its hilt with his right. *Who says a sword won't work against her?*

Hisama had had enough.

"Stop it, both of you!" he commanded. "Shinnosuke, go ahead and make your report if you must. I have no wish to interfere. But at least wait until I have fulfilled Sayo's request."

"What request?"

"To capture the monster who cut her down and left her for dead. If you'll promise me that, I'll tell you everything."

"Speak—I can promise nothing."

Sayo shot Obori a glance that made his blood run cold.

Grinning, Hisama gave his old friend a slap on the shoulder. "You're as stubborn as ever, I see," he chuckled. "All right then, this is what happened…"

It was two months ago that the rumor of the ghost that haunted the banks of the Okawa River had reached Hisama's ears. Now, your average samurai would have dismissed such a rumor outright, or perhaps wandered down to the river to have a look, just out of curiosity. But Hisama was different.

I'll *get rid of that ghost*, he thought to himself. And he meant it.

It wasn't that Hisama believed in tricksters, spirits, monsters or anything else supernatural. But since it seemed *something* was up to no good, he was determined to put a stop to whatever it was—that's as far as his thinking went. Even though *he* might not believe in such things, if they *did* exist, he wouldn't tolerate any mischief on their part. Fortunately, he'd been fired from his job, so, come what may, at least he wouldn't embarrass the clan.

Thus, late one night, about a month ago, Hisama had found himself down by the riverbank at the spot where the ghost reportedly had been sighted.

It was early autumn. There was a refreshing breeze, but the weather hadn't turned cold. Silvery moonlight glistened on the surface of the river. The only sound to be heard was the rippling of water. The houses on the embankment across the river were dark and quiet. Only a few scattered lights still shone in the distance from the direction of the red-light district.

As he was standing there, a long reverberating sound reached Hisama's ears. It was the bell of Jo'an Temple striking the hour—two o'clock in the morning.

Not much longer now, he thought, surveying his surroundings. Just then he caught sight of a figure standing upstream.

It was a woman in a white kimono. Her face looked unusually pale. A shiver ran down Hisama's spine. Even though she was a good forty to fifty feet away from him, he could clearly make out wisps of loose hair hanging over her forehead. And yet she was not holding so much as a lantern. The impression was too vivid to have been just the moonlight.

That must be her, he thought, setting his lantern on the ground. He nudged the hilt of his sword out of its sheath with his thumb. For a brief moment he wondered if it was possible to kill a ghost. Then his fighting instinct took over and the thought vanished.

The woman began walking toward him. Soon she broke into a trot. Before Hisama knew it, she was running flat out. The hem of her kimono fluttered behind her.

Her skirts parted to reveal an enticing glimpse of bare thigh. As he watched her racing toward him, pebbles scattering in all directions, a single thought flashed through Hisama's mind:

Holy shit!

At that instant the two collided.

Hisama was fast—very fast. He got off a good blow and his sword split the woman's chest in two. But to his astonishment, it was like swinging at thin air.

"Bloody hell!" he groaned. Turning, he watched the woman's pale shape receding along the riverbank.

It occurred to Hisama that he should go wake up a priest and have him recite sutras over him—or at least knock back a few drinks—to exorcise any evil spirits that might have rubbed off on him. Instead, he headed straight home and went to bed.

Next time, he thought as he prepared to turn in for the night, *I'll cut her to ribbons.* He hadn't found the apparition the least bit spooky or unsettling.

Upon entering his bedroom and lighting the lamp, something made him glance to his right. There, kneeling on the tatami with her back straight and eyes cast down, was the woman from the riverbank.

Anyone else would have jumped out of his skin. Hisama coolly leapt to one side and assumed a fighting posture, sword drawn.

"How dare you come here! Stay where you are, ghost!"

Without moving a muscle, the woman continued to stare down at the floor.

"No one can hurt me now," she said, not without reason.

"You're right," Hisama replied, sheathing his sword. "Wait here. I'll go fetch a priest." Turning his back, he began to leave, only to find her seated in front of him.

"Out of my way!" He didn't care if she *was* a ghost—she was beginning to get on his nerves.

Suddenly he kicked at her but his foot met nothing but air.

Hisama opened the shoji. She was seated in the corridor.

"Must you go?" she asked, her eyes still fixed on the floor.

"Of course. If you prefer, I could go out for a drink. But I expect you gone when I come back."

"I am afraid I cannot do that."

"Okay. A priest it is then. You're a pain in the neck, you know that?"

"Wait—I came here because when I saw you tonight I thought, 'At last, here is someone who can help me.' Won't you at least listen to my story?"

Struck by the imploring tone in her voice, Hisama looked down at the woman. She was young—sixteen, seventeen at most—a girl, really; a merchant's daughter from the look of her. That was evident from her clothes and manner of speech. She wore her hair in a high bun, as unmarried women did in those days. *There must be a good reason why she's come here*, considered Hisama. *She's no cause to torment me.* His logic was typical of his stubborn nature.

"First tell me your name," he demanded.

Hisama noticed the ghost's expression brighten.

"I am called Sayo."

"Are your parents still alive?"

"Yes. My family has a textile business in Sogacho. I was the eldest daughter."

Now that Hisama seemed willing to listen to her story, her speech assumed more politesse. He turned back toward the room. "Well, let's not stand around talking out in the corridor. Come in here."

THE FIRST THING Hisama wanted to know was why Sayo had come to see *him*—a complete stranger—of all people. After hearing her explanation, he shook his head several times. Beneath his bushy eyebrows, Hisama's eyelids flickered.

"You're one strange young lady, you know that?" Never had a truer word been spoken.

Sayo had been killed the year before last, in early autumn, after being attacked on her way home from visiting a friend, Otsune, in Yokogicho. Her attacker had hid in an alleyway and waited for Sayo and the shop boy escorting her home to pass by. Then he jumped out like an angel of death and slashed her from behind with his sword, killing her outright.

"So you see," said Sayo, "I never saw his face." Apparently a ghost had to know her killer's identify before she could haunt him.

"But what," Hisama questioned her, "were you doing down by the river?"

Sayo had been killed in town. If she had returned to the scene of the murder, she said, people would have quickly guessed her true identity. But not even *she* knew why she had ended up haunting the riverbank.

She confessed that she had been waiting for a samurai who was handy with a sword like Hisama to come along.

"You see," she explained, "there is a man I have loved since I was five years old. His name is Wahei; he runs a shop near ours, only much smaller. As children we vowed we would get married when we grew up; at the time my parents smiled on our relationship. But after Wahei completed his apprenticeship and returned to the neighborhood to open up his own shop, my parents changed their tune. How could they send their darling daughter to live in such a dingy little house, they said. I persisted. Wahei came to our shop practically every day to try to persuade my parents to let us marry. He was repeatedly turned away on the pretext they were out, but he never gave up.

"Then, during one of Wahei's visits, he begged my parents over and over to give us their consent. Still they refused. Unable to stand it any longer, I removed one of my hairpins and threatened to stab myself in the throat. Wahei grabbed my hand and begged me not to give up hope, saying he was willing to wait as long as it took. From that point on, my parents' attitude began to soften."

At last Sayo's parents had relented. As tears of joy streamed down her face, Sayo's father bowed his head and asked his daughter to forgive her parents for their obstinacy.

"I was killed three days later," she concluded.

Hisama sighed.

"Please avenge my death with your sword," pleaded Sayo.

"But how *can* I when you don't know who did it?"

To this the ghost replied:

"I may not know what he looks like, but I know he is a skilled swordsman. My body is testament to that."

As she spoke, she turned her back to Hisama, loosened her sash and let her kimono slip from her shoulders.

Hisama ran his eyes over the young woman's deathly pale but still fresh, smooth skin. There, across her back, was a deep, gaping wound, running from the nape of her neck to just below her left shoulder blade. Even as he watched, blood began to ooze from it.

It was all Hisama could do to keep from crying out in alarm.

"Watch out!" he shouted. "It's dripping onto the floor!"

Sayo quickly pulled her kimono over her shoulders. No blood seeped through the material, and when Hisama looked down, he saw the drops that had fallen to the tatami had vanished.

"I am no expert when it comes to swords," said Sayo, "but I shall never forget the excruciating pain I felt at that moment. Even *I* could tell that he knew what he was doing. I doubt there are many samurai in this fief who possess such skill. Perhaps you have some idea who it might be? If not, just show me all the great swordsmen in the fief and I will tell you which one did it."

"But how will you recognize him?" asked Hisama with understandable skepticism.

Sayo ignored his question. "You are no match for the man who killed me," she declared. "You must begin training at once."

"Now wait just a minute," objected Hisama. "I haven't agreed to avenge your death. Don't put this on me."

"But you are a samurai, are you not? Do you not find it vexing that there is another man who is a better than you at handling a sword?"

"Not especially. I've no illusions. If you need help attaining nirvana, go find someone better than me."

"But I don't know how to."

"Tough luck. Go back and wait on the riverbank. Someone else as crazy as me is bound to come along sooner or later."

"Or maybe not. I cannot go to the river every night."

"Then you'll have to give up."

As soon as he'd spoken, Hisama felt a peculiar sensation come over him.

"Hey! What are you doing?"

"You tried to kill me with your sword. Before you, there was another samurai who came out of curiosity—now he is an invalid. For you, I have devised an even crueler fate."

"Wait, this makes no sense. If you can track *me* down, why can't you find your killer? Go torture *him* to death."

"But I want *you* to kill him for me."

"Why?"

"Because he is someone who cannot bear to think there might be someone better than he is. That is why he killed me and his other victims—to hone his skill. A person like that deserves to be humbled by another man's sword and cut down like a dog, do you not agree?"

"Perhaps, but that's not my job. I understand how you feel, I really do. My heart goes out to you. You've every right to be angry. But I don't feel like sticking my neck out to settle your old score. Try someone else. Hey, how about that fiancé of yours—Wahei, or whatever his name was. How about explaining the situation to him?"

A silence fell over the room—a very awkward silence.

"I'm afraid that is impossible…"

A tear welled up in one of Sayo's eyes and rolled down her cheek.

Can demons—I mean ghosts—cry?

As Hisama stared at the tear glimmering in the light, he heard a voice that made everything she had said up until now seem in retrospect like lighthearted banter, so dripping was it with hatred.

"Wahei is no longer among the living. He was the killer's seventh and last victim… he died trying to avenge my death."

The following day, Obori Shinnosuke presented himself before Inspector Shoji and respectfully made the following report:

"I found no indication that any woman in particular has been frequenting former detective Sakakibara's house. The earlier reported sightings were probably of one of the neighborhood wives whom he employs to do housework. I will continue my investigation," he concluded.

How in the world did I get into this mess? Hisama lamented.

Out loud, he told Sayo:

"I can't promise to avenge your murder. But I'll help you track down your killer. If that's not good enough, go ahead and kill me."

Hisama had come to this compromise out of sympathy for the ghost's plight: two young lovers promised to one another, one of them, a beautiful young woman, mercilessly cut down from behind in the dead of night... this was not the act of a man who had devoted his life to the way of the sword.

Sometime later Hisama heard secondhand how the young shopkeeper, Wahei, the serial killer's seventh victim, had died. Carrying a cheap short sword purchased from a second-hand shop, Wahei set out one night for what he thought were the serial killer's likely stomping grounds. His body was later found with three severe wounds. "Whoever did this," a local sword instructor, whom the Magistrate's Office had called in to have a look at the corpse, told Hisama, "could have killed him with one stroke if they'd wanted—instead they made him suffer." Apparently, Wahei's sword had still been in its sheath; the honest shopkeeper had been cut down before he'd even had a chance to draw it. His only real weapon—his determination to strike at least one blow in revenge for his lover's death—had failed him.

The story made even the curmudgeonly Hisama burn with righteous indignation. But indignation was one thing; taking on the killer in man-to-man combat was another altogether. For one thing, Hisama's father and younger brother, Kazuma, were both government officials. It could well cost them their jobs, not to mention the family's honor, if it got around that Hisama were pursuing a vendetta on behalf of a ghost.

Even worse, popular opinion had it that the culprit was someone high up in the clan hierarchy. It was common knowledge that the killer was a master swordsman, and the names of several possible candidates were half-openly being bandied about.

Two names often mentioned were those of Suzuki Shohachi, captain of the Castle Guard Corps, and Sakurai Umon, an officer in the Light Infantry Corps. Suzuki, during his lordship's tenure in Edo, had studied the Onoha Itto style of swordsmanship, reportedly achieving remarkable results. Sakurai was an expert in the Taisha style, having honed his skills back home at the Sueki dojo. At thirty-nine and forty years of age, respectively, both men were in their prime.

A third suspect was Hisama himself. Many average students of swordsmanship tended to underestimate the importance of sword-drawing technique in deciding the outcome of a fight. But people knew that one had to be on one's guard with Hisama because of the quickness of his draw and his irascible nature. This gave rise to some loose talk:

"That Sakakibara—there's something no quite right about him."

"I wouldn't put it past that curmudgeon to wander around at night attacking people."

If Hisama caught people whispering together and casting suspicious glances in his direction, he would lay into them on the spot, suggesting they step outside to discuss it. That quickly shut them up.

There were two other men of comparable skill to these three: Moriwaki Satoji, also of the Castle Guard, and Sera Makube of the Minor Works Corps. But Hisama quickly eliminated them from his list of suspects. Several years earlier, back when he was still a detective, he'd been ordered to conduct a secret internal investigation of Moriwaki and Sera in connection with the disappearance of one of his lordship's swords. He knew they were not the type of young men to get involved in anything as nefarious as murder.

Then there was Tarumi Kamon, the Army Chief-of-Staff, considered a shoo-in to be appointed to the Ruling Council for the upcoming term. Hisama had a gut feeling *he* was the serial killer. His hunch was based on the same probe he had undertaken in connection with the daimyo's missing sword. In his youth, Kamon had been a prodigy of the Kyoshin Meichi style of swordsmanship; by the age of seventeen, his sensei had made him his assistant instructor. Within six months, however, Kamon had been relieved of that responsibility.

Hisama had heard the whole story from Obori, whose uncle trained at the same dojo as Kamon. According to the uncle, Kamon always said one could not know one's true ability until it had been tested on a real opponent. As if to bear this out, one day Kamon was walking down the street when, passing a group of hooligans, a hand—so he later claimed—brushed against the sheath of his sword. He cut down three of the youth's right there on the spot. A fourth, who survived the attack, denied the allegation, but as it was his word against Kamon's, that of the samurai carried the day. But *that*, it was said, was not the real reason Kamon's sensei, Sajihara Ryusai, had relieved him of his position as assistant instructor.

Kamon went on to distinguish himself more in the field of government affairs than in martial arts. His agricultural policies gained favor with his lordship, who rewarded him by raising his salary from fifty *koku* to one hundred, then one hundred fifty, then two hundred, and so on and so forth, until now it stood at a staggering four hundred fifty *koku*. If so powerful a figure as Kamon were even to get wind he were officially under suspicion, the Chief Inspector would likely lose his head, while the mere mention of Hisama's name in connection with the case would undoubtedly result in his family's property being confiscated. That was why, even though the name Tarumi Kamon popped into everyone's heads when the murders occurred, no one dared let his name cross their lips.

"Damn it," grumbled Hisama to himself, his obstinate streak rearing its head. "What have I got to lose now?"

But I wonder—can I still draw my sword as fast as Kamon?

It was well known that despite the demands of his official duties, Kamon had not lost his edge, taking time out from his busy schedule to receive training at home from the current master of the Kyoshin Meichi dojo. Rumor had it he typically won about half his bouts—two out of three on a good day—against his sensei.

Nah, I doubt it. On that point, Sayo had been right.

Sayo had said she would know the serial killer if she met him, but Hisama could not simply walk up to the Army Chief-of-Staff and arrest him on the say-so of a ghost. By now the case was already two years old. The trail was cold. Even if Hisama *did* get hold of some evidence, Kamon would have it suppressed.

The first thing to do, Hisama thought, *is to get Kamon and Sayo together in the same place.*

WITHOUT ANY CONSCIOUS decision on his part, Hisama's life began to undergo a series of changes.

Sayo enjoyed helping out around the house. Though she hadn't appeared moved by his offer to help track down his killer—which had not included a promise to avenge her murder—the ghost now behaved as though she owed Hisama a debt of gratitude. As soon as the glow of the setting sun began to color the western sky, she would suddenly appear and begin to bustle about the house.

Before Sayo came along, any casual observer wandering into Hisama's house could have been forgiven for assuming it to be derelict. Then, overnight, it was transformed from a seemingly unsalvageable mess into something livable. She put away the bedding, tidied up the books strewn on the floor, washed the dirty dishes stacked in the kitchen, and swept up the dust that swirled around one's feet. Now, at last, the house had at least one occupant who cared about neatness.

In the morning, breakfast would be on the table by the time Hisama had gotten out of bed and finished gargling; even before he opened his eyes, the smell of miso soup wafting into his room gave him the illusion he was at his parents' house, being coddled and cosseted by his mother.

Sayo waited on Hisama while he ate. The first time the ghost handed him a bowl of steaming rice, he hesitated for a moment before putting his chopsticks into his mouth. But the rice tasted perfectly ordinary.

"Do you appear during the day?" Hisama had asked Sayo one morning when he sat down at the table.

"Sometimes," she answered. There were times, as Hisama later found out, when she did not appear even at night.

I guess ghosts don't necessarily behave the way we in the world of the living think they ought to, he mused.

Sayo took care of dinner. The only drawback to the whole situation was Hisama found it off-putting to have a pale corpse hovering over him as he ate.

"Why don't you join me?" he finally asked.

Shaking her head, Sayo kept her eyes cast demurely downward and waited for Hisama to finish his meal.

I suppose ghosts don't need to eat, he thought.

Once, he half-jokingly suggested to Sayo that she try wearing a bit of makeup. The ghost glared at him and he quickly dropped the subject.

During the day, neighborhood children came by the house for their calligraphy and sword lessons. At least it kept a roof over his head and food on the table. Occasionally, someone from his old dojo would drop by and ask him to come back, saying he was wasting his talent.

"Funny," Hisama would reply sarcastically, his cantankerous streak coming out, "I don't remember you saying that when I was fired."

He was the same with his pupils. However much he tried to restrain himself, if he had a student who wrote Chinese characters well, he couldn't help pointing out all his mistakes, even while praising another child who wrote poorly. Once confident children would burst into tears and run straight home, never to return. As a result, at one point Hisama was left with only a handful of students. All this changed when Sayo came along.

One day, after Sayo's arrival, Hisama was berating one of his pupils in his usual perverse way. The child ran bawling from the room. That was nothing new. But after a little while the child came back and quietly took her seat. When the lesson was over and the girl was getting ready to leave, Hisama asked her what had happened. She replied that outside in the street she had encountered a young lady who happened to be passing by. Seeing the girl in tears, the lady asked her what was wrong and, upon hearing her answer, consoled her, saying that the teacher who lived there was a bit odd—he had a habit of praising his bad pupils and finding fault with his good ones. She should know, the young lady said, because she herself had once been a student of his and now she was a calligraphy teacher. "With him, it's better to be criticized than to be praised," she concluded. Heartened by this, the girl had decided to return.

Of course, Hisama knew at once that the "young lady" was Sayo. No doubt she approached the girl in the street rather than inside the house to avoid the child from spreading any strange rumors.

After hearing the girl's story, Hisama made an effort to rein in his cantankerousness—at least when he was around children. As a result, his pupil retention rate dramatically improved.

Meanwhile, Hisama's sword students were always getting their training uniforms dirty—those who could afford to buy them, that is.

The others just wore ordinary street clothes, which were always getting torn or splitting at the seams.

One evening, Sayo whispered to Hisama that next time he should tell his pupils to leave their outfits with him when they went home. He did so the very next day, and when the lesson ended there was a pile of sweaty, smelly clothes heaped on the floor. Sayo stayed up all night washing them. The next day, they were hanging on the clothes pole drying, and Hisama was flabbergasted to see that they had all been neatly mended. It was a superhuman feat. When word got around that the young sensei looked after his pupils like a mother, some of the more well-heeled parents began sending him tokens of their appreciation. The bean-paste buns and other sweets he shared with his pupils, while any alcohol he received he drank by himself. But if anyone sent him money he scrupulously returned every penny of it.

"Why do you return it?" Sayo once asked him.

"I'm not married. As it is, I make enough to live on," Hisama replied. "And it doesn't cost anything to keep you."

Sayo, her head lowered, cast her eyes up at him in that way she had that could make one's blood run cold.

"What a strange man you are."

He felt like snapping at her, W*ell, if that isn't the pot calling the kettle black, you ghoul,* but he kept his thoughts to himself.

Sayo even helped Hisama to get dressed when he had to go out, all the while making not-so-subtle suggestions about his personal appearance, such as how he needed to wash his hair and shave.

He dutifully complied, compelled by some uncanny force. But somehow the results did not sit well with him. Vowing that the next day he would start letting his beard and forelocks grow out, he was on his way home when he ran into a carpenter of his acquaintance.

"Gotten married again, have you?" the man remarked. "Well, if you ask me, I liked it when you looked kind of scruffy."

From then on, Hisama became fastidious about his grooming.

On a practical level, Sayo's presence in his house brought a certain richness into Hisama's daily life. But on those few occasions when she was spotted by someone on the outside, Hisama, as he'd always feared, found himself in hot water.

Obori's visit was one of those times. Worse still was when his own mother showed up at his door, having heard a rumor that her son was keeping a woman.

"So who *is* she?" she asked him, a twinkle in her eye, after taking one look at the tidy state of his house.

Knowing his mother as he did, Hisama realized that resistance was futile.

"The plasterer's wife down the street has been coming in to clean," he lied.

"I don't believe it!" she snapped. "I hear she's sixteen… Oh, Hisama, I can't believe you've forgotten Fumiyo already!"

"No, you're mistaken, Mother."

Fumiyo was Hisama's late wife. Though plain looking, she'd had a kind, gentle disposition. He had by no means forgotten her. That was why—in addition to not having a job—he hadn't remarried.

But Hisama knew better than to argue with his mother. Choosing the path of least resistance, he gave in and listened meekly—the sooner he let her have her say, the sooner she would leave. Outside the window, the sun was already starting to set.

A good two hours passed.

Finally, drawing her lecture to a close, his mother said in an imperious tone:

"One day you will be the head of the Sakakibara house—you must begin to act like it. Don't let yourself fall into the clutches of some undesirable woman."

"I understand, Mother."

"Good evening, Mrs Sakakibara…"

Startled by Sayo's voice, Hisama's mother spun round. Hisama felt like bursting into tears.

Sayo gave a polite bow.

"And who might *you* be?" Hisama's mother demanded, not the least bit frightened.

"My name is Sayo. Your son has deigned to treat me as he would a wife."

"Why did you have to have to come butting in?" demanded Hisama, dumfounded, after his mother had stormed out of the house. "I'd just about gotten rid of her!"

"But how could you sit there and take that?" she retorted, more forcefully than usual. "*I* was willing to put up with her abuse. But she made is sound as though you were gallivanting around with loose women."

"What?" Hisama gazed deeply into Sayo's pale face, which wore a bitter expression. "Are you upset because my mother was lecturing me?"

"No," replied Sayo, looking away.

Despite the awkwardness of the situation, a pleasant calm descended over the room.

It was Hisama who seized the initiative. "My mother didn't realize you were a ghost. Why is that?"

"I don't know. It happens with some people. Perhaps they are the beneficiaries of divine providence."

It was true—Hisama's mother was a devout follower of Tendai Buddhism.

"Anyway, she'll be back, I reckon," he said. "It looks like our carefree life is about to come to an end."

"Do you think your mother intends to get rid of me?"

"It would seem so. Not that she can send you back to your parents' house…" Hisama folded his arms and frowned. "Do you think you can manage her?"

"I'm not sure," replied Sayo. Her face was suddenly brightening—as much as a ghost's face can. She asked, "So… is it all right if I stay then?"

Hisama was momentarily taken aback. *I can't believe it—she's actually asking for my permission*, he thought.

"It's a bit late to be asking that now… Hey, I've got it! I'll ask Mother to bring a priest with her next time," he joked.

"How can you say such cruel things?" protested Sayo, sounding like the spoilt teenager that she was.

"It's settled then. We'll have an exorcism!"

"Just go ahead and *try*," said the ghost, trembling.

Hisama felt the atmosphere in the room turn suddenly cold.

Hisama's prediction was correct. His mother returned the next day—and every day after that.

"Where does she *go* during the day?" she asked him, hurriedly setting about washing the children's clothes as soon as they had gone home.

"Mother, Sayo can do that," protested Hisama. His mother was over sixty after all.

He regretted his words as soon as they were out of his mouth. He knew what was coming.

"What can *she* do? All she's got going for her is the fact she's young. Someone like you—who's never been anything but a burden to your poor mother—can do better than her. Not that I was exactly satisfied with Fumiyo either. Now, I don't mind if you see some girl who only appears at night and then vanishes like some ghost. But for the time being, *I* can look after you."

"But Mother! I can't have *you* taking care of me at this age—I won't be able to show my face in public!"

He had no doubt it would have been embarrassing if it were to become known that someone with his reputation was being looked after by his mother. But more to the point, it was evident she couldn't have cared less about *him*; she was simply trying to thwart Sayo.

When Sayo arrived that evening, she took one look at the clothes Hisama's mother had washed and said flatly, "These aren't washed properly. Really, Mrs Sakakibara, you mustn't take on more than you can manage."

"Is that so?" the older woman shot back. "Well, then—let's see how your cooking is."

When Sayo was done making dinner, Hisama's mother took one bite and put down her chopsticks. "Too salty," she declared. "In samurai families we prefer a more delicate flavor."

Sayo was unperturbed.

"Shall we ask your son to decide?"

Hisama, feeling two pairs of eyes fixed on him, folded his arms and stared up at the ceiling. Given the situation, he considered, there was more to be gained by taking his mother's side. Then his stubborn streak reared its head and told him to stick up for Sayo. But if he did, and if his mother took it into her head to go digging into her background, she'd find out she was a ghost. Then she'd probably show up at his door with a *thousand* monks. That would ruin his chances of punishing the person who had killed Sayo and Wahei.

"Humph!" muttered Hisama, standing up.

"Humph, humph!" he growled, stalking out of the room and leaving the two women in his life—new and old—seated there, steadfastly avoiding each other's gaze.

Things might have been fine if Hisama's mother had come only during daylight hours, but since her real objective was to have it out with Sayo, she insisted on staying right through until evening.

One day Hisama accidentally let slip that Sayo had been making breakfast as well as dinner for him. "Right," said his mother, and the next day she turned up at four o'clock in the morning and began cooking rice and grilling fish. Sayo, who was slow getting started in the morning, found herself with nothing left to do.

The ghost sat in a corner, staring at Hisama's mother as she folded the washing and prepared dinner. Her usual ghoulish expression was terrifying enough, but now she pulled out all the stops. A woman with more delicate nerves than Mrs Sakakibara would undoubtedly have fled at this point, but Hisama's mother did not flinch. Her enemy's resentment tasted to her like victory's sweet nectar, and it drove her to work that much harder.

"I can't take it any longer!" Sayo blurted out one evening after this had been going on for about a month. "Thanks to your mother I haven't got a *thing* to do. How can I ask you to track down my killer if I can't repay the debt I owe you?"

Though he was secretly thinking, *Great—now we're getting somewhere!* what Hisama actually said was: "C'mon now. Don't give up so easily. Don't tell me a ghost can be bested so easily by a living person. You must have a few tricks up your sleeve—a curse, a spell… *some*thing?"

While it might seem Hisama was going too far in suggesting the ghost actually curse his own flesh-and-blood, his words belied a conviction that Sayo was no match for his mother.

"Okay," Sayo said at last, "I'll give it a try." The look of intense determination on her face seemed to belong more to this world than the next.

Oh, no. What have I done? thought Hisama. His plan had backfired.

His fears were allayed when his mother turned up right on schedule early the next morning. Still, he couldn't help wondering if Sayo had attempted some form of retribution. So, with trepidation, he asked his mother, "I don't suppose anything out of the ordinary happened last night, did it?"

"No," she answered calmly from the kitchen, where she was already busy preparing breakfast.

There was a pause.

"But now that you mention it," she continued, "in the middle of the night I could have *sworn* I heard a woman sobbing. And a little while ago, on my way over here, I tripped on a stone and almost fell flat on my face… Oh, and one more thing. Everyone I passed in the street seemed to be looking at me strangely. Is there something on my face?"

It's not on your face, Hisama wanted to say, *it's behind you.* What passerby wouldn't have stared in horror at the sight of a genteel samurai matriarch walking down the street in the wee hours of the morning with a pale female corpse hovering behind her?

"How do you feel?" he asked solicitously. "Did your long walk tire you? Any indigestion?"

"Never felt better," she replied. "Just so as long as that young lady of yours doesn't go and put a curse on me."

A curse… muttered Hisama silently to himself.

Just then, his mother, crouching in front of the oven, toppled backward and landed on her bottom. Clasping her hand to her lower back, she rolled onto her side.

"Ah! Oh!" she moaned, trying to stifle a cry of pain. It still ended up sounding like a shriek.

"Mother!"

Hisama rushed to her side. *She must have strained her back.* It seemed Sayo was to have the last laugh after all.

"Pride cometh before the fall…" murmured Hisama as he stooped to pick up his mother.

She stopped groaning. "What did you say?" she demanded.

Hisama kept quiet. One thing was for sure: his mother was one tough old lady.

After helping his mother onto the futon that he had spread out on the floor of his bedroom, Hisama noticed Sayo seated next to the pillow, legs folded under her, staring down at his mother.

He felt a chill run down his spine.

"Did you—?"

For a brief moment, he imagined he saw a thin smile rise to the ghost's pale lips, which barely stood out from the pallor of her skin.

Sayo shook her head. "Don't be ridiculous. Did she hurt her back?"

"Yes," said Hisama. "She's getting old, after all."

"*Pride cometh before the fall.*"

Hisama's mother—silent until now—suddenly opened her eyes. "What did you say?"

"Nothing," said Sayo. "Does it hurt?"

Hisama's mother relapsed into silence.

"Would you like to roll onto your side? I could massage it for you," offered the ghost.

Hisama was about to speak but stopped himself. He was suddenly reminded of the old ghost story about a noblewoman whose place in her husband's affections is usurped by his new, younger mistress. The wife puts a curse on the mistress so that when the man caresses her breast, it leaves a mark that causes her unbearable agony.

As it turned out Hisama's fears were groundless.

With his help, Sayo turned his mother onto her side and began rubbing her back.

"Oh, my!" exclaimed Hisama's mother with a mixture of surprise and pleasure. "That feels so cool and nice! Ooh, ah! I can feel the pain leaving my body. You must be experienced at massaging your parents, I imagine."

"Yes. They both suffer from back pain—I used to massage them each three times a day."

"I knew it. It couldn't be otherwise. Oh! You're better than any masseur. It's not a matter of just being skilled with one's hands and fingers. One's heart has to be in it."

"I used to massage you quite a bit myself," chimed in Hisama, a bit miffed.

"Yes, but you were always too rough," replied his mother, giving herself rapturously over to Sayo's fingers. "Your father's the same.

The men in our family," she said to Sayo, "know how to handle a sword but not how to touch a women. Now, you and your father both—"

Hisama hurriedly got up and went to the next room.

After about half an hour he heard the peaceful sound of breathing coming from the other side of the sliding doors.

"She is asleep."

Sayo was standing behind him.

"Don't *startle* me like that," he chided her. "I wonder if Mother will be all right."

"You seem to be under a misapprehension. I did not—"

"Really?"

"You know, I asked her how old she was," went on Sayo. "She is only two years older than *my* mother. I felt like I was massaging my own flesh-and-blood."

"Maybe you should pop in at her place and massage her *there*," he said sarcastically. "She'd be *so* pleased; I don't think she'd even mind the fact you're a ghost."

"I wish I could but…" Sayo lowered her eyes.

So did even ghosts, he wondered, *have their limitations?*

"I'm sorry," he apologized. "I shouldn't have said that."

"By the way," she asked. "Do you have any leads on the identity of my—of Wahei's— killer?"

Hisama grunted. "Be patient."

He'd already asked Obori to dig up whatever he could on Tarumi Kamon. Without anything definite to go on there wasn't much he could do. If a big shot like Kamon, a future senior councilor, *was* guilty—and even if Sayo used her ghostly powers to exact her revenge—Hisama was still taking a big risk. Sayo had already been spotted by Hachiya. Who knew who *else* has seen her? If Hisama wound up on the wrong side of the law, his parents would not escape punishment either. He couldn't bear the thought of dragging them into this. He wanted to avoid that. He thought of his mother. No, he *had to* avoid it at all costs.

"Be patient," he repeated, avoiding Sayo's eyes. "I'll know something soon."

Obori came to see Hisama late that night. He'd found no evidence regarding the serial killer's identity.

"But one thing's for certain," he said. "There's something not quite right about Kamon. Last year, he fired one of his servants, a man by the name of Chuzo. On his way home to his village, Chuzo was murdered. The official conclusion was highway robbery but…"

"You think he was killed to shut him up?"

"Probably. And get this: the magistrate's report states that he died from a single diagonal stroke to his back—the serial killer's trademark."

"And Tarumi's technique?"

"He parries his opponent's blade with an upward stroke, then brings his sword down diagonally… like so—"

"Hmm, it fits, doesn't it."

"Yes, it does. But so far I haven't been able to connect Kamon to the murders two years ago. I've a feeling it will be impossible."

So the time has come, thought Hisama. The only thing left to do was to bring Sayo and Kamon together.

"Now, about my fee…" added Obori stiffly.

"Sorry—I don't have it right now."

"I know. But I've stuck my neck pretty far out for you. Plus, there's my wife's condition to consider, you understand."

"Of course."

Recently, Obori's young wife had been suffering from chest pains. Her doctor had recommended a period of convalescence at a hot spring, guaranteeing a full recovery provided her condition were treated immediately. This, in addition to his relationship with Hisama, was the reason Obori had undertaken a task that involved considerable risk to himself. But at the moment, friendship took a back seat to money.

After sending Obori on his way with a promise that he'd have the money ready in three days, Hisama felt a sinking feeling in the pit of his stomach. The sum he'd agreed to was nothing to sneeze at. *I'll manage it somehow*, he'd thought at the time, figuring he could always count on his father to help him out. But when he went round to his parents' house, his request had been flatly rejected.

"I've no money," his stubborn old man had said with a fierce scowl, "for a son with no wife and no prospects!"

Hisama had had no choice but to go around asking his friends, but so far he'd raised only half the needed cash. He considered offering Obori what he'd scraped together so far and promising to give him the rest later, but his pride wouldn't allow it.

He was just pondering his next move when he again heard Sayo's voice behind him.

"I overheard what you said just now."

Despite being ordered to remain at his mother's bedside, Sayo had apparently been standing there listening to his conversation with Obori all the time.

"What insolence!" Hisama barked in mock anger. "You'll pay with your life!"

"Gladly," shot back Sayo.

Their eyes met and they both laughed—Hisama not loud enough to wake his mother, Sayo somewhat eerily. Without actually being aware of it, their relationship had reached the point where they genuinely enjoyed each other's company.

"Forget what you heard."

Sayo shook her head. "Leave everything to me—I will find the money."

"It's none of your concern. What do you intend to do anyway? Make a pact with the lord of the underworld?"

"Never mind that. More to the point, this Tarumi Kamon of whom you spoke, is he the serial killer?"

"I'm not sure."

"I will know it when I see him. Please let me meet him."

"I will... soon. But we mustn't rush into it. He's very powerful."

"I will not cause you any trouble—I promise."

"It's not that simple. All *you* have to do is attain nirvana, but the rest of us still in the realm of the living have to obey the rules of *this* world."

"Very well. But when?"

"Soon."

"All right." Sayo nodded.

"So you're not ready to let go of your desire for vengeance?"

Sayo kept her eyes lowered. "Please do not forget your promise."

Hisama's blood froze. He'd never heard such an eerie voice.

"If you break your word, I will kill not only you, but your mother *and* your entire family. Do not forget that."

At that moment, Hisama's mother's pained voice came through the sliding door.

"Sayo, my back hurts."

"Coming," the ghost called back with a smile, turning toward the next room.

And she'll begin with Mother, thought Hisama with a shudder.

BY LATE AUTUMN everything was in readiness. For the past month, Hisama had been honing his sword-fighting skills at home.

There was more to swordsmanship than striking the first blow. One had to know how to react if one's opponent blocked or parried. Still, the essence of sword fighting was a lightning-fast draw.

The coming contest will be decided by speed, thought Hisama.

The only way to improve my speed is through tireless practice. If I practice enough I'm bound to get faster. The problem will be biding my time until conditions are right to strike—and overcoming my fear while I wait. If my opponent knows a duel is imminent, he'll try to make me draw my sword. Will he attack like a madman or with nerves of steel? I'll have to be prepared to block his blow, to dodge and parry—his blade going 'whoosh' over my head and around my ears—waiting for the perfect moment to strike.

I should go to the dojo to practice, but that might arouse suspicions.

Hisama had no choice but to prepare himself physically and mentally on his own.

A month ago, Sayo finally set eyes on Tarumi Kamon.

The ghost had given Hisama a list of places in town where it was possible for her to appear, and he compared this to the route Kamon habitually took on his way home from the castle, information Obori had provided Hisama only after he'd handed over the agreed sum, which Sayo had somehow managed to procure.

"Are you sure it's not going to disappear," Hisama had asked her skeptically, "or change into a bunch of leaves after I give it to him?"

"I'm a *ghost*, not a trickster," she shot back with a glare. He resisted the urge to ask her if she didn't conjure the money out of thin air, then where *did* she get it from?

It turned out there was no point along Kamon's usual route home where Sayo could appear. Fortunately, Obori found out the senior councilor had an alternative route.

Once a week, on a given day, Kamon stopped in at a teahouse for a drink on his way home. Afterward he went for a walk along the riverbank to sober up. Obori noted in his report to Hisama that Kamon's mother, who lived with him, could not abide the smell of sake. Upon hearing that the man who had taken Sayo's life went for walks along the very riverbank she had once haunted, Hisama couldn't help feeling that the invisible hand of fate was at work.

It was a clear moonlit night in mid-autumn—the night of the harvest moon. Hisama and Sayo were concealed, waiting, beneath a willow tree on the embankment above the river.

Shortly before eleven o'clock, Hisama saw Kamon approaching along the riverbank below. Despite his high rank, he was alone—without guards—a sure sign of his confidence as a swordsman.

"I'm going," Hisama heard Sayo say behind him.

He kept his eyes fixed on the approaching figure, grateful there was a full moon.

Kamon had walked about ten paces past the spot directly below Hisama's hiding place when he suddenly came to a halt.

Sayo was standing about six feet behind him.

Kamon turned. As soon as he saw Sayo the tension left his body and he spoke to her. She did not move, but just kept staring intently at him. A casual observer might have taken it for a secret rendezvous between two lovers. But even from his vantage point, Hisama sensed the weird aura that surrounded the two figures.

Kamon sensed it too. His entire demeanor changed; stiffening, he took two steps backwards. His right hand reached for his sword and there was a flash of light, different from the light of the moon glinting on the water. A cry of "Hell fiend!" reverberated in Hisama's ears.

Kamon raised his sword into striking position over his right shoulder and brought it down. For a man who was both drunk and scared out of his wits, there was no denying it was a beautiful stroke.

His blade passed through the ghost's body as though she were made of snow.

By the time Hisama realized Sayo was gone, he heard a voice behind him.

"He cut me exactly as before," she said. "There can be no doubt it was him." Sayo's voice was the same as always.

At such a moment, do ghosts feel anything? he wondered.

"Let's go," he said. He began walking down the path they had come along, which shone white in the moonlight. After a short way, he turned and looked down again at the riverbank. Kamon's sword dangled limply from his hands; his shoulders heaved with each breath. But what Hisama had seen of Kamon's swordsmanship was enough to convince him Sayo had been right: he was no match for her killer.

For the next month, Hisama continued his relentless daily training. To his surprise, he found he hadn't lost his touch. He practiced drawing and striking, drawing and striking, over and over again, for two straight days, and his quickness and agility returned. But his fear did not abate. The source of that fear was the blade he'd seen Kamon brandish above his head that night by the river.

Hisama was by no means confident he could block or parry such a strike. A dark foreboding settled in the pit of his stomach. In an attempt to dispel it, he threw himself into his training.

"Hisama! Hisa—ma!"

Suddenly aware of someone calling his name, Hisama let go of the hilt of his sword with one hand and turned around.

His mother was standing in the corridor that ran along the veranda overlooking the garden. It would seem she had come for another of Sayo's massages.

Hisama found it astonishing his mother still hadn't cottoned on to Sayo's true nature. "Have you *always* had such a poor complexion, my dear?" his mother would ask at mealtimes while Sayo waited on them.

"Come inside, Hisama," she called to him, interrupting his thoughts. "I want to talk to you."

As soon as they were seated facing one other, she got right down to business.

"So how long," she asked with a stern look, "do you plan to string Sayo along?"

"Huh?"

"Don't just say 'Huh?' What would people say if word of your relationship got out? Sayo's family must be beside themselves with worry. I wouldn't blame them if they began to suspect their daughter had fallen into the clutches of some unscrupulous samurai."

"I see."

"I'm not saying to break up with her. I've taken a liking to that young lady. She's a far sight better than any samurai's daughter *I've* ever come across. It's for that reason I've spoken to your Honden uncle about finding a family to adopt her."

"Mother!"

Hisama's "Honden uncle" was his mother's elder brother, the commander of the clan archery corps.

"And he's arranged," she continued coolly, "for Sayo to be adopted into the family of one of his junior officers, a man by the name of Naito Hangoro, who has an income of one hundred and twenty *koku*."

"B-b-but…" objected Hisama, lurching forward in alarm, "that's impossible!"

His mother did not flinch. "Why is it impossible? Is there something wrong with the girl?"

"No, there's nothing wrong with her *per se*…"

Just that she's a ghost, he thought. He'd realized the two women had grown close, but he never foresaw that it might come to this—that she would go and arrange to have Sayo adopted into their family without consulting her or her parents first. He'd been wary of his mother getting involved to begin with, and now she had justified his fears.

"Tomorrow I'll send someone round to Sayo's house to tell her parents the good news. I'd like you to speak to her about it today."

"Tomorrow? I'm sorry. Tomorrow is out of the question. It's too soon."

This argument, at least, seemed to hold some sway with his mother.

"All right then. When would be a good time?"

If, ultimately, Hisama found himself in the position of having to kill one of the clan's senior samurai, he'd need more time to prepare.

"Just wait a while."

"A while? Hisama, please be more specific."

"A month. Please give me another month."

"Fine. But make sure you keep your word," his mother said pointedly.

In reply, Hisama could only grunt.

That night, Hisama sat down with Sayo and explained the situation.

"—So, in other words, Kamon has to be killed within the next thirty days. Now remember, I never promised *I* would do it."

"That said," he went on, "I *will* kill him. Not just because I feel sorry for you and Wahei, but, more than that, because a monster like *that* shouldn't be allowed to live."

Sayo bowed. "Thank you," she said. "It gives me great joy to hear you say that. I will do everything in my power to show you my appreciation."

"You will, huh?"

Sayo tilted her head and looked at him questioningly.

Hisama found his own words deeply unsettling. *What am I looking for from this woman?*

He didn't want to let on what he was thinking. Rising, he bid her goodnight and slid aside the door to his bedroom.

The weight of soft flesh on top of him made Hisama open his eyes. He could tell right away it was a woman. She spread her bare thighs and straddled him.

There was only one woman in the house it could be.

She's warm, he thought, *for a ghost.*

"I've apologized to Wahei."

Sayo's voice was near and seemed to be drawing nearer.

"I've been happy while I've been with you," she went on. "And now that happiness is to last one more month."

Hisama moved his right hand and felt it brush against something warm and heavy. *It must be her breast.* With his other hand he reached around her back. The tip of his finger touched something rough and sinewy. It was the gaping wound in her flesh. He wanted to stop but his finger kept moving of its own accord.

As it traced the edge of the wound, he felt something warm and moist.

"That's how I died," she said.

In life she was flesh and blood, and now—though a ghost—she was still flesh and blood.

"It hurt," she went on. "It hurt terribly."

It must have, he thought. *It must be unbearable*. Hisama drew her bloody body more tightly to him.

Suddenly, he was reminded of his late wife.

He could not picture her face.

The last part of the plan left to figure out was when and where to kill Kamon.

The answer literally turned up on Hisama's doorstep late one night, three days before the one-month deadline, in the form of two of Kamon's household retainers, Izubuchi Shinjuro and Sagawa Seikichi.

"Our master would like to question you about your recent activities, which he deems suspicious. Please come with us."

Hisama could tell by the way the men held themselves that they were both accomplished swordsmen. Kamon had no doubt gotten wind of the rumors going around the castle—started by Hachiya, the detective who went mad—that Sayo had been seen at Hisama's house.

"Is that an official order from his lordship?" asked Hisama. "If not, I refuse."

"Do you *want* it to be?" countered Sagawa, a thin smile rising to his lips. "If it comes to that, it'll be a matter between your family and the clan. Is that what you want?"

"Just try it," Hisama wanted to reply, but checked himself. "Wait a minute," he said instead.

"Bring along the woman too," said Izubuchi, peering into the house. "We know she's here."

"There's no one here but me."

"Mind if we search the house?"

"Go ahead," dared Hisama. "But if you don't find anything, I'll kill you both."

Hisama meant what he said. He smiled wryly to himself, realizing he didn't want Sayo to get hurt. But then again, who was he to try to protect a ghost?

The two samurai looked at one another. "Okay," relented Sagawa, "have it your way."

Had his bluff worked? Or—as was more likely—did they, and Kamon, know the truth about Sayo?

Hisama went to his bedroom to get ready to go out. He had a feeling he'd reached the end of the road. The only glimmer of hope he could see was that Kamon and his men didn't seem to be acting on orders from his lordship or the Chief Inspector. Nor did they appear to have a warrant. Even so, now that his name had come to Kamon's attention, Hisama knew his fate, and that of his family, was sealed.

Though the situation seemed hopeless, Hisama had no regrets. Even if he'd had it to do all over again, he wouldn't change a thing—either about what he had done, or what he was about to do.

Hisama was just tucking his swords into his sash when Sayo appeared. His eyes grew wide. The top half of her kimono was soaked with blood.

"You're going to meet Kamon, aren't you?" she said. "I shall come with you."

"Impossible. His house is outside your haunting grounds."

"Then I'll come with you as far as I can."

She gave him an imploring look. Hisama could only nod. Together they left the house. The two samurai, it seemed, were unable to see Sayo, who walked a few paces behind Hisama.

There was no palanquin to take them. Sagawa walked in front while Izubuchi brought up the rear. With Hisama and Sayo in between, they set off walking south. The hour was a little past eleven o'clock. It was a moonless night. The only light came from the two samurai's lanterns, which glowed dimly in the dark.

They had passed Yashikicho and were entering Hanayacho when Sayo suddenly vanished. They had reached the edge of her haunting grounds.

So this is goodbye, thought Hisama. *Whatever happens to me, before the night is through, Kamon will be dead. If we're lucky, perhaps we'll meet again in the next world. Until then, ghost, farewell.*

They turned west when they reached Kibikicho, and Hisama began to grow suspicious. Kamon's house lay in the opposite direction. But Sagawa, walking ahead of him, said nothing. Izubuchi, too, followed along in silence.

Then he heard the sound of running water. "We're heading for the river," he blurted out.

Did Kamon intend to get rid of him on the same spot where he'd encountered Sayo's ghost? *What's he got up his sleeve? If he's going to kill me, it'd be better to do it at his own house, where there's less chance of witnesses and where it'd be easier to dispose of the body.*

They turned left at a narrow crossroads and came out onto the familiar path that ran along the embankment.

Lights twinkled in the houses across the river, enabling his eyes to just make out the river's silvery serpentine thread.

Down below them on the riverbank stood a samurai, arms folded across his chest. He had no lantern with him. Descending the embankment, Hisama and his companions approached. At last, in the light of Sagawa's lantern, Hisama made out the visage of Tarumi Kamon.

Suddenly, behind him, Hisama sensed the presence of a blade. Leaping to his left, he heard Izubuchi scream. Turning and drawing his own sword, he saw a ghostly female figure dressed in white standing before him.

"Die, ghost!" screeched Izubuchi, bringing down his sword. Meeting with nothing but empty air, he lost his balance. Hisama's own blade flashed in the darkness and Izubuchi's head toppled from his shoulders, attached only by a thin flap of skin. Then, propelled either by the force of the fall or the blood spurting from its stump, the head rolled along the riverbank.

"My turn," murmured Sagawa, stepping forward. "Stand back, my lord," he said, moving in front of Kamon to protect him. No sooner had he spoken, however, then Kamon's own sword shot from its sheath and bit deep into Sagawa's shoulder. A scream of agony arose from Sagawa's lips. Kamon, as though annoyed at this disturbance, plunged his blade into Sagawa's neck with surgical precision, severing his carotid artery.

"What the hell," Hisama couldn't help from asking, "are you doing?"

Without answering, Kamon lowered his sword so its tip nearly touched the ground.

To Hisama—fighting back the urge to scream—Kamon's serene assurance could just as well have been a full-throated battle cry.

Hisama wiped his blade on the sleeve of his kimono and sheathed his sword.

"I'm going," he said, kicking the ground. His righteous indignation at the injustice Sayo had suffered had vanished. In his hands Kamon held the power to decide life and death.

Kamon looked only at the tip of his sword.

Suddenly his blade flew up, describing a gentle arc. Hisama tried to jump to his right, but he was too slow. He felt a sharp pain bite the inside of his left thigh. He shifted his weight to his right leg and fought to retain his balance, barely managing to prevent himself falling forward.

Having wounded Hisama with an upward stroke, Kamon was now brandishing his sword over his head. The sight of his exposed torso made Hisama's heart leap with joy.

In unison the two men cried out and lunged at one other. Even as he was aware of Kamon's sword descending with a *whoosh* past his left shoulder, Hisama executed a flawless body strike, splitting Kamon's chest in two.

A deathly cry carried across the water and lingered there before being swallowed up by the sound of the river. Planting the tip of his sword in the ground and leaning on it for support, Hisama gasped for breath, too tired even to deliver the coup de grace. His throat felt incredibly dry.

Someone placed a warm hand on one of his shoulders, which heaved uncontrollably. It remained there until his breathing had returned to normal.

"Sayo"—his voice was hoarse—"are you leaving?"

Hisama's eyes followed her warm, soft hand as she withdrew it. In front of him, face down on the dark ground, lay the body of Tarumi Kamon. Beyond it stood two pale figures, a man and a woman.

The young man, standing to Sayo's right, smiled guilelessly at Hisama. Sayo loved that smile.

"This is Wahei," she said.

Suddenly Hisama understood—Kamon's seeming madness, the swordfight... While Sayo had been visiting Hisama's house, Wahei had possessed the body of his killer. Suddenly Hisama understood why Kamon had chosen the riverbank and why he'd murdered his own retainer, Izubuchi.

"Sir," said Sayo, "no one but us three knows of this. It would be best if you left at once."

"I'll do as I please," Hisama retorted. For the first time in a long while, he felt himself again. "Anyway, it's *you* who should leave at once," he went on. "Go to nirvana and don't come back to this world. But if you do, don't come to *my* house. You won't be welcome."

The two lovers looked at one another. A wry smile—one an older sister might give a naughty younger brother—rose to Sayo's lips. It made Hisama feel unbearably sad. The memory of Sayo's warm home-cooked miso soup and white rice flashed in his mind's eye.

"Go on," he spat, "get out of here—haven't you given me enough grief already?" He shut his eyes. He wondered how long he should keep them closed. *Maybe when I open them only Sayo will be there*, he thought.

Hisama opened his eyes.

He was alone. Only the sound of the river, the night breeze, and the three dead bodies remained.

"Good riddance."

Feeling as crotchety as ever, Hisama stood up, leaning on his sword for support.

Hisama informed his mother that Sayo had left him.

"Some son you are," she cursed on her way out the door, though not before adding: "And don't darken our threshold ever again!"

After an official investigation, it was determined that Kamon—who had been acting rather strangely for some time—had lured to two samurai to the riverbank to kill them, and all had died of wounds inflicted on one another. Kamon's strange behavior, and the fact that, as the investigation revealed, his blood was found on Sagawa's sword, were no doubt both Wahei's doing.

Back in his empty house, Hisama had begun to think about getting married again. The only thought which troubled him was a rumor that a rich textile merchant in Sogacho had recently discovered a large sum of money missing from his strongbox.

A Consultation

IT WAS LATE one night in mid-October when Tatebayashi Jinzaemon's nephew, Kisaburo, turned up at his uncle's residence in Dohocho, not far from the Yushima Shrine.

Once Kisaburo had been shown through to an inner room, the first thing Jinzaemon asked his nephew was what on earth he was doing calling at such an ungodly hour.

Kisaburo's response surprised him.

About a fortnight earlier, Jinzaemon, a high-ranking vassal of the Shogun, had sent a young manservant of his to work in his nephew's house. Kisaburo's wife, Onei, had a frail constitution and had long complained of needing help around the house. Several days later, Kisaburo and Onei had stopped by Jinzaemon's residence and left an expensive box of sweets as a token of their appreciation for providing them with such a good servant. The young man's name was Mosuke.

"Where did you find him, Uncle?" Kisaburo asked abruptly, without answering Jinzaemon's question.

Though somewhat taken aback, Jinzaemon quickly replied, "You know, I can't quite recall… I must be getting senile. Why? Has he done something wrong?"

Jinzaemon gave his nephew an awkward smile. *Great, just what I need*, he thought to himself. When a man comes barging into someone's house in the middle of the night on account of a servant, it spells just one thing—trouble. Mosuke must have committed some unpardonable offense and been punished by his master, and now that Kisaburo had calmed down he was here to ask his uncle to settle the matter.

So instead, when Kisaburo blurted out, "He's not human," Jinzaemon—who looked much younger than his fifty-seven years—could only give his nephew a puzzled look.

"He's not human?" he asked after a moment's pause.

"That's right."

"Then what is he?"

"I don't know. All I know for sure is that he isn't human."

Jinzaemon took a sip from a cup of tea his manservant had placed before him. Of the two chambermaids in his household, one had recently returned home because her mother had passed away, while the other would not be woken from her evening slumber come hell or high water.

"Do you have proof?" he asked his nephew, putting down his cup. The hot tea seemed to have lent his voice a certain huskiness.

"I do," replied Kisaburo, nodding. He began to relate everything that occurred over the previous fortnight.

As he listened, Jinzaemon's expression gradually changed from skepticism to shock, and finally, by the time his nephew had finished his story, to one of absolute horror, the color draining from his face.

"I… I can't believe it. If what you say is true, uh… err…"

"I'm Kisaburo, Uncle."

"Right, Kisaburo… If what you say is true, Kisaburo, it's like one of those ghost stories you read about in comic books."

"Exactly."

Jinzaemon folded his arms thoughtfully. By now, it had grown very late indeed. "I still can't believe it…" he muttered. Just then the manservant, from the other side of the shoji, announced Kisaburo's wife had arrived.

Jinzaemon expressed his astonishment that Kisaburo's wife, too, should be calling at this hour, but his nephew only stared down at the floor, saying nothing. Jinzaemon had no choice but to instruct his servant to show her in.

Onei, now twenty-six years old, was the younger daughter of Oyada Einoshin, a lower-ranking vassal of the Shogun with an income of one hundred *koku*. She entered the room with silent tread and knelt on the tatami behind her husband.

"What is it?" asked Jinzaemon on behalf of his nephew, who remained quiet.

"Nothing," Onei replied, keeping her eyes fixed on the floor.

It could hardly be anything that had caused a samurai's wife to leave her house in the dead of night.

"Perhaps there's something," Jinzaemon prompted her, "you wanted to tell your husband?"

"No," Onei replied before falling silent again.

Even for someone as famously good-natured as Jinzaemon, this was a bit much. With rising annoyance, he turned to his nephew and asked, "What's the matter with Onei?"

Kisaburo informed his uncle that Onei had been going through a period of melancholia this past couple of weeks.

Even so, that didn't begin to explain her behavior. Women suffering from depression didn't go jumping into palanquins in the middle of the night, racing over to their uncle's houses, and then acting as though it were nothing unusual. "Melancholia" indeed!

Jinzaemon began to think the problem wasn't with Kisaburo's servant but his wife.

"At any rate," said Jinzaemon, wanting to bring an end to the conversation, "this warrants looking into. I'll come over tomorrow and find out from Mosuke what it's all about."

"He's not there," said Kisaburo, still without moving a muscle.

"Not there?"

"I sent him away the day before yesterday."

"In that case, everything's taken care of, isn't it? Do you mean you came barging in here in the middle of the night to talk to me about a servant you've already dismissed?"

"That's correct."

Outside it was pitch dark. It seemed to Jinzaemon the darkness that had enveloped the corridor, and everything beyond the thin paper doors, was trying to push its way into the room.

"So what do you want me to do?" he asked his nephew. He felt like throwing up his hands in despair.

"I need you to tell me where he comes from. I want to settle this once and for all."

"You mean kill him?"

"If I let him be, he'll just go and find employment in some other house. I can't allow that to happen."

"But what guarantee is there that he's gone back to his hometown?"

"He's hasn't—he's somewhere else."

Jinzaemon gave Kisaburo a long, hard look. To be sure, this was the same young man he'd doted on ever since he was a small boy.

"Where then? And if he hasn't returned home, why go looking for him there?"

"He told me once that his parents were still alive. I intend to kill them."

"What!"

"No human being could have given birth to such a monster. But if they *are* human, they deserve to die a thousand deaths."

"Well, let me see now…" Jinzaemon racked his brain for the name of Mosuke's hometown, which he vaguely recalled having been told once. "No," he said at last, "it's no good. I can't remember."

Kisaburo remained silent.

Just then Jinzaemon's manservant returned and announced yet another visitor—this time it was Kisaburo's son who had arrived.

Jinzaemon stared at Kisaburo and Onei, but neither of them showed the slightest reaction.

Sangoro, Kisaburo's son, was eight. His parents doted on him to such an extent that Jinzaemon had often feared for their sanity.

The boy, dressed in kimono and hakama, politely entered the room, keeping his eyes cast down at the floor, and went and knelt beside his mother.

"You were lonely, I dare say, without your mother and father. Well, that doesn't surprise me one bit. What's gotten into you two? You must be mad coming here in the middle of the night and leaving a young child like this at home alone with only a maidservant for company."

Kisaburo replied, "I've sent the maid away too."

Jinzaemon was on the verge of asking when this had happened when he stopped himself and stared hard at his nephew and his family. Finally, as though a thought had just occurred to him, he asked, "Kisaburo, why won't you look at me?"

Suddenly, Kisaburo, Onei, and Sangoro rose to their feet.

"We'll be leaving now," Kisaburo announced. There was no need for him to bow his head.

Jinzaemon tried to call for his servant, but before he could get the name out, the three figures disappeared into the darkness of the corridor.

Before closing the shoji behind him, Kisaburo turned and said, "I'll leave Mosuke to you, Uncle."

Once the three mysterious figures had gone, the room suddenly felt cold and empty.

Feeling in desperate needed of a drink, Jinzaemon called for his servant. This time the name rolled right off his tongue.

"Mosuke!"

Mosuke is somewhere else. I'll leave Mosuke to you, Uncle.

Suddenly Jinzaemon remembered: yesterday he'd taken Mosuke back into his employment.

"You called, my lord?" a familiar voice asked from the corridor. A shudder ran down Jinzaemon's spine.

"Never mind—it's nothing," he said, desperately trying to act natural. "You can go to bed now."

Mosuke was not fooled by his charade.

"No thank you, my lord."

The shoji slid open.

Metamorphosis

NEVER WAS THERE so eccentric a character as Chitsugi Gembei, who worked in the clan accounting department. Now that the world is at peace, among the samurai it is only the accountants in charge of the fief's finances who swagger about like merchants, flaunting their power both inside and outside the castle walls.

Now, in any profession one tends to find that men suck up to their bosses and look down on their subordinates, but accountants look down even on their bosses. When Chief Accountant Sakuma Shuzen went before the Ruling Council, he was always careful to speak deferentially, but there was nonetheless a touch of arrogance in his demeanor. Everyone who worked for him followed his example toward their peers in other departments. As a result, they were widely disliked.

But Gembei was hated more than any of his colleagues because he treated *everyone* the same regardless of whether they ranked above or below him. His eccentricity exceeded all bounds. He never smiled nor spoke a pleasant word to anyone.

As he sat silently hunched over his abacus, rapidly flicking the beads back and forth and jotting down figures in a ledger, the expression he wore on his face suggested not so much that he'd grown weary of the world, but that he'd been born without the ability to experience joy. So miserable did he look in his work that once, when a new employee remarked on it to his boss, the man, who had entered the accounting department alongside Gembei twenty years before, replied, "Yup, hasn't changed one bit." Gembei was now thirty-eight years old.

Today people talk of drawing a line between one's public and private lives. Some will immediately stop what they are doing and kick back as soon as they hear the sound of the drums echoing through the castle at day's end. Or you may see them passing through the castle gates, the corners of their mouth turning upward from a frown into a smile the moment they step outside, as they raise an invisible cup to their lips in invitation to a colleague.

But Gembei experienced no such transformation. Spring, summer, winter and fall, the sour expression he wore never faded. That expression, so it was said, could cause a cherry tree in full bloom to drop its petals, a clear blue summer sky to cloud over, golden ears of grain to wither on the stalk, and powdery flakes of snow to turn to lumps of ice in midair.

It was no surprise, then, that Gembei got on badly with his colleagues. He never smiled at his boss, got drunk with his peers, or bantered with his subordinates. By this point, his colleagues no longer even bothered inviting him out for a drink after work. So Gembei traipsed silently back and forth between his home and the castle, the same dreary expression on his face, day in and day out.

So bad was his reputation that once Nakasu Ryohaku, a member of the Ruling Council, asked Chief Inspector Motomura Shozo to investigate Gembei's private life. Motomura assigned Hada Shinsaku to the case.

Several days later, Motomura reported Hada's findings to Nakasu. He summed up Gembei in one word:

"He's a misanthrope."

"A misanthrope?"

"Yes. A hopeless case, it seems. You see, for the most part misanthropes aren't born that way; the vast majority of them don't start out hating people; they just end up that way due to their personality or physical appearance. However, this Gembei character is a misanthrope right down to the very core of his being. According to Hada's report, from the time he was seven, whenever another person approached him he'd quickly move away—even his parents, it seems. When relatives came to the house he'd refuse to come and greet them. His whole family was worried about his future. That's undoubtedly why, at thirty-eight, he's still unmarried. No, all in all, it's fortunate he found a job where he has to deal with numbers, not people."

"I see. Well, at least he seems to be good at his job," the senior councilor replied vaguely.

It wasn't because anyone had accused Gembei of wrongdoing that Nakasu had ordered the internal probe into the accountant's background. It simply had been a personal request, as it were, on Nakasu's part: "Because he's so unpopular around the castle," as he'd explained to Motomura, adding, "but only if you have time." The result, however, merely confirmed what everyone already knew: that Chitsugi Gembei was a most singular character. And that, as far as Nakasu was concerned, was the end of the matter.

Normally, once the Criminal Investigation Division, for whatever reason, was called in and uncovered such an undesirable character, the Personnel Division would have felt compelled to take action to remove him from his post.

In this case, however, the unseen hand of the powers-that-be was held in check by Gembei's genius for overseeing the clan finances. For twenty years he had been crunching numbers on his abacus and never been wrong once. Not a few times, in fact, he had been in the position of uncovering the mistakes, or outright fraud, of others.

About fifteen years ago, for example, Castle Chamberlain Mitaka Shusuke, had been caught taking kickbacks from a rice merchant in exchange for selling stores of rice from the castle's warehouses at illegal prices. It was Gembei who, instantly spotting the skillfully doctored invoices, had unmasked the deceit. He'd brought to light several more cases of minor fraud, which for a while had made him famous around the office.

But Gembei did not let this go to his head. On the contrary, he made no attempt to hide his annoyance whenever one of his colleagues mentioned the matter.

As a result of Gembei's actions, some—but by no means all—of those involved in fraud, including a number of senior samurai, had been put under house arrest or banished from the fief. But others who deserved to go to jail had managed to escape punishment and hold onto their jobs by feigning ignorance of wrongdoing.

Afterward, most of them kept their heads low and remained quiet, but others secretly began plotting revenge. To those who disliked him, Gembei's personality offered the perfect means for bringing about his downfall.

In time, a malicious rumor began making the rounds of the castle, and eventually the entire fief came to hear of it. The reason Gembei still wasn't married at his age, the gossips said, was that he had a mistress—more than one in fact. What's more, he'd been cooking the books and pilfering funds in order to support them.

At first, Chief Accountant Sakuma, Gembei's boss, paid no heed to these slanders. But after a while he could no longer ignore what everyone in the office—everyone who had never cared for Gembei, that is—was talking about it. He decided to personally conduct an audit of Gembei's work.

Sakuma was flabbergasted by what he discovered.

The malicious rumors, it turned out, were true. That very day a detective was sent into town to investigate; he came back with the names of two women Gembei had been supporting.

A committee of inquiry was immediately convened and Gembei called in to testify. Presented with the charges, the accountant humbly prostrated himself before the committee and acknowledged his malfeasance, uttering nothing throughout the entire proceedings but the words, "It is as you say, my lords."

Gembei even remained silent at the very end when Senior Councilor Kamoeda Shigefusa announced, "You shall receive our verdict in due course." It was only at this point that the members of the committee realized Gembei had lost consciousness. The act of prostrating himself on the floor all that time had aggravated his chronic lumbago, and he had passed out from the pain.

A fortnight later, when his lordship handed down his verdict, Gembei still had not fully recovered. Two messengers from the castle arrived at the door of his ancestral home, and Gembei came crawling across the floor like some insect to meet them. They informed him he had been banished.

But that was not the end of the matter.

"I cannot accept the sentence," said Gembei, still groveling on the floor.

The messengers' eyes grew wide.

"*What* did you say?" one of them demanded, bristling.

"For twenty-one years, I have faithfully served his lordship and the fief. Who was it, I ask you, who, fourteen years ago, procured the funds for the land reclamation project in Koganeki village that brought an end to the peasant uprising there? Who scoured the ledgers and memoranda for the past fifty years and found a moneylender in Edo who would give us a low-interest loan? Chitsugi Gembei, that's who! And who was it who—"

Gembei proceeded to rattle off the various accomplishments of his career, which were more than one could count on the fingers of both hands, and to decry his unjust sentence. He railed against the messengers, his lordship, and the entire clan.

The messengers listened, their faces flushed with anger and the veins popping out on their necks. Gembei continued:

"I cannot submit to the orders of a lord who would refuse to overlook the inconsequential pilfering of a vassal with such a distinguished record of service. Such as my condition allows, I shall resist. I will not leave this house come hell or high water. If that displeases you, then send your assassins to kill me. If you want a bloodbath, I'll give you a bloodbath—even if I have to crawl on all fours to do it."

"You'll eat those words," spat one of the messengers as they turned and left.

After careful deliberations, the clan officials decided to send assassins to kill Gembei. No one spoke up in defense of his twenty years of loyal service. Burned into their memories was the image of Gembei seated at his desk, turning his face away with an annoyed look whenever someone spoke to him.

Five assassins were chosen—which some thought too many considering Gembei's physical condition. One was Hada Shinsaku, the man Chief Inspector Motomura had earlier given the task of investigating Gembei's private life. Though he'd only just turned thirty, Hada was regarded as an expert swordsman, having studied the Itto style during his lordship's tenure in Edo. Early one morning, four days after the messengers' visit, the five assassins burst into Gembei's house.

It was a large house for someone of such humble station. Though Gembei had employed a maidservant and an elderly steward, he had sent them away after the messengers' visit.

The men found Gembei in the sitting room.

His condition did not seem to have improved in the least. He lay sprawled face down on the tatami, eyes glowing feverishly from his shriveled face, like some hideous giant insect in human form.

Pathetic wretch, thought Hada.

"Leave this to me," said Niimura Zentsuke—the most senior and hardcore of the five assassins—stepping forward.

For an old hand like Niimura, who had mastered the Mu'nen style of swordsmanship at the Myokokan, the clan's own school of martial arts, it must have seemed killing Gembei would be as easy as skewering a bug. But the situation took an unexpected turn.

Aiming the tip of his sword at the figure crawling toward him on the floor, Niimura suddenly realized he was not in a good position. His blade was too low. A sword is designed to be wielded upright; that is the essence of all sword-fighting technique. In this sense, as an opponent Chitsugi Gembei presented a challenge Niimura had never before faced.

Nonetheless, Niimura calmly began to circle around Gembei. After all, his opponent's stance was not in accordance with any recognized style of swordsmanship; it was simply the result of his disability.

Look out—thought Hada—*he's moving!*

At astonishing speed, Gembei spun around on his stomach one hundred and eighty degrees. A horizontal streak of light shot out several inches above the floor as Gembei's sword mowed through Niimura's defenseless ankles, cleanly severing both of them.

Though dumbstruck for a moment at the sight of their companion writhing on the floor, blood spurting from the raw stumps of his legs, the other four assassins quickly rushed at Gembei, blades gleaming. But Gembei's sword flashed out continuously as he crawled back and forth, holding them at bay. He eventually retreated, still on his stomach, through the open sliding doors that led into the corridor running along the east side of the house.

"Leave him to us," barked Higaki Chojuro, the next most senior of the assassins, "you look after Niimura!" Hada was actually relieved. Though Niimura had been struck down in the blink of an eye, Hada was still reproaching himself for not having acted somehow to prevent it.

As his companion writhed on the floor, still clutching his bloody sword, Hada took out two handkerchiefs and made tourniquets for Niimura's legs. Then he applied a medical balm he'd been given especially for this purpose. By the time the bleeding had stopped much time had passed, not least because Niimura was half mad with pain and would not stop thrashing about for an instant. As Hada was coaxing and cursing him in turns, two of the three other men who had gone after Gembei returned.

I don't believe it, thought Hada, noting their disgruntled looks. He glanced at their swords. They were smeared with blood, but not much.

"Did you kill him?" he asked.

"We got him," nodded Higaki. His body language suggested he was to convince himself as much as Hada. "Between the three of us we must have struck fifteen or sixteen blows. But somehow he managed to crawl to the north end of the corridor and disappeared over the edge of the veranda. Tawara's still looking for him now."

"You mean you can't find him?"

Higaki looked away. Sekine Hashizo—the fourth assassin—gave a grunt and nodded. "We searched everywhere. There's blood on the ground where he dropped from the veranda, but that's where the trail ends. It's as though he just melted into the earth."

"That's enough," said Higaki. Then, as the three of them were lifting Niimura up, Tawara Tamotsu, the fifth assassin, returned. As Hada expected, he had found no trace of Gembei.

AFTER MAKING a full report, the assassins, apart from the wounded Niimura, were grilled by their superiors for several days. Some suspected them of having conspired to let Gembei escape. The stench of corruption hung over the affair.

In the meantime, Gembei's house and vicinity were subjected to a thorough search, but no trace was found of the supposedly mortally wounded accountant. Nor did the blood-streaked corridor vindicate their version of events, as it was pointed out that they could have used animal blood for that purpose. But while the interrogations continued, Hada was cleared of suspicion early on, as all the assassins testified he had stayed behind with Niimura.

The day after he was released, Hada was permitted to return to work. But though Chief Inspector Motomura thanked him for his good work and things quickly returned to normal, Hada could not help brooding.

It was not Gembei's strange disappearance that worried him. It was the fact that he was the only man in the fief whom the accountant—who was eight years his senior—had ever invited out for a drink.

Hada could not quite remember when it was that the two of them had started frequenting a bar called *Nokeya* in Sakashitacho. There had been nothing memorable about their first meeting. All he knew for certain was that it was Gembei who had issued the invitation.

The sake served at the bar was nothing to write home about. Hada was by no means melancholy by nature, but he found that his drinking companion's disposition put a damper on his enjoyment of alcohol. It was Gembei's habit to drink in silence. He never touched food, unlike Hada, who liked to nibble on little dishes of this or that or order a nice piece of grilled fish. But Gembei just sat there gulping down his sake from a chipped cup without any sign of pleasure. It must just have been his nature.

But if that had been all, Hada might have borne it knowing that at least there was a drink in it for him, albeit a bad one. But what he could not abide was what came next. Once he had a few under his belt, Gembei would begin grumbling to the younger man about this and that. Listening to others complain was always depressing, but when Gembei complained it was especially so. Worse, the more he drank the more inarticulate he became. He droned on and on, slurring his words and staring off into space as a pall descended over the table.

Most of what Gembei had said on those occasions was now a fog to Hada, but there was one thing he still remembered clearly. Ironically, it was not so much a complaint as a lament:

"I've spent my whole life crawling around, kowtowing to my superiors. Once, my boss ordered me to redo an entire ledger because he found a stray spot of ink. Then there was the time I drew up an expense sheet detailing the entire history of our clan's income and expenditure, only to be told I had to start over from scratch because someone had lost it. It's because of my nature that I have to put up with such crap. The higher-ups don't like me. They find my very presence repugnant. But they won't fire me because I'm too *useful* to them. So they just go on tormenting me. Is that fair? Okay, so I'm not Mr. Congeniality. But I greet my colleagues when I arrive at the office. I do my job. Isn't that enough? In the workplace it's a mistake to measure someone based on anything other than their ability to get the job done."

In principle, Hada agreed with this sentiment. But Chitsugi Gembei took things to a whole different level.

"I know I'm a social misfit," Gembei went on, as though reading Hada's mind, "and that's why people don't like me. I don't even *try* to make people like me. The only way for a man like me to get by is to keep kowtowing. The world will always get its revenge on men like me."

Then, with an upward glance, Gembei concluded, "I know this is just sour grapes. It must be tedious to listen to. You know, I don't expect people to try to understand. I don't even care if you forget everything I've just said. But I think you *do* understand, Hada. Even if later you don't remember a single word, you'll still have understood—because you're just like me. That's why I invited you out for a drink tonight."

Lucky me, Hada had thought at the time, suppressing a rueful smile. But looking back on it, he couldn't remember ever having refused one of Gembei's invitations or having made any effort to avoid the accountant. Gembei said he'd invited him for a drink because they were birds of a feather. Had Hada perhaps secretly enjoyed Gembei's company?

Impossible! Hada suddenly felt a gut-wrenching sense of denial. *No offense to Gembei*, he thought, *but we're completely different. I have friends and a wife and mother to look after. Sure, we're of similar rank and status, but that's about it.*

Gembei and Hada both came from low-ranking samurai families. Gembei had an income of fifty *koku*, Hada forty. True, in terms of his domestic circumstances, Gembei, with no dependents, was quite a bit better off than Hada. While some might have found living alone in a big house very lonely, for the misanthropic Gembei it was perfect.

I've got nothing in common with him, thought Hada. *I wonder why he treated me as a friend.*

It was a downright imposition, that's what it was. Still, having more than once shared a drink with the man, he couldn't help feeling somewhat sorry for Gembei. The thought weighed on his mind like a pool of dark, stagnant water.

Late one night, about two weeks after the attack on Gembei's house, Hada was summoned to Chief Inspector Motomura's residence. It was early autumn and the clear moonlight made the wind feel cool and crisp.

In addition to Motomura, Senior Councilor Nakasu and one Captain Goto were also present. As he surveyed their faces, Hada had a feeling there was something familiar about their expressions, but he couldn't quite place it.

Hada went and kneeled on one of five empty cushions that had been laid out facing the three senior samurai. At first Hada thought he must have been the first to arrive, but as soon as he sat down four other men entered the room: Sekine, Higaki, Tawara, and one other whom he did not recognize.

All of a sudden Hada realized why his superiors' expressions seemed familiar: it was the same look Higaki had given him that day at Gembei's house when he told Hada that Gembei had disappeared.

"Thank you all for coming," said Goto. "Let me introduce everyone."

He proceeded to rattle off the names and positions of the five men. The new face turned out to be a samurai by the name of Nashimoto Kippei assigned to the Minor Works Corps. He was twenty-two years old. When it was his turn to be introduced, he spoke up of his own accord, confidently adding to what Goto had said the fact that he was trained in the Itto style of swordsmanship. Hada's three colleagues from the attack on Gembei's house had their own affiliations: Higaki was an assistant to the local government agent while Sekine and Tawara were both attachés on his lordship's staff.

Of the five men, Nashimoto was clearly the odd man out. The Minor Works Corps was tasked with miscellaneous minor construction and repairs. Within the clan military bureaucracy it was the most physically demanding and least respected unit. Perhaps to compensate for this, Nashimoto behaved with unusual formality, sitting bolt upright on his cushion and speaking in a stiff manner.

"The reason I've called you all here," continued Goto when he was done with the introductions, "is rather, shall we say, extraordinary. I imagine at least four of you can guess what I'm referring to."

Hada's and his companions' face registered surprise.

"Apparently there's been a sighting at Chitsugi Gembei's house."

The four men exchanged glances. Nashimoto said nothing but looked on knowingly.

"A *sighting*?" asked Higaki on behalf of the others. "You mean Chitsugi's been spotted?"

Goto looked at his two colleagues seated beside him, as if seeking their permission to proceed. But Motomura and Nakasu made no reaction. It appeared the meeting was entirely in Goto's hands. With a look of resignation, he turned his gaze back to the five men seated before him.

"Four nights ago," Goto went on matter-of-factly, "three intruders broke into Chitsugi's house. How do we know this? Simple: they were found dead outside the front gate the next morning—all had had their feet cleanly severed from their ankles." Goto explained that the men appeared to have crawled there from inside the house before expiring from loss of blood.

Hada shuddered at the gruesome thought of the robbers clawing at the ground even as they clung desperately to the life force quickly draining from their bodies.

"And Chitsugi?" asked Higaki without giving Goto time to catch his breath. Given the nature of the attack, he'd obviously concluded Gembei was responsible.

"The civilian authorities have been conducting an investigation for the past three days. At first the clan stayed out of it. We informed them that Chitsugi had been disciplined, you see. They think it was a falling out among thieves and believe a ronin might be involved. Or rather I should say *thought*."

"You mean," blurted out Hada, "that's not the case?" Higaki turned and glared at him as if to say, *Let me ask the questions*.

Hada waited for Goto's answer. All this time, he'd been assuming that Gembei was dead; that after being wounded he'd crawled into some secret hiding place and later died. *The manner of the thieves' murder is just a coincidence—wasn't it?*

But Goto said differently. "The authorities searched the house from top to bottom but found nothing. So, yesterday, after they had left, we sent three of our own men to the house to have a look around. They were all first-rate swordsmen. I heard nothing back from them all day…"

Goto explained that one of the three men had reported back to him in the middle of the night. He could see at a glance that something extraordinary had happened, for the man was trembling like a leaf.

According to his story, the three samurai had stayed at Gembei's house all day without incident. Then, at about eight o'clock that evening, from somewhere inside the house, they heard what sounded like someone crawling across the floor. Having been informed of the outcome of the previous attempt to assassinate Gembei, they drew their swords and searched every corner of the house, but to no avail. Afterward, they went to separate rooms to wait, determined not to let Gembei escape should he reappear. Finally, at about eleven o'clock, they heard the same noise again, this time coming from the corridor on the east side of the house. It was undoubtedly the sound of clothing sliding across the floor.

Thinking they had their man, the three dashed out into the corridor. All they saw there was a long streak of blood, as black as ink. Whoever or whatever had made it was nowhere to be seen. The three men were thrown into confusion. "He must be underneath the house!" shouted Goto's interlocutor, jumping off the veranda into the garden and looking around for more traces of blood.

There were none. He turned back to the corridor and was just about to call out to his two companions when he heard their screams and saw them fall to the floor, one after another. There was nothing visible below their ankles. The man in the garden immediately bolted for the front gate.

"You can't blame him," said Goto. "They had orders to return at once if the other two were killed—with or without ascertaining the identity of their attacker." What Goto omitted to mention was that *he* was the one who had given the orders.

"So what was it," asked Higaki, "that attacked the other two men?"

"He had a fleeting impression of some shadowy shape darting past their feet," replied Goto. "That's all he said."

"A shadow... that's it?" exclaimed Higaki, angrily raising his voice. "You mean they died in vain?"

Two samurai had had their lives snuffed out and for what? The third hadn't even been able to determine the identity of their attacker. Why had Goto sent them in the first place?

Nakasu broke his long silence. "They're not *dead*," he said in a bored tone.

A hush fell over the room. The senior councilor's creased face would not have looked out of place on a giant Buddha statue. He was known as the shrewdest of the clan's leaders.

"We sent help," continued Nakasu, "as soon as we received word. The men were still alive. It seems they managed to stanch the bleeding themselves. They'll survive."

"So," asked Hada, leaning forward, "what did *they* have to say?"

In his mind was a vivid image of Chitsugi Gembei, cut to ribbons, crawling along the corridor. *Was he dead or alive?*

"The first had his feet cut out from under him before he knew what hit him. The second reported seeing a man sliding across the floor towards him like a lightning bolt."

"Is he *sure* it was a man?"

"He is. Though he didn't get a good look at his face—what with being taken by surprise *and* in incredible pain—he did see the man's clothing. It matches our description of what Chitsugi was wearing at the time of the previous attack. Plus his kimono was slashed to pieces. It was definitely Chitsugi."

"His kimono... how did you—?"

"From Niimura."

Ah-hah, thought Hada.

"So," continued Nakasu, "now it's no longer a question of whether Chitsugi perpetrated these attacks. We *know* he's still in the house and will attack anyone who enters. Now we have proof he's no longer human."

"Not human?"

The five men exchanged glances. Earlier Goto had used the word *sighting* in reference to Gembei. Was *this* what he'd been hinting at?

"It's not just a question of Chitsugi taking down two men all by himself," insisted Nakasu. "It's the *speed* with which he appears and disappears, and the fact that he cut clean through their legs. Our man swears no human being could have done that."

To punctuate his point, Nakasu stabbed his knee with the handle of his fan he was holding so forcefully that it visibly dug into his flesh, belying his measured tone and calm expression.

"And *that* is why you five have been chosen," solemnly intoned Chief Inspector Motomura, the only person in the room who had remained absolutely silent throughout the proceedings.

TWO GROUPS of dark figures hurried through the streets. To their left and right stretched the walls of high-ranking samurai residences.

There were five men in all—one group of three, the other two. Hada was with Nashimoto. It had not been a conscious decision on Hada's part. He'd just naturally gravitated to the younger man.

He understood why. He could tell Nashimoto was of low status like himself; he had that air about him. The other three came from rich families with incomes of over one hundred and fifty *koku*—two hundred in Higaki's case. With just forty *koku*, Hada did not even come close. The trio of high-ranking samurai forged silently through the darkness without even attempting to include Hada and Nashimoto.

"Nakasu's being unreasonable," spat Higaki, breaking the silence. "'Just kill it,' he says. Hell, he doesn't even know if it's human or not."

His voice was loud enough for Hada, walking briskly about ten feet behind him, to overhear.

"What can it be but a ghost?" Higaki continued. "It's like the Inspector said: Chitsugi's returned from the grave."

"You mean to exact revenge?"

It was Sekine's voice.

"Do you have a *better* explanation?" retorted Higaki. "Look, I know both of the men who were attacked last night. They trained at the Shirasaka dojo—there aren't five men there better than those two. Even if they *did* let down their guard for a second, they'd never let a single assailant cut their feet right out from under them. Nakasu knows that perfectly well, but what does he say? 'If *it* can get them, you can get *it*; with five of you, you shouldn't have any problem.' No, believe me—we won't be coming out of there alive."

Hada seemed to feel the darkness closing in and tightening around the three men ahead of him.

"You don't know that for sure," he suddenly heard himself blurt out. It made him uncomfortable to hear Higaki talk this way, especially to Sekine and Tawara, who were only in their mid-twenties.

"Hey, look who's talking!"

Higaki stopped and turned around. Sekine and Tawara followed suit, but seemed unsure what to do.

"Are you saying," Higaki asked scornfully, "*you* could kill Chitsugi's vengeful ghost?"

Uh-oh, now I've gone and stepped in it.

"All I meant," stammered Hada, "was that we don't know for sure that 'it' is Chitsugi's ghost,"

"What!" shot back Higaki. "Didn't you see the way he cut off Niimura's legs? Chitsugi trained at the Hado dojo in Musakacho over a decade ago—word is he was so good they made him assistant instructor. Or maybe you didn't know that, *Mr. Detective*?"

"Err, no," Hada replied feebly. The fact was that although Chief Inspector Motomura had asked him to investigate Gembei, Hada had not dug all that deeply into his background. Stupidly, it had not even occurred to him the accountant might have had some sword training. It was an inexcusable blunder.

Higaki did not try to conceal his contempt.

"You call yourself a detective!" he sneered. "So who's going to stand in Chitsugi's way? Slithering across the floor like some sword-wielding fiend from hell. Hey, don't give me that look. Don't tell me you think he's still alive? Oh, that's right—you weren't there when he was flailing around on the floor. You weren't with us when we were cutting him to ribbons. I must have severed his backbone and I reckon Tawara split his skull in two. But he just crawled off into his hole like the wretched worm that he is."

"That's enough!" Venom welled up in Hada's breast and spilled into his voice. He knew if any more of it came out he would end up crossing swords with Higaki.

"Well, well," said Higaki, glaring at Hada. "Just as I always suspected—you've got a soft spot for Chitsugi, haven't you?"

"That's not—!" The last word—*true*—stuck in his throat. After all, he'd never, not even once, refused Gembei's invitations.

Higaki seemed to read his mind.

"You know what *I* think?" he said, his refined, aristocratic features curling into a cruel sneer. "*I* think you've been in secret contact with him. After all, it makes perfect sense—birds of a feather."

Hada heard Sekine and Tawara gasp. He felt the venom in his chest begin to stir again and fought to keep it under control.

"And what exactly," he demanded, "do you mean by *that*?"

"Just what I said. People like you and Chitsugi will never amount to anything in this clan. You'll crawl around like bugs your entire lives—"

Hada was conscious of his own hand reaching for his sword.

"Hada!" shouted Tawara. He and Sekine moved away from Higaki.

"Hey—you wanna fight?"

Higaki nudged the hilt of his sword out of its scabbard. By all accounts, he was no mean opponent. Hada slowly moved his right hand to the hilt of his own sword.

The darkness spun a thread between the two men, connecting them in their bloodlust.

About an hour later, when Hada returned, Yae was still up.

He was still feeling keyed-up as she helped him change into something more comfortable. Only once he was seated cross-legged on a cushion in the sitting room did he at last come to a resolution.

It seemed to Hada his wife wanted to say something.

"What is it?" he asked.

"Your mother—" began Yae.

She was not complaining. If only she were. At least *then* there would have been some emotion behind it, be it anger or frustration. *Then* there would have been hope. But when Yae came to him with a grievance about her mother-in-law, Toki, it was like a very able official delivering a progress report to his superior. Her emotionless account invariably cast a pall over Hada's mood and the entire house.

Eight years earlier, when Yae, then a demure, kind-hearted girl of eighteen, had married Hada, his mother had been very taken with her. In fact, it was Toki who had chosen her as his bride.

No doubt the clever Toki, in making that choice, had been looking far ahead to a time when she was old and infirm and would need looking after. She hadn't calculated on being laid low by gout just three years later. The intense pain that accompanied her periodic attacks turned the bedridden Toki into a difficult, nagging old woman.

Not a day went by when Yae was not upbraided for every little thing, from her housekeeping to her care of the invalid herself. Hada could only sit by, filled with a kind of awe, watching silently as his cheerful young bride slowly morphed into a stern, tightlipped woman.

If Hada tried to say anything to his mother about it, she would invariably choose that moment to have an attack of gout. So he'd resigned himself to his wife's fate. As a result, every morning and night, including tonight, he was forced to listen to Yae taking her mother-in-law to task.

But as his wife rattled off her usual litany of grievances, like someone monotonously intoning a libretto from a Noh play, Hada cut her short. The tension of the near life-or-death showdown with Higaki at last ebbed from his body. He was in no mood to listen to his wife's grumbling.

"Is something wrong?" asked Yae, finally noticing the change in her husband.

"Well, as a matter of fact…"

Hada explained the situation. Nakasu had ordered the five samurai to make a thorough search of Gembei's house in three days' time. If he failed to return, Yae would have to deal with everything on her own. When that day came, he had no doubt she would be angry with him. At least he wouldn't be around to bear the brunt of that anger.

"Nashimoto is a good man," Yae observed in an unusually demure tone, once her husband had finished speaking.

It was Nashimoto who had stepped in at the last moment to prevent Hada and Higaki from coming to blows, placing a restraining hand on Hada's shoulder a fraction of a second before Hada's own right hand reached the hilt of his sword.

"Hada," he said forcefully. "Stop it."

Nashimoto's words were a warning to both men to come to their senses.

"Tawara, Sekine—" he added, "please restrain Higaki."

Thus prompted, the other two samurai rallied to Nashimoto's aid: "Yes, Higaki," they chimed in, "don't do anything rash."

Hada and Higaki had had no choice but to sheathe their anger and their swords.

After Hada had apologized politely, Higaki stalked silently off, followed by Tawara and Sekine, leaving Hada and Nashimoto standing alone in the street.

Hada thanked Nashimoto.

"What for?" the younger man replied, waving his hand dismissively. "I've got a good deal more in common with *you*," he laughed, "than that lot!"

Hada smiled and said goodnight, but inwardly the encounter left him feeling despondent. Nashimoto had that slightly seedy, impoverished air of many low-ranking samurai. From the look of him, Hada figured his estate couldn't be worth much more than twenty *koku* a year. And yet he had treated Hada as an equal. Was that how *he* looked to others?

But here his wife—far from sharing his indignation, as Hada had expected—was actually *praising* Nashimoto.

"About this search you mentioned," continued Yae when Hada remained silent, "it sounds as though Senior Councilor Nakasu plans to cut his losses."

More than the coldness of her tone, it was the thin smile on Yae's lips that deepened Hada's despair.

"That's right," he muttered gloomily, "we're going to kill Chitsugi."

"No, what I meant was it appears the senior councilor intends to wash his hands of this whole affair by sacrificing you to that ungodly *thing*."

"What are you talking about?"

"You four—not counting Niimura—failed to kill Chitsugi the first time. If you ask me, his wrath is directed at you."

"In other words," said Hada, "once we're dead, his desire for vengeance will be satisfied, is that it?"

"Exactly," his wife nodded coldly, as though it was *she*, not Chitsugi, who was the vengeful spirit. "If the deaths continue much longer, people will start to talk. 'Why'—they'll ask—'does Chitsugi's ghost bear such a strong grudge? Did the clan treat him unfairly? Is his lordship not a good ruler?' People are always gossiping. The senior councilor wants to avoid that at all costs. That means getting rid of Chitsugi's ghost—and the four of you. Nashimoto was probably just chosen to divert attention from his true intent—more's the pity for him."

Hada sat with his eyes closed and arms folded across his chest, still saying nothing.

"But even if the others are killed," continued Yae, hammering home her point, "*you* must escape. If not, the Hada name will die with you. I'm sure you don't want to take the blame for that, even if your estate *is* only worth forty *koku*."

Not that again! thought Hada, anger welling up inside him. *Even at a time like this, she can't open her mouth without slandering my family!*

Yae's father came from a long line of district magistrates. Until her grandfather's generation, her family had controlled an estate worth four hundred *koku* a year. But she'd never boasted of her family's wealth until Hada's mother fell ill.

Over the next two days, Hada was forced to hear the words "forty *koku*" over and over again. Therefore, when the appointed day finally arrived, he actually greeted it with a sense of anticipation.

HADA REACHED Chitsugi's house slightly before the agreed-upon time of four o'clock.

A young couple was standing in front of the gate, bathed in the evening glow that seemed to envelop everything. As he rounded the corner, Hada stopped and began to observe them. Judging from appearances, they belonged to the merchant class and were either engaged or recently married. On the young woman's chest, a splash of color peeked out beneath her kimono.

The pair stood looking up at Chitsugi's gate, which was made of bamboo poles lashed together at right angles. Suddenly they turned and anxiously surveyed their surroundings. Hada quickly drew back out of sight. Their eyes passed over the place where he was standing without noticing him.

Hada took a couple of breaths and poked his head out again. The young woman stooped over, surreptitiously inserting a bouquet of flowers she'd been holding into a gap in the wall between the door and the gate.

He saw sadness in the girl's slender, attractive profile. Hada was puzzled. Did she understand where she was and what she was doing? The young woman stood up, took a step backward, and, together with the young man, joined her palms together in prayer. Hada approached within about six feet of the couple. The pair noticed him before he could open his mouth. They froze, their faces frozen in fear.

"It's okay," Hada said. "Relax." At his gentle tone, their expressions softened. "Are you aware," he asked, "that this is the home of a man condemned to death by his lordship?"

The couple exchanged glances. "Y-yes," they replied simultaneously.

"What are those flowers for?" asked Hada, coming straight to the point.

"Um, err…"

The man tried to speak but no words came out. Hada ignored him. It was the girl after all who had placed the flowers in the gate.

"Well, young lady. How about it?"

For several moments, a hush fell over the three figures while the girl seemingly tried to make up her mind. Finally, a sound as though she was struggling to swallow something emanated from her throat.

"I heard Mr. Chitsugi had been killed. So I thought the least I could do was offer some flowers at his grave."

"Who exactly are you two?" asked Hada, taking a slightly different tack.

"Allow me…"

This time it was the young man, submissively rubbing his hands together, who answered.

As it turned out, he owned a haberdashery called the *Okada* in Hanakagecho. His name was Sokichi and the girl's, his wife, was Otsuta. They were newlyweds, married just two weeks earlier. But in order to bring about their nuptials, a significant obstacle had had to be overcome. The *Okada* was mortgaged to the hilt.

Sokichi's father, Eikichi, after handing his business over to his son, had taken to drinking and gambling heavily, as though to celebrate his newfound freedom. At first Sokichi had not been all that concerned, knowing full well that his father was honest and prudent by nature, traits he assumed would carry over into his new pursuits. Sokichi naively believed the pain of losing a little bit of money was the only medicine needed to cure his father of his gambling addiction. In the end, that medicine had cost him dear—two hundred *ryo*, to be precise.

Not bold enough to dip into the till of the store, Eikichi had borrowed from a bookie, putting the store and its land up as collateral. The bookie had lent him as much money as he needed. Then, two weeks before Sokichi and Otsuta's wedding day, some men had shown up at the *Okada* grasping a handful of IOUs.

"Father took to his bed while I ran around trying to scrape together as much money as I could," Sokichi told Hada, "but I knew the amount was far more than a tiny shop like ours could come up with. So, reluctantly, I asked Otsuta here if we could put off the wedding."

Otsuta had asked Sokichi the reason for the postponement. "If you have a good reason," she'd said, "I'll wait as long as it takes." Sokichi had been moved by her fortitude.

In the end, it was Otsuta who had resolved the crisis and saved his family's shop.

Otsuta worked at a bar across the river. One of her customers was a rather dour samurai who always drank there alone. She'd heard it said by another group of samurai who frequented the bar that he had loads of money stashed away and was in the habit of loaning it out at usurious rates.

"So *that's* what Chitsugi was up to!"

Disappointment and anger darkened Hada's face.

"No," Otsuta hastened to add, "you've got it all wrong. Yes, I did come here to Mr. Chitsugi's house and ask him to lend me money. He wanted to know why I needed it, so I explained the situation without holding anything back. He nodded and said he'd lend me the money. You can't imagine how relieved I was to hear that. But then, being a woman, I immediately started worrying about the interest rate, so I asked him how much he wanted. 'I won't charge you anything,' he said."

Hada was dumbfounded.

"Of course, I was skeptical too," continued Otsuta, "so I asked him, 'Really? Do you mean that?' After all, you hear all sorts of stories about people who borrow money and when it comes time to pay it back the lender says, 'The reason I didn't say anything about interest was because I *assumed* you understood,' or something like that—"

Otsuta had become quite excited. Sokichi tugged on her sleeve.

"But it's true," she protested. "Among our class of people, there're plenty of folks who'll stoop to that sort of thing. But no matter how I pressed him, Mr. Chitsugi just shook his head. 'I'm a samurai,' he said. 'I've saved money and I like to lend what I can to those in need. Just be sure you return it—that's all I ask. I don't want your gratitude. It's enough if you pay me back by the agreed upon date.' Well, I felt so bad about it that I offered to pay *some* interest, even just a little. But Mr. Chitsugi wouldn't hear of it. 'If you worry too much about such things at *your* age,' he laughed, 'you'll grow old fast!' Now, I don't know what Mr. Chitsugi did to incur his lordship's wrath, but after what he did for *us*, what's wrong with offering him some flowers? Why, even my own flesh-and-blood turned their backs on us. Only Mr. Chitsugi agreed to help, and he did so gladly. It's thanks to him the two of us are standing here before you today."

A tear rolled down Otsuta's cheek.

"I didn't say," said Hada, his mood brightening, "there was anything *wrong* with it. Leave the flowers; they'll make Chitsugi happy. Now be good to each other and stay well—I'm sure he wouldn't want to see his efforts go to waste."

The pair realized Hada was quietly ordering them to move on. Otsuta wiped her tears and, together with Sokichi, bowed to Hada. Then they turned and began to walk away. When they reached the next corner they turned again, as though on cue, and bowed to Hada once more. Then they disappeared. Hada was left alone with the flowers in the gloaming.

He suddenly became aware that the unpleasant lump in his chest had disappeared. It no longer mattered to him whether the thing lurking beyond the gate was a man clinging to life or a vengeful ghost.

Chitsugi Gembei had disliked other men and been disliked in return; their schemes had been his downfall. Not a single person had stood up and protested his punishment—and yet here were these pretty flowers placed as an offering before his gate.

"Hold on, Chitsugi," Hada cheerfully called across to the other side of the gate. "I'm coming to perform your last rites."

As soon as he'd spoken he heard the sound of footsteps behind him. He turned to see Tawara and Sekine walking toward him side-by-side. The other two samurai would undoubtedly be along shortly.

Hada took the bouquet in his hand and, after greeting his comrades, walked around the corner whence the young couple had disappeared and placed it upright on the ground against the wall. He knew if Higaki saw the flowers he'd tell him to throw them away.

Returning to the front gate, Hada saw, in the distance behind the figures of Tawara and Sekine, the older samurai approaching.

Darkness had fallen rapidly once the five samurai were assembled, as though it had been waiting for them.

Hada and Nashimoto were stationed in the drawing room at the back of Chitsugi's house where Niimura had been attacked. Dark bloodstains stretched across the tatami as though someone had dumped ink on the floor.

Higaki took up his position in the ten-mat room next door that had served as Chitsugi's bedroom and study. Tawara and Sekine patrolled the corridor which ran all the way around the house and stopped at the entrance hall.

Somewhere in the distance a bell tolled, signaling the hour.

"Eleven o'clock," said Nashimoto. "If he's going to appear, it'll be soon." He glanced at the shoji facing onto the garden and rapped his ankle with his hand, making a strange sound. As Hada looked down, Nashimoto lifted the hem of his hakama up to his knee, revealing a series of dark lines running down his calf to his ankle. Hada realized he was wearing chain mail.

"I thought of asking a blacksmith to make some iron leggings for me," explained Nashimoto, "but no matter how thin they were they'd be too heavy. One doesn't want to be weighed down *too* much. These are light, plus I was able to have them made at home."

Now that was smart, thought Hada, impressed.

But while he admired the young man's foresight, he couldn't help wondering whether such lightweight mail would really provide sufficient protection against Chitsugi's lightning-fast, razor-like ankle strike. Hada had seen what Chitsugi's sword had done to Niimura's legs. It had not only cut clean through the flesh but even the bone, leaving a wound so smooth it was hard to believe it was the work of a mere mortal. Chitsugi's life, reflected Hada, hinged on that one blow, a fact that seemed to give him a strength defying human comprehension.

"Just to be on the safe side," continued Nashimoto, "I've also been honing my technique for parrying an upward blow. But try as I might, I just can't figure out a method of defending against a horizontal strike low to the ground. How about it, Hada—do you have any suggestions?"

"Nope," Hada answered. It was a lie—and yet not a lie. No school of swordsmanship said anything about how to counter a sword strike low to the ground and aimed directly at one's feet. The best one could hope for was to try to read one's opponent in time to parry or jump out of the way. But when one's opponent moved with demonic speed, faster than the human eye could follow, one could only resign oneself to death.

At home in his garden, over and over again Hada had practiced jumping aside and lunging forward, but he knew ultimately it was just a makeshift technique.

"What style?" asked Hada, trying to be sociable.

Nashimoto flashed his white teeth. "Shinko Itto."

"Any good?"

"Not bad," replied Nashimoto, oozing confidence.

Just then they heard footsteps. Tawara and Sekine had returned. Their relief at returning unscathed was clearly visible on their faces. Hada didn't blame them—who wouldn't have preferred the relative safety of the room to patrolling the dark, eerie corridor?

Hada nodded silently.

"Anything?" he asked.

Shaking his head, Sekine replied, "Nothing unusual." He, like the others, was ready for battle, his sleeves tied back with a sash that crisscrossed his chest.

"Well, there *was* one thing," said Tawara with a chuckle. "I heard something moving about in the long grass and threw my dagger at it, but it turned out to be just a stray cat."

After exchanging polite bows with the other two samurai, Hada and Nashimoto left the room.

The wind outside was pregnant with autumn.

The two men walked together as far as the corridor on the north side of the house. There they bowed to one another and headed off in separate directions. Hada was to walk to the end of the corridor on the east side of the house and then double back to where he started. Nashimoto would do the same on the west side.

At that point, the two men would check the other was safe before exchanging roles, this time Hada patrolling the west side and Nashimoto the east. This was the plan all four samurai had agreed upon beforehand. The corridor was only about twelve yards long on each side of the house. Two candles would have provided sufficient light to see the length of it. As it was, three circles of light quivered in the breeze of the corridor.

In any similar situation, when on patrol, one would keep one's eyes peeled in all directions. But in this case Hada focused his attention only on the floor directly in front of and behind him.

Chitsugi had crawled off into his hole like the wretched worm that he was—those had been Higaki's words. But surely he was dead by now. It was his vengeful ghost that was haunting the house. In which case—strange as it might sound—he'd attack them as he had before: crawling on all fours, as though the humiliation he endured in life continued even after death.

HADA HAD REACHED the entrance hall without incident and returned halfway along the east corridor when he heard the sound of the shoji to one of the rooms opening behind him. He spun around and saw Higaki standing there.

"Seen anything?" asked the older man in his usual intimidating tone.

"No," Hada replied curtly, "nothing."

Without another word, Higaki stepped back into the room. The shoji slid shut behind him as though of its own accord.

By the time Hada had returned to the north side of the house Nashimoto was waiting for him.

"Any sign of Chitsugi?" asked Hada.

"No. Not yet."

"Well, be careful, especially in the dimly lit areas."

"I know."

Hada could clearly hear the determination in Nashimoto's voice. He thought, *This young man wants all the glory for himself.* Of course, the Ruling Council was bound to offer a reward to whoever killed Chitsugi and—if that person really distinguished himself—maybe even an increase in pay. For a confident and ambitious young man like Nashimoto, one could hardly wish for a better opportunity.

But something was nagging at Hada.

As he headed off toward the west corridor in the direction of the entrance hall, he felt a sudden urge to use the toilet.

It was then he heard the scream.

Hada's hand was on the shoji before he'd even realized it was Higaki's voice. He opened it and charged into the room. Tawara and Sekine had just risen to their feet.

On the opposite wall, a pair of sliding doors adorned with a Chinese landscape painting closed off the ten-mat room where Higaki was stationed.

"Move!" barked Hada as he barged past the two men and slid open the doors.

Hada had the sensation of something brushing past his feet. His momentum carried him three steps into the room.

Higaki lay convulsed on the floor in his final death throes, blood spurting from the twin stumps of his legs. Just then Hada heard another scream behind him, or rather, two overlapping ones.

That thing just now—at my feet, thought Hada as he whipped around.

He was just in time to see Sekine, on the threshold between the two rooms, and Tawara, standing behind him, crumple to the floor, screaming as they fell. Their feet had been cleanly severed, their right hands clutched their sides, just below their ribcages, fresh blood trickling from between their fingers.

This time it intends to kill us all!

Hada felt a shiver run down his spine. It—the thing on the floor—was consumed with bloodlust. Before it, ambition and fighting spirit meant nothing; all their efforts—the patrols, the candles in the corridor—had been in vain.

Nashimoto called out behind him. "Hada!"

Hada turned and cried, "Check if they're alive!" before adding, "No, wait—let's shut those doors first before it gets in!" He stepped around Tawara and Sekine, whose breathing was growing shallower, and closed the shoji leading to the east corridor.

Hada had just realized something:

Higaki had stepped into the corridor to speak to him only moments before being attacked. It must have been lurking outside in the corridor and slipped into the room when the shoji was opened. The same thing had happened to Tawara and Sekine. Hada had unwittingly unleashed the bloodthirsty fiend on them when he opened the sliding doors to Higaki's room.

As long as the doors were closed, it couldn't get inside. Hada didn't know why, but he was sure of it. In order to move about, it needed someone else to remove any obstacles in its way.

Hada checked Tawara's and Sekine's pulses and examined their pupils. Both were dead. The angled thrusts delivered below their ribcages must have reached their hearts.

He called to Nashimoto. "Where's Higaki?"

There was no answer. Behind him he heard the sound of rapid heavy breathing, but it didn't appear to be Higaki's.

Hada turned. *Just as I feared.*

Nashimoto was slouched against the shoji, his body racked with sobs. The paper screens rattled violently with each convulsion.

"All three... *killed*... just like that!"

Nashimoto appeared to be almost in a state of shock. Despite years of training in the dojo, he'd never witnessed death face-to-face.

"We're the only ones left... just the two of us... I can't... Hada, I wanna go... let's get out of here."

"That's not an option," replied Hada sternly. "If we leave now without fulfilling our duty we'll be forced to commit seppuku. We have to stand our ground. In the morning they're sending more men from the castle. Everything's been arranged."

"You mean we have to wait here until morning!" shrieked Nashimoto. "Just the two of us!"

This was exactly what Hada had been afraid of. The young samurai's overweening self-confidence had been based on pure numerical superiority—five of them against one adversary. Now, with three down and two to go, the odds didn't look quite so favorable, and Nashimoto's bravado had turned to cowardice.

"I can't wait—I'm going to get help *now*!"

Holding onto the shoji with both hands, Nashimoto stood up. Hada sprang toward him, but the two bodies on the floor blocked his way.

The shoji closed in front of Hada's outstretched fingers.

"Nashimoto—*stop*!"

It was only a matter of seconds before Hada reached the shoji and opened it. In that short amount of time he heard a scream. It was Nashimoto's death cry.

As he bounded into the corridor, to his right Hada saw Nashimoto's body convulsed in the final paroxysms of death. His legs were severed in exactly the same place as the others, and his right hand was clasped over the fatal wound just below his ribcage.

Hada closed the shoji and went over to where Nashimoto lay. He knew it was too late to do anything for him. As Hada bent over, Nashimoto's convulsions grew smaller and then abruptly stopped. At that moment, his throat relaxed and a torrent of blood came gushing out.

"*Whom the gods love dies young…*" murmured Hada.

He glanced at Nashimoto's ankles. The young man's chainmail leggings had been cleanly cut through.

Hada stood up and walked around to the east corridor. He followed it to the end—the place closest to the entrance hall.

"Are you listening, Chitsugi? It's me, Hada—I've returned," he called out.

There was no answer. His words were swallowed up by the darkness. "At this point it's useless talking, I suppose," Hada continued, "I take it you've let me live this long because of some good will you feel toward me. But I can't very well go waltzing back to the castle as though nothing has happened after letting four comrades die. Seeing as you're a samurai, too, I'm sure you'll understand. Now, I'm going to start walking toward the north corridor. Do me a favor and attack me before I get there, and I'll do my best to defend myself. Only the war goddess Marci knows who shall prevail. Okay, are you ready?"

Without waiting for a reply, Hada nudged the hilt of his sword out of its scabbard with his thumb and headed down the corridor.

"Here I come!" he called out.

He proceeded halfway along the corridor without incident. Of the three candles that had been lit, one had gone out. The area around his feet was wreathed in shadows.

Though Hada had been listening intently for any sound from inside the house, suddenly, down by his right foot, he was startled to hear, quietly but clearly, someone call his name.

He looked down in astonishment. There on the floor, staring up at him, was the pale face of Chitsugi Gembei. He was crawling on all fours, his body pitch black from the neck down. His right hand, holding the naked blade of his sword, was twisted behind his back.

"Chitsugi!" Hada's first instinct was to run, to put as much distance as he could between him and *it*.

Suddenly, something tugged at his hakama. Hada toppled inexorably forward. Breaking his fall with his hands, he turned his head. There, right in front of him, was Gembei's face. Instead of being pale, though, as he'd expected, Hada saw that it was smeared with blood.

"Kill me, Hada. Only you… may kill me… you and I… are the same."

"No!" protested Hada. "That's not true!"

Holding his sword, Hada raised his right arm above his head. The image of the young woman at the front gate and the flowers she'd left there flashed through his mind. He had to put the flowers back… He brought his arm down. He was astonished at how fluidly it slipped through the air.

He wouldn't have thought it possible given his position, but somehow the blade of his sword connected with Chitsugi's neck, severing it at a single stroke.

Hada was overcome by a fit of coughing. He had the sensation he was sinking into a bottomless pit.

As he drew nearer Chitsugi's corpse, what he saw made him shut his eyes: Chitsugi appeared to have been dead a long time. The stench of decaying flesh assaulted his nose.

Hada was overcome by fatigue.

Chitsugi's words came back to him:

"You and I are the same."

To this was added another voice:

"I've got a good deal more in common with *you* than any of that lot."

And then one more:

"…even if your estate *is* only worth forty *koku*."

No! I'm not like them. I'm different from Chitsugi and Nashimoto.

Then—was it the body and the blood around him that triggered it?—another memory crept into his head.

When Hada was fifteen or sixteen years, he'd joined a gang of similarly disaffected young samurai of low rank and run around getting into trouble. Later when he'd become a detective and gone to work in the castle, no one had been more surprised at his transformation than his family. His mother had cried with joy.

But it wasn't what people thought. I hadn't changed. I know that now. I just gave in. I didn't give a damn about my relatives or my mother—always going on about what would become of our wretched family. They could all go to hell for all I cared. If I could have chucked it all and sold my services to the highest bidder, I'd gladly have done so. But I realized if I abandoned my family and the clan I couldn't survive on my own. The world's a cold place to those who deviate from the norm. I dreaded the price I'd have to pay for my rebellion. So I gave in and decided to get a job and go on the straight and narrow. Perhaps Chitsugi chose the same path.

For twenty years, Hada had been keeping the fire inside him tamped down.

Chitsugi was right—I am the same.

He struggled to picture the face of the young woman with the flowers but couldn't.

Resentment never dies—it's merely passed on. Chitsugi's grudge falls to me now—the grudge of one who crawled about his entire life, never bothering anyone, and was unjustly condemned to death.

Hada readjusted his grip. He would never sheathe his sword again.

If anyone enters this house, I'll cut off their feet. Until I find a new Chitsugi—a new Hada.

Hada waited in the corridor for a while before heading back to the sitting room. He was unaware that he hadn't stood up since killing Chitsugi.

I'll just wait here until dawn.

That would be when the men from the castle came.

Gripping his sword, Hada crawled along like a bug.

On Plovers' Legs

OTSUJI Gensaburo, an officer in his lordship's horse guard in one of the Akita clans, was a famous practitioner of the Shinden style of swordsmanship. Though the outcome of a swordfight is usually determined by timing rather than power or speed, in Gensaburo's case his success as a swordfighter came down to brute strength.

Since the age of three he'd been training with a practice sword meant for an adult, swinging it back and forth a thousand times a day. As a result, his body was hard as chiseled rock. It was said he could cut clean through bone wielding only a stick, let alone a real sword. Not split or break it, mind you, but actually cut right through it.

That this was something of an exaggeration was borne out the time he accidentally beat two opponents to death while practicing at the clan dojo with a wooden sword. He did not actually manage to cut right through their bones, but merely tore their flesh to pieces and broke a number of ribs.

Though it is not known who first told Gensaburo the ghostly story of Plovers' Pool, it undoubtedly must have been some frivolous young comrade of his, who, even if he foresaw the result of his actions, clearly had not considered their gravity.

At any rate, one night in early autumn, shortly before the annual clan festival, Gensaburo found himself in the unenviable position of having to walk the lonely, deserted path around Plovers' Pool all by himself, knowing full well the eeriness of that godforsaken spot.

A hundred years before—when all of Japan was engulfed in civil war and the thundering of horse's hoofs and the clanging of steel resounded throughout the fief—a battle so bloody had taken place on the plain near Plovers' Pool that it was said not so much as a blade of grass grew there for ten years afterward.

To the victors went the spoils.

One of the samurai on the losing side fled the battlefield with the enemy in hot pursuit and sought refuge at a nearby farmhouse. Taking pity on him, the farmer agreed to lead him over the border of the fief to safety. However, as they were passing the pond, which was on their left, they encountered a handful of enemy soldiers. In vain they pleaded for their lives. Both lost their heads.

Supposedly, before he died, the vanquished samurai uttered these parting words: "Beware all who tread past this pond on a rainy night!" It was presumably on one such damp night that he met his end, his head lying on the rain-soaked grass, staring lifelessly up at the dark fateful sky.

Afterward there were occasional rumors of a headless samurai haunting the path at the edge of the pond, or reports of people seeing travelers being dragged into its waters by some unseen hand. But in the hundred years that had passed since then, the immediacy of these events had faded, so now it seemed no more than one of those quaint old legends one is apt to come across just about anywhere.

In fact, it is only in the past ten years or so that the spot has come to be known as "Plovers' Pool." Before it was not called anything at all; but it did not earn that name on account of the sight of those pretty little wading birds taking off and alighting by it, but rather because it has the dubious distinction of being close to a local watering hole, from which a succession of inebriated samurai emerged, tottering around "like plovers" (as the saying goes), only to stumble and vanish into its murky waters.

However ignominious, these events were what had led the clan's best swordsman to the predicament in which he found himself.

The story, as Gensaburo heard it, went as follows:

A couple of months earlier, two of the clan's scribes, Tomono Hachizaemon and Sakata Seiichiro, had been drinking together at a tavern not far from Plovers' Pool. The sun was setting and it was raining heavily when they got up to leave. Brushing aside the tavern keeper's entreaties to wait until the downpour let up, the two samurai set off for home. Walking north, they reached the pool a half hour later. All was quiet.

Although, over the course of time, the pond had shrunk to about half its former size, the bamboo thickets and tall grasses that surrounded its murky waters gave a sense of desolation that still lent credence to the old legend. Even in the early evening when the lights of the town still twinkled in the distance, let alone late at night, an eeriness pervaded its dark edges. Even stray dogs steered clear of it.

This then was the place where the two samurai now found themselves. According to Sakata, who lived to tell the tale, the subject of the old legend had come up as they were about to leave the tavern. "Must have been a night just like tonight," said one of them. "What do you say we go over there and have a look around?" They were both quite drunk.

But stepping out the door of the tavern and gazing out at the rain from under the eaves, Sakata had had second thoughts. "Perhaps," he was on the verge of suggesting, "we should wait until the rain lets up a bit." But his companion's enthusiasm prevented him. "Last one in is a rotten egg!" cried Tomono, opening—with exaggerated panache—the oil-paper umbrella the tavern keeper had lent him and plunging headlong into the downpour. The rain beat down loudly on the umbrella. Steeling himself, Sakata had had no choice but to follow.

They walked along side-by-side, the edges of their umbrellas bumping against each other. Finally, in the dim, flickering light of the lantern—also courtesy of the tavern keeper—the murky waters of Plovers' Pool came into view. Tomono, perhaps to pluck up his courage, began singing a verse from a popular ballad. He'd drunk twice as much as Sakata and was very unsteady on his feet.

At the far end of the pond the path curved and continued around the water's edge; another part branched off across the fields and emerged behind the temple of Ryogan-in. It was this second path that Sakata intended to take, and he assumed his companion had had the same idea.

They were about halfway along the path when Tomono cried "Oh!" and suddenly lurched to one side. Sakata inquired if he was all right but received no reply. Reeling drunkenly, Tomono wildly waved his umbrella and his free left hand about in the air, desperately trying to regain his balance. But before Sakata fully realized what was happening, Tomono's umbrella had fallen into the water, followed by Tomono himself.

Though Sakata knew he should dive in and try to save his companion, he did not. The thought of the old ghostly legend held him back as surely as if he were bound hand and foot.

Later, for his negligence, Sakata's superiors ordered him to commit seppuku. After recounting the entire story from beginning to end for the examining magistrate, Sakata dutifully ended his own life.

If the story had ended there, the whole affair might simply have been put down to Sakata's cowardice, but in the years that followed three more drunken samurai disappeared into the murky waters of Plovers' Pool, never to be seen again, under precisely the same circumstances.

"The pond must be haunted…"

"…No, it's just a coincidence. It might have been cursed *once*, but that was a hundred years ago. Why should all this happen *now*?"

Samurai and commoners alike were split between these two opposing points of view.

Despite the clan authorities' issuing strict orders that no one was to speak of what had happened, news of the strange events leaked out and spread like wildfire. It was not long before people began to whisper that it was the work of a mischievous water sprite.

This, then, was the prevailing state of affairs when the clan's best swordsman appeared on the scene.

At last, the appointed day—a rainy day—arrived. Until now, Gensaburo had not taken any of it very seriously. Like any truly intrepid samurai, he believed that ghosts and monsters were just so much foolish nonsense.

"If I see a *kappa* I'll cut it to ribbons with my sword," laughed Gensaburo. "But if it turns out to be the ghost of some samurai who can't reach nirvana because of an attachment to this world, then I'll shout: 'Stop this effeminate nonsense and be a man!'"

It was late autumn. Since morning of the day in question the town had been soaked in a cold rain that stung one's skin.

At Plovers' Pool, the sound of the heavy drops striking the water echoed loudly over the vicinity.

Gensaburo made his way to the pool with two colleagues. When they reached the point where the path approached the water's edge, Gensaburo waved his hand as a signal for his companions to stop. Then he continued on alone. The other men watched him go, intending to run after him should anything untoward happen. As Gensaburo's figure receded, his massive frame became shrouded in a veil of falling rain.

Halfway along the path his feet got tangled up (in order to replicate the same conditions as before, Gensaburo had downed a dozen flasks of sake, for that was how much it took to get him drunk). His companions were about to run to him when he managed to recover himself. He continued on, teetering on the brink but just managing to keep his balance. The two other samurai remained frozen, afraid lest they cause him to fall in by calling out to him.

More than once Gensaburo lurched all the way to the edge of the path, his two companions watching on tenterhooks, but he at last made it to the end of the pond and stepped off the main path onto the one that led to the temple.

Suddenly he stood up straight.

When his two astonished and terrified companions reached him, Gensaburo, who was for some reason opening and closing his umbrella, said only:

"Let's go back."

Cutting through the precincts of Ryogan-in, the three samurai returned to town and entered a tavern. There, Gensaburo told them exactly what had happened.

The reason he'd lost his footing, he said, was because he had suddenly felt a tremendous weight on top of his umbrella. But Gensaburo had not let go. He *could* not let go. As the weight bore down on him, he heard a voice say:

"Go on. Drop it!"

Just then Gensaburo recalled the farmer in the old legend who had lost his head.

Behind him he could hear his colleagues shouting but was unable to reply. They were unable to see what was on top of his umbrella.

Whatever was pressing down on him—be it the farmer's severed head or some other poltergeist—Gensaburo knew he couldn't let go of his umbrella. As it violently shook and swayed back and forth, he desperately tried to control it with the hand that held it. He couldn't understand why his free left hand wouldn't move, but one thing was clear: if he dropped the umbrella he would end up in the pond like the four hapless samurai before him.

The moment he stepped onto the side path leading to the temple, Gensaburo sank to the ground in a heap like a drunkard, exhausted and relieved. The sinews in his legs and his right arm bulged to the point of bursting.

"I suppose one has to admire that farmer's determination in holding a grudge for a hundred years," he said, raising his sake cup to his lips. Then he paused and gave a wry smile.

Though he'd solved the mystery of Plovers' Pond, Gensaburo still had no idea why the farmer's ghost had appeared after a hundred years and dragged those samurai into the water.

A few days later, Gensaburo and his companions returned to Plovers' Pond and placed flowers on the spot where the poltergeist had landed on his umbrella.

When they were done, they turned and walked home.

The Return of Juzaburo

ONE EVENING in early autumn, as dragonflies flitted about in the street outside his parents' house, Yomiya Ryosuke received a visit from Setsu, his elder brother's fiancée.

Ryosuke was taken aback to say the least. From the very first time Setsu had come to the house to meet her future in-laws, he'd sensed a bad vibe. For whatever reason, they just didn't hit it off. The feeling appeared to be mutual, for although Setsu was always perfectly charming to the rest of her betrothed's family, the smile she gave Ryosuke was blatantly false.

"Okay," his brother, Kango, finally asked him in an accusatory tone, "what did you *do*?"

"Nothing—I swear," Ryosuke replied defensively. "I know she's your fiancée and all, but we just don't seem to click. I try to hide it but it's as plain as the nose on her face. It's a question of personalities. It's beyond my control."

"I see…" said Kango, crossing his arms. "So you're not taken with my future bride, is that it?"

Well, we'll see about that, his tone and the look in his eyes seemed to say.

Just as Ryosuke was about to protest, Kango continued:

"Right. From now on, when Setsu comes to the house you better make yourself scarce. That's an order," he said arrogantly.

Being the younger son, Ryosuke lived in a small outbuilding on the family's estate, a bit removed from the main house. He belonged to that category of samurai whom people uncharitably referred to as "parasite sons." Unless he managed to have himself adopted into another samurai family through marriage, he'd have to remain in his parents' house living off a small allowance for the rest of his life. And, since his brother would succeed their father as head of the family, if he couldn't get along with his sister-in-law, a bleak future lay in store for him.

That was why ever since Ryosuke had been secretly praying that his brother's nuptials, which were to take place the coming winter, would somehow fall through. So it was no wonder he was taken aback when Setsu suddenly turned up to see him.

"I've come to ask you a favor," she said, adding to his astonishment.

Maybe I was just imagining *she doesn't like me*, thought Ryosuke. *Maybe she likes me* more *than my brother?*

Perhaps, if one had been in his shoes, one might have had the same thought.

After all, he reasoned, if she needed a favor she could have asked his brother. The fact that she had come to see him could mean only one thing: she fancied him.

Ryosuke glanced cautiously in the direction of the main house.

"So where's Kango?" he began. Ryosuke knew he'd be run out of the house on a rail if he stepped on his straight-laced brother's toes.

"He went out a little while ago to meet some colleagues from work. He asked me to wait for him."

"Isn't it a bit... well, *unseemly* for an engaged woman to be alone with her fiancé's brother?"

"But your parents gave me leave to come and speak with you."

"Is that so?—I mean, they did, did they? Well, then, what's this favor you wanted to ask?"

What a pain in the neck, groaned Ryosuke inwardly. *What's she got against me anyway?*

Setsu's expression suddenly changed. Her pale ethereal beauty, usually the color of polished wood shining in the moonlight, assumed the luster of porcelain.

"First swear you won't breathe a word of this to anyone," said Setsu with a glint in her eye. Ryosuke felt his pulse quicken. In spite of Setsu's off-putting personality, ever since their first encounter Ryosuke had found his manhood aroused by her beautiful countenance and the voluptuous limbs, swathed in her silk kimono.

"I swear," replied Ryosuke, regretting his promise immediately. But Setsu then said something that made him forget everything else.

"I want you to kill someone for me."

"Come again?"

"Another samurai. His name is Shindo Juzaburo. I was in love with him until three years ago."

Ryosuke was flabbergasted, that Setsu should sneak around behind his brother's back and ask him to kill someone; that it should be her former lover beggared belief.

A look of blank amazement subsumed his chiseled, unshaven face. Then, with a thin, unconcealed smile, his future sister-in-law fixed him with a dreadful stare and proceeded to explain the whole story. He listened raptly as the waning sunlight began to engulf the white kimono-clad figure before him.

Setsu had first met Juzaburo about three and a half years before. She'd been sixteen at the time. From the very beginning Setsu's beauty had attracted men like moths to a flame; she'd had no end of eager suitors, but none stirred any feelings in her young heart. Then one day, a colleague of her father's—the captain of the castle guard—had come to the house.

"This is my son—he's in his lordship's bodyguard."

The moment she'd laid eyes on the young man, Setsu had fallen head over heels in love.

"He was over six feet tall and built like Hercules, but there was a feminine gentleness to his face."

A smile flickered across Setsu's radiant moon-like face at the memory of those bygone days. So much did the incipient pale glow of early evening enhance her beauty that an exclamation inadvertently escaped Ryousuke's lips.

I must be careful, he warned himself, *she's trying to beguile me.*

"—in appearance," Setsu continued, "Juzaburo resembled *you* more than your brother."

Suddenly, Ryosuke's caution evaporated like a puff of smoke in the wind. *C'mon, snap out of it,* he thought.

"But why do you want him killed?" he asked. "Did he say something spiteful to you when he found out about your engagement? And where is he now?"

How troublesome love is, reflected Ryosuke heavy heartedly. Things were fine so long as both parties fell in and out of love at the same time, but in this day and age it was not unheard of for unrequited love to end in bloodshed. Perhaps Setsu considered their relationship over and Juzaburo was unwilling to let go.

Maybe, he thought, *even since becoming engaged to my brother, she and this Juzaburo have*—

Setsu seemed to read his mind.

"Don't misunderstand me," she said, her words cutting into his thoughts like a scalpel. "Juzaburo and I parted after six months. He left the fief to go to Edo to hone his sword-fighting skills at one of the large dojos there. He didn't say anything about what would happen when he returned."

Whatever promises might have passed between the two lovers, those words meant nothing now that his lordship had personally given his consent to the matrimony of Takahashi Setsu and Yomiya Kango. Juzaburo might reproach his former lover for her faithlessness, but the planned union would go ahead with the clan's full backing. Once something like this had been decided the feudal system did not permit for objections from former lovers.

Without taking his eyes off Setsu's face for a moment Ryosuke searched his memory.

Any salaried samurai needed his lordship's permission to leave the fief to receive sword training, and such permission was by no means easy to obtain. There was any number of dojos one might attend without leaving the fief. To shun these and go off to Edo must mean that this Juzaburo was so accomplished a swordsman that there was nothing anyone here could teach him.

Ryosuke wracked his brains trying to recall if he knew of anyone of such high caliber. He could think of no one. The dojo he himself attended taught only the rudiments of the Muso Shinmyo sword style, but he'd competed against students from the other three major schools represented in the fief. He'd heard the names of all the good swordsmen and knew most of them by sight. There was no one who fitted Setsu's description of Shindo Juzaburo.

As for Juzaburo being in the castle guards—well, as Ryosuke had no official position himself, that was beyond his ken.

I hear his lordship is quite fond of young men, Ryosuke reflected. *Setsu says this beau of hers has a feminine way about him… perhaps his lordship sent the lad to Edo for training, planning to bring him back here and give him his own dojo, like a rich merchant setting his mistress up with her own shop—*

Ryosuke's mental wanderings had reached the point where, if anyone had been able to read his mind he'd undoubtedly have been forced to commit seppuku. Just then he heard Setsu's voice beside him.

"Juzaburo has not returned from Edo. In fact, he never arrived."

Apparently, the ambitious young man had set off for his lordship's Edo residence accompanied by a servant. Along the way, both had vanished into thin air. When the clan officials in Edo reported that he had failed to turn up a large search party was sent out after him. They were able to trace his footsteps as far as the inn where he stayed on the third night of his journey, but there the trail went cold. It was as though he'd been swallowed up by the mountain mists or spirited away by some supernatural being.

"Well, this is news to me," said Ryosuke. "Even though I have no official position, I should think I'd have heard of it."

"My father told me that on his lordship's orders the search was conducted in utmost secrecy."

So I was right, thought Ryosuke. *He was his lordship's lover.*

"But if you want me to kill him," he said out loud, "then I take it he's returned now?"

"Yes."

"And he's objected to your impending marriage?"

"No."

"Then what?" Ryosuke furrowed his brow.

"He has returned to the fief but he has not yet been home to his parents' house, nor has he come to reproach me about my marriage."

Ryosuke said nothing.

The setting sun, as though summoning its last remaining strength, suddenly swallowed Setsu in a burst of light. Just before she melted away, Ryosuke saw for the first time a shadow of fear pass across her beautiful countenance. "It was about ten days ago," she continued, "that I realized he was back. I was returning from Daizen Temple having paid a visit to my grandfather's grave when I had a strange feeling someone was following me. I turned around and saw him standing about ten paces away. His left hand was clasped to his chest... like so... and he was dressed in traveling attire. His clothes were in tatters and his face was filthy, but I knew at once it was he."

Then, she said, she murmured his name. The young man seemed to hear, for he took two steps closer. Then he abruptly turned and disappeared to his right down a side street.

Due to the unexpectedness of the encounter and its strange and abrupt conclusion, for a moment Setsu stood rooted to the spot not knowing what to do. Then she turned back in the direction she'd been heading.

As she did so she saw a man dressed like a laborer strolling toward her with a toolbox on his shoulder, nonchalantly humming a tune. As he hadn't been there a few moments earlier, Setsu assumed he must have come out from one side or other of the cross street just ahead of her.

Setsu did not go to Juzaburo's family home. More than nostalgia or surprise, the encounter had left her with a vague sense of terror that made her skin crawl. For the next three days she did not leave the house. She sent one of her servants out to talk to Juzaburo's neighbors and find out what he could, but there was no indication Juzaburo had returned. Nor did her father say anything about it.

Finally, on the third day, having reached the conclusion that it all must have been her imagination, Setsu went out to her aunt's house in Sakashitamachi on an errand.

On her way back, as she was passing the Santai Shrine, whose precincts were thronged with people celebrating the autumn festival, "...I felt the same strange presence behind me and turned around. Standing there, again, was Juzaburo."

At a glance Setsu could tell his appearance had not changed the slightest in three days. Where had he been during those three days, she wondered, since he clearly had not been home? And what had he been doing these past three years? But above all, what was behind that vacant stare of his that seemed to express neither happiness nor bitterness? Under the stare, she felt the blood in her veins turn to ice.

Setsu desperately tried to summon some of the tenderness she had once felt for him, but there was none left.

"Why… why…" she muttered to herself as though in a delirium, standing there in front of the candy stall, "did you come back?"

Setsu felt she was on the verge of blacking out. Juzaburo grinned.

Then, very faintly, Setsu heard a woman calling her name and she came back to herself. Her savior was none other than her aunt from Sakashitamachi. Juzaburo was gone and the aunt was standing just beyond where he had been only a moment before. Far away Setsu could hear the lively cries of the hawkers and plate-jugglers calling to her.

Setsu was now walking about six yards ahead.

Watching her long, voluptuous legs moving rhythmically beneath the skirts of her kimono, Ryosuke imagined that he caught a whiff of her feminine scent.

C'mon, get a grip, he admonished himself.

As a "parasite son" Ryosuke had little to occupy himself other than wine, women, and gambling. For someone normally so strict, his father, an army captain, was surprisingly indulgent with his profligate younger son. Jinnai gave Ryosuke just enough money to have a good time, provided he asked for it politely. His brother, on the other hand, could be a royal pain in the neck. But Kango's nagging was like water off a duck's back to Ryosuke.

Thanks to his father's money, Ryosuke had spent a lot of time cavorting in teahouses and had had more than his share of women. Some had been as ugly as sin, others had made him groan with pleasure. But for raw sensuality none could touch Setsu.

From the front it's like she's wearing a Noh mask, he thought. *But from the back… What a woman! If I were to get my hands on her, first I'd—*

Suddenly cold water was thrown on his lascivious thoughts.

RYOSUKE AND SETSU were proceeding along the west bank a tributary of the Chofu River, which ran more or less north-south through the fief. To their left the embankment fell away sharply. Ahead of them lay Myoken Temple, famous for its fall colors. When the maple leaves were at their peak the temple's grounds became so packed with sightseers one could scarcely move. But today there were few people about as the wind had just turned cold.

It was Ryosuke who had proposed that Setsu take a stroll by herself in some lonely, out-of-the-way spot and that he follow her at a discreet distance. Setsu had agreed—on the condition that *she* chose the spot.

In the end Ryosuke had acceded to Setsu's astonishing request. But not from a desire to remove an impediment to his brother's upcoming nuptials. Rather, it was Setsu's strange and extraordinary confession that had convinced him:

"Juzaburo is... no longer among the living," she told him.

As Ryosuke gaped at her she explained that two days ago she'd hired some men—three down-and-out ronin she'd found through a merchant who did business with her family—to follow her. They'd done exactly as she and Ryosuke were doing today. As expected Juzaburo had appeared behind her for a third time as she passed through a lonely and wooded part of Rinzocho.

"It is a pleasure to see you again, Juzaburo," she'd said, bowing. Raising her head, she'd found him standing right in front of her and had had to suppress the urge to cry out. Then she informed him of her engagement.

Juzaburo listened, holding his clenched left hand to the center of his breast. When she was done speaking, he suddenly reached out his right hand and grabbed her wrist.

"His hand felt like ice," she told Ryosuke.

Silently, Juzaburo tried to lead Setsu away.

"Where are you taking me?" she asked. "Where you are going, I cannot follow."

The two had struggled.

Then the three ronin who'd been following her the whole time had appeared and surrounded Juzaburo.

Juzaburo fixed Setsu with so eerie and unsettling a glare that she fainted on the spot. When she came to, the merchant, who'd observed the proceedings from a safe distance, was shaking her.

Around her the three ronin lay moaning amidst pools of blood. One gruesome look at the mortal wound each had received was enough for Setsu to grasp the awesome skill of their adversary. They had faced the Grim Reaper himself.

Leaving the merchant to take care of the bodies, Setsu quickly left the scene.

"Now you understand the reason for my request."

Ryosuke looked fixedly at Setsu. *There's something not quite right about this woman*, he thought for the first time.

"Only the clan's best swordsman," she continued, "stands a chance against such demonic power. You must seek him out and ask him to help me. I will be eternally grateful to you."

Setsu bowed and, as she did, reached out and rested her right hand on his knee. Her meaning was blatantly clear. Ryosuke didn't need any more convincing.

A ghost or a dead person couldn't kill a living, breathing human being. Juzaburo must be alive. Ryosuke told Setsu he would follow her, as the three ronin had, and wait for Juzaburo to appear. Then he would question the other samurai, prepared to draw his sword if need be. She agreed. Though she *said* Juzaburo was a ghost, she didn't really seem to believe it. After all, one didn't hire ronin to fight a ghost.

Which means, thought Ryosuke, *she merely wants Juzaburo eliminated so he won't get in the way of her marriage, and to do in such a way that Juzaburo's family won't find out. She* says *she only hired those ronin as bodyguards to protect her so she could talk to Juzaburo, but I don't buy that. Damned temptress! She's like a black widow that preys on men. And now I'm caught in her web too, lured by her bewitching beauty.*

Ryosuke came to a halt.

Up ahead stood the temple with its colorful maples, and along the riverbank ran a row of cherry trees. Suddenly, from out of the shadow of one of these, a samurai in traveling attire stepped onto the path in between Ryosuke and Setsu. How long had he been waiting there and how could he have known they were coming?

Ryosuke did not move. Setsu stopped too and turned around. Then her beautiful countenance froze. She cast Ryosuke an imploring look.

Juzaburo turned to face Ryosuke. His appearance and expression were just as Setsu had described. He didn't look very dead to Ryosuke. For one thing, there was a shadow on the ground at his feet. Admittedly, it *was* a bit odd the way he held his left hand, clenched in a fist, to the middle of his breast.

"You, sir, are Juzaburo I take it," said Ryosuke. "Allow me to introduce myself—my name is Ryosuke, second son of Lieutenant Yomiya Jinnai. I agreed to accompany Miss Setsu here today so that she might have the opportunity of speaking with you. I humbly beg your indulgence."

"This gentleman," added Setsu, "is the brother of my betrothed."

Now why did you have to go and say that? thought Ryosuke, glaring at Setsu. *Are you trying to piss him off?*

Just as Ryosuke had feared, Juzaburo's left hand moved from his chest to the hilt of his sword and nudged it loose from its scabbard. The movement had a sudden awkwardness to it, as though some unseen force were wrenching his hand out of the position in which nature held it.

"Wait," said Ryosuke. "I haven't come here to fight you. All I wanted was to give you and Miss Setsu a chance to talk in peace without being interrupted."

Juzaburo drew his sword and held it out before him, its tip pointed directly at Ryosuke's face. One look at his opponent's eyes was enough for Ryosuke to realize that further talk was futile.

My god—what form! he thought as he gazed admiringly at Juzaburo's stance. *I reckon he's worth ten average ronin rolled into one. But if not Edo, where on earth did he learn such technique?*

As Juzaburo advanced toward him, Ryosuke drew his sword. When they were only a few feet apart Juzaburo, with a quick backward flick of his sword, struck at Ryosuke's throat. Ryosuke had no time to step out of the way. Without flinching he parried Juzaburo's blade. The tremendous force of the blow sent Ryosuke reeling backward. Having taken several steps, he was still struggling to regain his balance when Juzaburo charged at him with his sword high above his head.

"Shit!" rang out Ryosuke's voice as he fell to the ground.

Juzaburo's blow, aimed at Ryosuke's shoulder, sliced only through air. At the same moment Ryosuke lashed out sideways and felt his sword bite into Juzaburo's right knee. *So he is human!*—the contact of steel and flesh left little room for doubt.

The right side of Juzaburo's body crumpled to the ground like a marionette whose strings have been cut. Ryosuke watched as his adversary slowly raised himself to his feet, supporting his entire weight with his left leg. Then, dragging his right leg, Juzaburo set off running in the direction of the temple. On the way he passed Setsu who was standing stock-still. Juzaburo looked at her but did not say a word. He kept running and turned down a side street.

Setsu rushed to Ryosuke's side but before she could reach him he was already on his feet again. He was trembling violently, however, as though gripped by fever, and could not even manage to sheathe his sword.

"Are you hurt?" she asked.

"I'll be okay," he replied. "I've never been in a real fight before—it's a natural physical response. It won't happen next time."

"There, what did I tell you?" she said. "I *knew* you could do it."

Enough already, Ryosuke felt like saying. He knew he couldn't claim victory. If his instincts hadn't told him to let himself fall, he had little doubt his opponent's blade would have cut clean through his collarbone and into his chest cavity. Instinct alone had saved him.

"Well, now one thing's clear—Juzaburo's made of flesh and blood." He glanced down at the ground, where several drops of fresh blood lay scattered in the dirt like flower petals. "Ghosts and dead men don't bleed," he added, looking to Setsu for agreement.

But she only shook her head slowly. "Who knows?" Her voice sounded old and weary.

Sighing, Ryosuke sheathed his sword. Perhaps thanks to Setsu's presence he'd finally stopped trembling.

"Well, we can't keep quiet about this any longer. That wound I gave him might be life threatening. You could say he came to see you, insanely jealous, and pestered you to break off your engagement. You agreed to speak to him alone, wanting to spare his family embarrassment, but asked me to come along, afraid there might be trouble. It's not the whole truth, but at least it's consistent with the facts."

"But Juzaburo won't return to his parents' house," said Setsu. Her voice was uncharacteristically subdued. "He only appears to *me*. Why would his family believe our story without having laid eyes on him? No, I'm quite sure he's not of this world."

"But what about the blood?"

"Who said ghosts can't bleed?"

Ryosuke had no reply to this.

After seeing Setsu safely home Ryosuke wandered about for a while. His feet eventually led him to Miyoshicho, reputedly the most popular entertainment district in the fief.

Though the sun was still high on the horizon when he arrived, the teahouses, restaurants, and taverns lining the main street were already full of customers. Ryosuke made for one with a sign over the door that read *Mutsukiro*. Upon entering the teahouse, he immediately called an attendant over and made a request.

He was on his tenth flask of sake when his request was fulfilled.

A man wearing a staid brown kimono jacket entered the room and slid the door shut behind him. Then, being careful not to step on the edges of the tatami mats, he knelt down and bowed deeply to Ryosuke. He looked to be about forty and was the very picture of a wealthy merchant.

"It's a pleasure to see you, sir. It's been a while."

"Sure has. Let's dispense with the formalities, shall we? Here—have a drink. I've got a favor to ask you. This is a job for someone of your—how shall I say?—*unique* abilities."

"You're too kind."

Holding out both hands, the man took the proffered teacup and watched as the samurai filled it to the brim with sake. Then, gulping it down at one go, he sighed and wiped his mouth with his handkerchief.

"I see you haven't lost your taste for drink," observed Ryosuke.

"Forgive me—my throat was parched. Now, sir, what sort of favor is it you wished to ask?"

"Well, I need you to help me track down a samurai. His name is…"

Ryosuke proceeded to describe Juzaburo—his approximate age, manner of dress, and general appearance. He explained that he'd left for Edo about three and a half years ago but disappeared on the third day of his journey. He even mentioned the name of the traveler's inn where Juzaburo was last seen.

"It seems the clan officials poked around a bit but got nowhere. But you know how samurai are—they're blind to the dark underbelly of their privileged world. That's where you come in. I need you to find out what's really going on."

"I understand."

Wearing a cold, hard expression that bespoke the world from which he came, the man's face broke into a broad smile, making the deep scar that ran down his right cheek twist and coil itself up like a snake.

It was a sight that had made many a gangster recoil in fear.

"LAST NIGHT I heard a rumor that that guards captain who disappeared a few years ago—Shindo something-or-other—has returned," Ryosuke said nonchalantly to his brother the next day after the latter had returned from the castle.

Kango, clearly taken aback, looked blankly at his foolish younger brother.

"How do *you* know about that?" he demanded, blanching as though he'd seen a ghost.

"Oh, is it supposed to be a secret?" asked Ryosuke innocently, thinking: *So the rumors are true! His lordship's fondness for young men is behind this—the whole thing's a cover-up.*

"How much do you know?"

"Nothing—just what I told you."

"*Who* told you?"

"Just someone."

"Okay, now listen. That person could bring ruin on this family. You mustn't mention him to anyone. Understand? Not a word."

"Okay."

"Do you swear?"

"Huh?"

"Swear to me you won't speak of it—or I'll personally see that you're punished."

Ryosuke looked at his brother's face. *He's actually serious*, he thought. "I understand," he replied, bowing deferentially to Kango, who squirmed uncomfortably. Ryosuke could hardly stop from bursting into laughter. He wanted to say: *Don't tell me you're afraid of a namby-pamby young man!*

"Have you actually *seen* Shindo?" Kango asked, stiffening.

"Of course not."

"How about this 'someone' who told you?"

"Hmm, I don't know…"

His brother glared at him angrily, then closed his eyes.

He's trying to decide whether he should report this to his superiors, thought Ryosuke. He'd run afoul of his brother's warped sense of loyalty before, but in this case he was quite sure Kango would keep quiet.

As it turned out, he was right.

"I'm going to forget what you just told me," Kango said, opening his eyes. "And you should too, if you know what's good for you. And don't—"

"—tell anyone. Yes, I understand. I won't—I haven't. I swear… By the way, is it true? Has Shindo returned?"

"Don't ask stupid questions!"

"Forgive me."

With a bow, Ryosuke left the room.

It was clear from his brother's answers that Juzaburo hadn't shown up at the castle. And judging from his shabby appearance, the errant samurai couldn't have been home yet either. So what was he playing at? Ryosuke was puzzled.

That evening when Ryosuke dropped by his dojo in Kagamicho, everyone there—from Assistant Instructor Soma Kinbei on down—greeted him enthusiastically. A year earlier Ryosuke had earned their undying praise and admiration for his brilliant performance in the tournament against their rival dojos, decisively winning all twelve of his bouts.

"To what do we owe this unexpected honor?" asked Soma, walking over to Ryosuke with a smile on his face.

"I came to get some exercise. Nothing wrong with that, is there?"

After changing into his training uniform, Ryosuke stepped into the practice area. Immediately, several familiar faces came over and asked him to spar with them.

"Well, now. You gotten any better?" he asked.

"Yeah, a bit." They all nodded in unison.

Ryosuke felt his spirits rise. At the same time, after his recent brush with death he couldn't help feeling that his sparring companions were hopelessly naïve. In the past three years there had been only a handful of cases of swords drawn in anger in the entire town. One real swordfight had taught Ryosuke what twenty years of practicing with a bamboo sword had not: actual fear. The conscious desire to kill someone was a form of madness. The stronger that madness was, the easier it was to kill without hesitation.

A few moments later—after Ryosuke had dispatched three challengers in quick succession with decisive blows to the face and forearms—Mitsujo Samon, the master of the dojo, called him over. His challengers walked away, shaking their heads in disbelief at the ease with which Ryosuke had batted away their bamboo swords.

"I *saw* that," said Samon. "You've been in a real fight, haven't you?" he asked, cutting straight to the chase.

"You don't miss a thing," laughed Ryosuke.

Though his sensei had lost his sight six years ago, Samon was the one person Ryosuke couldn't deceive.

"I doubt those three even knew what hit them. But there's a big difference between playing with sticks and fighting with a real sword."

"It's true, I *was* in a fight. But I only wounded my opponent in the knee. I didn't kill him."

Samon stroked his grizzled beard thoughtfully and turned his unseeing eyes on Ryosuke.

"Who was he?" he asked at last.

"Just some young buck—but no mean swordsman."

"Hmm... well, we'll see about that."

"Huh?"

With a quickness that belied his blindness, Samon went to the door leading into the garden and opened it. For a second, Ryosuke thought he meant to summon Juzaburo. Instead he ordered all the other pupils to step outside to practice. "And no peeking!" he added.

Without giving the astonished Ryosuke a chance to ask what was going on, Samon removed his kimono jacket and tied his sleeves back with a sash. Then he grabbed a sword from the rack next to the wall and strode into the practice area ahead of Ryosuke.

A man of few words, Samon had always believed one had to learn by doing. Normally, Ryosuke might have dismissed his behavior with a sigh of "Here we go again." But today was different. His sensei's manner wasn't just unusual, it was downright eerie. As he prepared to face off against Samon in the silent dojo, that feeling of strangeness only intensified.

For it was not a bamboo sword Samon was holding. Seeing his sensei pick up a real sword, Ryosuke followed suit. *So that's why he asked the others to leave*, he thought.

A year ago Samon had turned seventy. There was not the least bit of wasted effort in the way he moved, and he parried rather than blocked his opponent's sword. When he struck, he aimed not for the shoulders, the chest, or the waist, but the carotid artery. One might almost say he played dirty. Ryosuke would be lucky to block three out of five such blows.

Thinking for a moment it all might be some sort of joke, Ryosuke peered at his sensei's face, but he saw no sign that such was the case. For one thing, Samon was not a man to brandish a real sword about in jest.

It crossed Ryosuke's mind he was about to die.

Without a word, Samon assumed the "Floating Cloud" position with his arms lowered and his sword pointed downward. In response, Ryosuke adopted the "Fast Ship" stance holding his sword pointed upward from waist height.

It was Ryosuke who made the first move.

Shifting his weight to the balls of his feet, he sidled slowly to his right. Samon did not move. Then, without crying out, Ryosuke lunged forward. Samon sidestepped his blade, opening up the right side of his body.

"Stop!" the sensei said. "You're still holding back. Come at me as though you intend to cut me down."

Twice more Ryosuke attacked, and twice more he was reproached in the same way. He'd just begun to grow discouraged when, on the third attempt, Samon casually gave his sword a flick with his right hand. The suddenness of the attack took Ryosuke completely by surprise. Though he managed to parry his sensei's sword in the nick of time, he felt a sharp sting on his cheek.

Once Samon had lowered his sword, Ryosuke reached up and touched his face. He felt something warm and wet on his fingers. Examining them, he saw they were stained bright red.

On the fourth attempt, Ryosuke was like a different person. Samon attempted to block his strike and was knocked off balance. Just as Ryosuke was about to bring his sword down on his opponent's shoulder blade, a thought flashed through his mind. But it was too late. As Samon tumbled to the floor, Ryosuke felt the cold touch of steel on his right knee.

"I've lost!" he cried.

A moment later, Samon rose to his feet. He still was not even breathing hard. Ryosuke on the other hand was drenched with sweat. He bowed to his opponent. By now he'd realized what had just happened. The bout had been a replay of his fight with Juzaburo, only the roles had been reversed. It was as though they had planned it beforehand. How had Samon known? Uncanny was the only word to describe it.

"Sensei—" Ryosuke wiped the sweat from his forehead before it dripped into his eyes.

Samon fixed him with a long, penetrating stare. "That was no ordinary man you fought," he said at last before stepping over to the window. Then he called to the other pupils, "Come in here—I want to see you all break a sweat!"

Ryosuke realized he was being dismissed.

"So he *is* a ghost after all?" he asked over the clattering of feet, as the other pupils filed back into the dojo.

But Samon appeared not to have heard. Ryosuke watched as the still imposing figure strode away with his usual calm and disappeared into another room.

Days passed without any further sign of Juzaburo.

The cool autumn wind, once a refreshing relief from the heat, now brought scowls to people's faces. In the towns and villages, summer's lush greenery gave way to reds and yellows. The peaks surrounding the castle town—Mount Azumi, Mount Shikamine,

Mount Hakuryugen, and Mount Kokuryuni—seemed to burst into flame, giving truth to the old legend that the forest breathed fire.

From time to time, Setsu and her betrothed paid visits to one another's houses. Whenever his future sister-in-law was due to call, Ryosuke, feeling on edge, made sure to be out of the house.

His encounter with Juzaburo had done nothing to endear Setsu to him. Not only that, it irritated him that her still lusted after her.

"It doesn't matter whether or not he's a ghost," he muttered on several occasions to himself as he sat drinking alone at home or in his usual watering hole. "He's her former lover, for crying out loud. No young lady ought to go slinking around behind people's backs like that, even if she did it to protect her engagement and her family name. She came to me for help to hush the matter up because she believed he's a ghost. But dead men don't bleed. She knew that and still she swore me to secrecy. Well, I suppose it's my fault for getting involved. Anyway, the problem now is Juzaburo. I don't think he'll give up on her that easily. He'll be back—that's for sure. And when he does, I hope I'll be ready for that ghost sword of his."

It had been ten days since Ryosuke's encounter with Juzaburo. He left the house shortly before lunchtime. The gambling houses in Teramachi where Ryoske like to play craps opened at night. Until then he planned to wander about the amusement quarter a bit and drop in at one of the teahouses for some lighthearted banter with a girl he knew there.

He'd just stopped at one of the stalls in front of the Santai Shrine to buy a cheap hairpin as a present when he heard someone call his name. Turning, he found Setsu's attendant, Heisaku, standing behind him. The young man whispered in his ear that his mistress had come in search of him and was waiting in the shrine compound. Not wanting to attract unwanted attention, Ryosuke instructed Heisaku to tell Setsu he would meet her at *Mutsukiro* in Miyoshicho.

About an hour later, Setsu and Ryoske were seated in a private room looking deeply into each other's eyes.

"There's been no sign of Juzaburo since that day by the river," she told him.

"Good," he replied curtly.

"Do you suppose he'll appear again?" There was contempt in Setsu's voice.

A guy can't get a break, thought Ryosuke, suppressing a rueful smile. "What about his parents' house?" he asked.

"There's no sign he's been back."

"Perhaps," suggested Ryosuke, "he's gone off somewhere to nurse his wound."

"So you still don't believe he's a ghost?"

"To be honest, I don't know. A samurai is taught to believe in reason, not the supernatural."

Setsu lowered her eyes and let out a deep sigh. Was she simply exhausted from her ordeal or was it some deeper emotion, nostalgia perhaps? Ryosuke suddenly felt the urge to know.

For a long time, Setsu did not look up. Finally, pity prompted Ryosuke to speak. "There's no turning back now. The next time you go out, send for me and I'll follow you to ensure you come to no harm. If anything were to happen to you, Miss Setsu, my brother would be heartbroken."

Setsu raised her head. Her beauty gave her face a certain severity, especially when she was angry. She glared at her future brother-in-law.

"Yesterday I… I followed you when you went out. I was waiting for you at the shrine, just like today."

"Oh?" was all Ryosuke could manage in reply. When suddenly faced with such a situation, sometimes even the best of men will freeze up. He was no exception.

Setsu edged closer and took Ryosuke's hand. Her brazenness was shocking.

"I wanted to see you. But I hesitated about whether I should try to speak to you. In the end I followed you all the way to Miyoshicho."

"But why?"

"I wanted to thank you for what you did the other day."

"You already have."

"That wasn't enough. You risked your life for me. I wanted to do more. I wanted to show my gratitude—"

Before Ryosuke could stop her, Setsu had draped a warm, voluptuous limb over his knees.

This can't be happening. What is she thinking? So she did *like me...*

His mind raced. Though usually fairly confident with women, Ryosuke was at a loss.

"Ryosuke," purred Setsu, "I've been waiting since yesterday..."

Did she realize how bewitching she was Ryosuke wondered, as he struggled to restrain the hand on his shoulder, pulling him toward her.

"EXCUSE ME," called the innkeeper's voice from the other side of the sliding door.

Setsu hurriedly turned away from Ryosuke and straightened the front of her kimono. Picturing beneath her thin under robe the heaving bosom on which his eyes had been fixed, Ryosuke felt his arousal grow.

"What do you want?" he asked in annoyance.

"A gentleman by the name of Shindo Juzaburo is here to see you," came the reply.

Setsu turned to stone.

Ryosuke reached for the sword that lay beside his pillow and inched the blade out of its sheath.

"When did he arrive?" he asked.

"Just now. He's waiting to see you."

Ryosuke stared at the sliding door. He imagined Juzaburo waiting on the other side, fully aware of what was going on inside the room.

Setsu was trembling.

"Ryosuke—"

"Just a moment," Ryosuke called through the door. "I'm coming." He was afraid Juzaburo might barge into the room at any moment.

It seemed to take him longer to get ready than he imagined. Beside him Setsu was still straightening her clothes. As soon as he saw that she was ready, he took a deep breath and slid the door open.

Juzaburo was standing in the narrow corridor. His appearance was exactly as before. His right hand was clasped to his chest, holding something Ryosuke couldn't see.

Ryosuke glanced automatically down at his right leg. Juzaburo's hakama was torn horizontally above the knee and a dark red stain ran all the way down to the hem of the tattered garment. But from the way he was standing he didn't appear to be injured.

One look was enough to let Ryosuke know that Juzaburo wasn't going to attack him then and there.

"My," Ryosuke exclaimed sardonically, "look what the cat dragged in!" He was about to ask Juzaburo how long he'd been following them when the other samurai turned and began walking back toward the front door. Ryosuke noted that he wasn't even limping. It was inconceivable such a wound should have healed in less than ten days. *So Setsu was right after all*, he thought, stepping into the corridor after him.

"Don't go!" he heard Setsu cry out behind him in a voice raw with emotion.

Ryosuke suddenly felt at peace. "Don't worry," he said soothingly. Sliding the door shut, he followed Juzaburo down the corridor.

At first, upon emerging from the teahouse, Ryosuke saw no sign of the other samurai. Then, looking up and down the street, he caught sight of Juzaburo's back about fifteen feet away to his right, disappearing in the direction of the Santai Shrine. Ryosuke calmly began walking after him. He observed that passersby in the street turned and stared at Juzaburo.

Clearly I'm not the only one who can see him, thought Ryosuke, relieved. At least it would be a fair fight.

The two passed through the gateway at the entrance to the shrine. A chill wind blew, sucking the warmth of the sun from Ryosuke's body.

Juzaburo passed the shrine office where charms and fortunes were sold and turned past it, disappearing from view. Ryosuke did likewise. Behind the shrine office he emerged into an open area with woods on one side. In the middle of the clearing stood Juzaburo.

"Tell me something," said Ryosuke, tying back his sleeves with the sash he'd brought with him. "Are you among the living or the dead? And why have you returned now, after all this time? Is your training complete, or have you come to haunt Setsu?"

In reply, Juzaburo's left hand, hanging naturally at his side, slowly moved to the hilt of his sword and nudged it from its sheath. Ryosuke followed suit.

"Somehow it seems you're more interested in *me* than her," he said. "That's fine by me."

Two swords flashed in the sunlight. For no apparent reason, Ryosuke's body went cold. His opponent was like a man possessed by a demon. They exchanged blows, parrying and striking at one another again and again. Juzaburo's shabby appearance belied a tremendous inner strength, and he at last succeeded in knocking Ryosuke off balance and lunged at him. A searing pain shot through Ryosuke's left thigh and elbow, and he went into something like a trance. As in their previous meeting, Ryosuke tried to draw Juzaburo out, but his opponent refused to take the bait. He had clearly learned his lesson.

It was only a slight wound, but the loss of blood made Ryosuke's body feel cold again despite his exertions, and his breathing quickened. *I can't keep this up very long*, he thought. He attacked Juzaburo with renewed determination, channeling every ounce of training he'd received into his blade.

On his third strike, Ryosuke split Juzaburo's left shoulder. Seeing he'd drawn blood, Ryosuke stepped boldly forward. That was a mistake. Before he knew it, Juzaburo had circled deftly around to his right. A split second of heart-stopping fear was followed by an excruciating, burning pain in his right thigh. Juzaburo's face seemed to loom up before him as his deadly blade hovered over the nape of Ryosuke's neck. In desperation, he hurled a taunt at his opponent.

"That Miss Setsu—what a woman, eh?"

Juzaburo reeled back as though he'd been slapped in the face. In the fraction of a second that it took for Juzaburo's astonishment to turn to anger, Ryosuke plunged a less-than-perfectly executed thrust into his exposed solar plexus. With a backward toss of his head, Juzaburo wrenched his body away from Ryosuke's blade and lashed out with his sword. It connected with Ryosuke's left shoulder, which felt as though it had split in two. *This is the end*, he thought.

Just then he heard a voice. "What's going on?" it seemed to be saying. All he knew for sure was that Juzaburo was running toward the woods.

A Shinto priest rushed to his side, panting.

"He's a fiend from hell!" Ryosuke murmured in the priest's ear as he collapsed to the ground.

Upon Ryosuke's return home pandemonium broke loose.

His mother and father nearly fainted when they saw the state he was in. They immediately called to the servants to send for a doctor. Ryosuke quickly reassured them, showing them his wounds had already had been stitched and bandaged.

"I got into a bit of a dustup with another samurai over a girl at the teahouse," he lied to his wide-eyed parents. "Fortunately," he added, switching to a more truthful version of events, "both the priest who witnessed the fight and the doctor who fixed me up are gambling buddies of mine, so I swore them to secrecy. By the way, I thought it best to give them each five *ryo* to ensure this doesn't prejudice brother's wedding. So if you don't mind…"

That night Ryosuke came down with a high fever and lay unconscious for two days and nights, but his family did not call a doctor. He had forbidden it before passing out.

Ryosuke had always had a strong constitution. By the third day he'd regained consciousness, his fever had abated, and he was cracking jokes with the servants as usual.

"Ryosuke," said his brother Kango sternly upon returning from the castle that evening, "I thought you said you'd make sure this wouldn't get out."

"I did—why, what's happened?"

He wondered if someone else had witnessed the fight. He hadn't seen Setsu since leaving the teahouse, but since his parents hadn't mentioned her, he assumed she'd returned home safely. The only other possibility was an unconnected third party.

"Since yesterday there's being a strange guy hanging around outside the house," said Kango. "I didn't get a good look at his face but he's dressed in dusty traveling attire. Yesterday and today he beat a hasty retreat as soon as he saw me, but I'm sure he's been spying on the pace. What have you gone and done?"

"Nothing."

At this point Kango would usually have scowled at Ryosuke and abandoned his interrogation, but not today.

"You understand what'll happen if you go stirring up trouble now, don't you?"

"Yes, I understand." Ryosuke's voice lacked conviction. The news that Juzaburo had returned had sent a shiver down his spine. He wondered if he should tell his brother the truth and get everything off his chest.

With a faraway look in his eye, Kango reminded his brother what a favorable alliance his impending marriage represented to their family. He warned Ryosuke that he risked incurring the displeasure of his lordship and his chief vassals, and, if worst came to worst, being placed under house arrest. The wedding between the two families had his lordship's direct sanction, and therefore to derail it would be a grave affront to his dignity. Drastic measures would have to be taken.

Ryosuke listened to his brother in silence. Personally, he was more worried about Kango finding out what had been going on between him and Setsu, but fortunately the matter didn't come up. He reflected, not without irony, that she'd done an expert job of concealing her feelings even from *him*.

At last Kango—either satisfied that he'd had his say or simply tired of talking—got up and left the room with a parting, "Well, if you *do* know him, get rid of him!" Ryosuke was left wondering what he'd do if Juzaburo were suddenly to burst into the house.

He didn't know how Juzaburo had found out about his secret rendezvous with Setsu but it was obviously jealousy that had brought him to the teahouse. Now he'd followed him to his very doorstep. It'd have been one thing if just *he* were threatened, but now Ryosuke's entire family was in danger. He'd have to be extra vigilant. Fortunately, he could still use his right arm, though his leg would take a while to heal.

Surely even a dullard like Kango would have sense enough to be on his guard. But Ryosuke doubted his brother could keep such a fiend out of the house if he was determined to enter.

Perhaps I should get away from here, he thought. There wasn't much else he could do. Tomorrow he'd look into finding a place to stay.

If he asked around among the merchants and workmen who came to the house, he was sure to find something. The decision put his mind at rest.

But he was already too late. In the middle of the night he heard a shriek that seemed to blow the sliding screens and doors off of the house. It came from his mother's room. Without waiting for the servants, he dragged himself out of bed and limped hurriedly to her room. He found her cowering in his father's arms.

"A man—there, staring down at me. Oh, his face—his *face!*" she cried again and again, pointing a trembling finger at her bedside.

Kango glared at his brother.

"This man—was he wearing traveling attire?" he asked.

Nodding her head vigorously, Ryosuke's mother gave another shriek and fainted.

"What? Who was it?" asked his father, furrowing his white brows.

Without answering, Kango ordered some men standing in the corridor to search the premises. Then he left the room.

Over the next five days Juzaburo appeared frequently at Ryosuke's house.

Once one of the maids, Oshina, spotted him in the garden in broad daylight and let out a scream. Another time a manservant named Shosuke bumped into him rounding a corner in the corridor and was scared out of his wits. Then one day while reading a book, Jinnai, Ryosuke's father, sensing someone watching him, turned around and saw Juzaburo entering the house through the shoji that faced onto the garden.

"How dare you!" shouted Jinnai, jumping up and brandishing his sword. Juzaburo easily parried it and retreated into the garden, but not before closing the shoji behind him. Ryosuke's father, carried forward by his momentum, ended by putting his head through the paper screen. His cries brought his sons to the room.

"For certain that was a man," said the father, crossing his arms, "but no ordinary man."

Predictably, Kango became more severe in his accusations of Ryosuke following these incidents. Ryosuke, for his part, kept up a vigilant patrol of the house—hobbling along on his bad leg—but never once ran into the intruder.

Juzaburo's trying to harass me, pure and simple, he thought. *He's furious I slept with Setsu. Well, I can't say I blame him.*

On the evening of the fifth day, Ryosuke received a message from a merchant whom he'd asked to search for a vacant house for him to rent. The merchant reported he'd found the perfect place near the plum orchard on the western edge of Miyoshicho. As Ryosuke could now walk without difficulty, he set off the next morning accompanied by a servant loaded down with his worldly possessions.

His spirits rose as they approached the orchard. *Not bad—not bad at all,* he thought, surveying his surroundings. Through the plum trees, their cold naked branches waiting for spring; there was a fine view of Mount Azumi.

The house, he'd been told, was no more than a small caretaker's cottage that the owner of the orchard had had built five years ago. For a time the man's nephew had decided to live there and so it had been extensively renovated. It was large enough for a family of five and strong enough to keep out the elements.

Once the servant had finished putting his belongings neatly away, Ryosuke sent him home. At last he could relax and breathe in the fresh morning air. He felt ready for anything.

Less than half an hour later Setsu arrived. She was alone. It was unlike her to take such a risk; if she'd been spotted walking about in such a place without her attendant, tongues would wag. *She must be really crazy about me,* Ryosuke thought narcissistically. Then he suddenly noticed that his brother's fiancée looked like she'd seen a ghost.

"What's wrong?" he asked.

"It's Juzaburo... he came to my house." Setsu sounded as though *she* were a ghost. Without further prompting, she proceeded to explain that about two hours ago she'd awoken suddenly to see Juzaburo standing by her bed, his arm raised and his index finger extended, as though pointing to something she couldn't see. She was about to scream when suddenly her mind went blank. Then, as though in a trance, she'd gotten dressed and followed him out of the house, unable to stop herself.

"I kept thinking, 'I mustn't go any further—I must return to the house.' But it seemed he could read my mind, and each time these thoughts got stronger he'd turn around and beckon to me to keep following him. My mind was still in a daze and I just kept walking. This happened again and again until I found myself here."

Ryosuke had to admit it appeared Setsu had been right all along about Juzaburo's being a ghost. He seemed to know everything that went on. He'd undoubtedly followed Ryosuke from his house and then gone and dragged Setsu out of bed and brought her here. That being the case, his intention was clear.

So this is the final showdown, is it?

Ryosuke untied the cord holding his sword to the sash around his waist and looked at Setsu. He supposed that after killing him, Juzaburo intended to take her back to wherever he came from. Even if he could do nothing else, Ryosuke had to prevent that. His feelings for Setsu were more than just brotherly. But why had Juzaburo chosen this moment?

"Ryosuke—" said Setsu, clinging to him.

"Don't worry. Whatever happens, I'll see you get back safely to my brother."

"For three years Juzaburo's been away," she said. "I'd forgotten all about him." Ryosuke placed his right hand on Setsu's shoulder and gently tried to push her away. She did not budge. "It was my parents who decided I should marry Kango. Then, when I saw you for the first time, I felt my heart beat faster."

Without the slightest pang of conscience, Ryosuke stopped pushing her away and instead pulled her towards him. He began to fantasize that he would not have to live out his life as a penniless second son in his brother's house; that he would marry this beautiful woman and they would live together there in the plum orchard.

A knock on the door brought him abruptly back to reality.

"Juzaburo," he called out, his arms still around Setsu. "Is that you?"

The sound stopped. Setsu gave a slight shudder.

Ryosuke slowly untangled himself from her embrace, stood up, and walked to the door. Each time he placed his weight on his right foot he felt an unpleasant stab of pain in his thigh. His leg was not what he would have hoped.

He slid open the wooden door. Outside an area of black earth stretched away to the orchard with the sharp outline of Mount

Azumi beyond. Juzaburo stood there with his left fist clasped as usual to his breast. As soon as he saw Ryosuke he drew his sword.

What's his hurry? wondered Ryosuke, feeling something wasn't quite right. He assumed Juzaburo had brought Setsu here so she could watch him die. So how come he was so eager to get started?

"Why the rush?" asked Ryosuke as he drew his sword with his right hand. Then, casually positioning his left hand on the lower part of the hilt, he raised his sword above his head. Having assumed his stance, he endeavored to read what Juzaburo was thinking from the expression on his face. *Well,* he thought, *if that's the way he wants it, he's doing me a favor. I'd rather not take the offensive. Against so skilled an opponent, it's easier to sit back and wait.*

As Ryosuke had anticipated, Juzaburo rushed at him with the hilt of his sword in front of his right shoulder and the blade pointing straight up. Ryosuke had no intention of stepping out of the way. With the injuries he'd sustained to his arm and leg, even if he managed to parry one or two of Juzaburo's strikes it'd be impossible to hold out for very long, and moreover he couldn't retaliate in kind. He intended to stand his ground and wait for his opponent to strike the first blow. At that moment Ryosuke would bring his sword down. He'd decided from the outset that as long as he had to die, he'd make sure he took Juzaburo with him. In one sense, that for a true samurai was the ultimate thrill.

Ryosuke kept his eyes fixed on Juzaburo's blank face, waiting for that split second before he struck when bloodlust would flash across it. That moment would decide Ryosuke's fate.

Juzaburo's face drew closer and closer until it completely filled Ryosuke's field of vision. Suddenly, a sneer rose to Juzaburo's lips. Rising up on tiptoe, Ryosuke brought his sword down with all his might. His blade went in at a sharper angle and bit deeper than he'd expected. He felt it cutting clean through Juzaburo's vertebrae.

As Juzaburo's decapitated body fell at Ryosuke's feet, a stream of blood spurted across the ground. Ryosuke did not dare so much as breathe. It wasn't until he'd stropped trembling and his breathing returned to normal that he realized what he'd actually done. He retched violently. He'd been prepared for death, and for a moment his body had shut down as though he truly *had* died.

Setsu rushed over and flung her arms around him. Even that must have taken a considerable effort on her part.

"What happened?" he asked, shaking his head as he gazed down at the severed head lying on the ground beside Juzaburo's right shoulder. Blood was still gushing from the body. Ryosuke felt the autumn chill beneath his skin.

He replayed the scene in his mind: just as Juzaburo had been about to strike he'd suddenly toppled forward, clutching at his chest with his left hand. As a result, Ryosuke's blade, aimed at the middle of Juzuburo's shoulder blade, had made direct contact with his neck. What on earth had happened to cause his opponent's body to react in that way?

"I don't understand it," he muttered.

"I do," said Setsu. "Just now Juzaburo died."

Just now Juzaburo died... She repeated the words four times.

It wasn't until two days later that the whole affair was truly laid to rest. That evening a man with a scar on his cheek visited Ryosuke's little house in the plum orchard.

"I was just at your house—they sent me here," he explained. Ryosuke had left instructions with his servant that if anyone came to his parents' house looking for him, he should send them to the cottage.

"Thanks for your help," he replied. "Shall we have a drink?"

They headed out to Ryosuke's regular haunt in Miyoshicho and were shown through to a private room. Once they were seated, Ryosuke's companion opened the door slightly and peeked out to make sure no one was eavesdropping before launching into an explanation of his investigation.

"You were right—this went very deep. I've never come across such a hard case before. Well, it's not surprising really—it *has* been almost four years. The guys who attacked him and left him for dead must have had a rude awakening, I should imagine. They went to great length to make sure nobody would talk."

"You mean he *was* killed during his journey?"

"You see, there was a gang of young hoods that worked that post town where he was last seen. After arriving at the inn he was foolish enough to show one of the maids what was in his wallet and she went straight to tell her boyfriend, who was in the gang. They decided to use her as bait to get the money. The next morning she lured Juzaburo to a nearby cave, no doubt having propositioned him. Her accomplices told me she was a real hot number, though she's since been chased out of town following a separate run in with the law… Anyway, they even killed his servant, who was waiting for him back at the inn."

Marveling at the means the man must have used to extract this information, Ryosuke held out the flask of sake for his fearless companion. "Ironic, isn't it?" he said. "There he was on his way to Edo for sword training, and he fell prey to some young thugs who wouldn't know one end of a blade from the other… Anyway, what happened next?"

Suddenly the man's eyes assumed a far-off look. His gaze was no longer focused on Ryosuke but something else—something in the past.

"He was still in the cave when I found him," the man said.

Ryosuke gave a start. He clearly sensed terror in the man's voice.

"They really did a number on him," he continued. "One of them cut him down from behind with a sword, then they all piled on and began slashing him to pieces. They finished by running him clean through the chest with a bamboo spear. He was pinned to the wall of the cave with the spear sunk in about a foot."

"Was he holding the spear like this?" Ryosuke suddenly asked, gesturing to his chest with his left hand.

"That's right."

"I see. That explains… never mind. But if Juzaburo's body was in the cave, who or what exactly did I kill?"

"What did you do with the body?"

"I sent for my brother and together we dug a hole and buried him. I think he recognized his face, but he didn't say anything."

"I understand—you have to protect your family name. But how strange… Shall we dig up the body and have a look?"

"No—let dead men lie. Anyway, I think I know why Juzaburo returned. After the way they killed him, I suppose his soul couldn't rest."

"I suppose so…" the man said, giving Ryosuke a strange look.

"Plus he was still in love with Setsu. She *said* they'd ended their relationship, but I don't think he saw it that way. When he found out she was engaged to my brother, he came back."

The man looked contemplative.

"At any rate, it's over now," continued Ryosuke. "By the way, did you dispose of the body in the cave?"

"Yes, but... I think you've misunderstood something, sir. I should have mentioned it sooner."

"What's that?"

"It's so horrible I can barely bring myself to speak of it, but... when I found him in the cave he was still alive."

"What!" The sound of rushing blood filled Ryosuke's ears.

The man continued:

"The morning sun was streaming in through the mouth of the cave, but in the gloom at the back I could just make out a wasted figure, his mouth opening and closing like a fish, as though he were saying something. I crept closer, thinking I might not come out of there alive, and I could hear what he was saying. It was the same word over and over—'Setsu... Setsu...' To think he'd been there for nearly four years, like a bug with a pin through its guts, clinging to life... The obsession of the human heart is truly terrifying!"

Ryosuke shook his head, as though trying to drive the image of Juzaburo impaled on a stake from his mind.

"I couldn't bear to see him like that, so I pulled the spear out. And then..."

The man described how Juzaburo's body had slumped to the ground and broken into pieces like a rotten rag doll. There was nothing more he could do. Leaving the cave, he went straight to the nearest temple and told the priest where to find the body. Then he headed home.

"What time of the morning was it when you pulled the spear from his body?" asked Ryosuke. "Was it—?"

Ryosuke specified a time.

The man nodded. "Yes, that's right. There's a temple bell that sounds at dawn to awaken the travelers at the inns; I heard it just as I was entering the cave."

That had been the exact moment when Juzaburo, poised to strike Ryosuke down, had toppled forward clutching his chest. Ryosuke knew it wasn't simply a coincidence. "Yes," he murmured, "that must be it..."

He recalled how Juzaburo had seemed in an unusual hurry to cross swords with him that morning. Had he somehow sensed the approach of the man coming to release him from his suffering? Killing his rival in love had been even more important to him than the salvation of his soul. To that end, he'd spent over three years in that cave unbeknownst to anyone, honing his swordsmanship in his mind.

"Torn between love and duty... How difficult is man's lot."

For the first time, Ryosuke began to look at his young adversary in a whole new light.

The nuptials of Yomiya Kango and Takahashi Setsu took place on an auspicious day in the first lunar month. Even the snow that had been steadily falling for days paused for a short time in honor of the occasion.

Since leaving the plum orchard that morning, Setsu had called several times at the house of her betrothed, but she did not stop by to see Ryosuke in his garden pavilion to which he had since returned. Nor did the lovers meet in a teahouse or anywhere else.

Nevertheless, whenever Ryosuke went out on one of his jaunts to the pleasure quarters, he would turn and look over his shoulder often, half expecting to see Setsu following him. But the cold ethereal beauty was nowhere to be seen.

The last time he saw Setsu was at his brother's wedding. Even then, however, she did not so much as look at him.

Hell hath no fury like a woman scorned, he thought. *Poor Juzaburo...*

The day Setsu officially became the new mistress of the Yomiya household, Ryosuke was not there to greet his sister-in-law.

Over the next six months there were occasional reports of him being spotted around the neighborhood or in Miyoshicho, but after that nothing.

Whenever the subject of Ryosuke came up, his older brother would click his tongue and mutter, "That ne'er-do-well..."

To which his beautiful wife would respond, "Indeed, dear... indeed."

The Cuckoo's Child

RETURNING from the castle at his usual hour and in his usual good humor, Gorota was surprised to find his wife in anything but her usual mood.

She looked daggers at him. If there ever was an expression that foreshadowed an impending explosion, this was it.

"Well, what is it?" he asked her.

His wife stated her case.

"You must be joking," Gorota blurted out.

At about two o'clock that afternoon, a woman with a shawl over her head—to all appearances the wife of a samurai—had come to the house. She was carrying a baby wrapped in an ornate gold brocade swaddling cloth.

"This child belongs to your husband," declared the woman, thrusting the baby into the arms of Gorota's astonished wife, who had come to receive her. Then the woman had abruptly left.

"She was a *very* beautiful woman," his wife said to him in a voice dripping with sarcasm. A shiver ran down Gorota's spine, but not before Gorota had begun searching his memory. He came across several possible candidates.

Reading him like a book, his wife rose abruptly and disappeared into another room, soon returning with the baby in question. Gorota was still not ready to concede defeat.

Gorota's eyes opened wide when he saw the sumptuous swaddling cloth, which was stitched with gold and silver brocade. A man on his income—a mere 150 *koku*—could never afford such luxury.

Whoever bought this must earn at least a thousand koku, he thought.

"Here, take a look at the child," his wife said icily, interrupting his thoughts. "He's a darling little thing, really. See how peacefully he's sleeping. Why, look, dear—he's got *your* eyes."

Gorota at last found his voice. "I haven't the foggiest idea what this is all about. It's preposterous—there must be some mistake."

"Is it?" she asked.

"What's wrong with you, anyway?" Gorota struck back. "How could you just take this woman's groundless accusations at face value and go and accept some stranger's child? That was very imprudent, if you ask me."

His wife's composure crumbled. "Yes, dear, you have a point…"

She confessed how, as she stood facing the woman, she'd been unable to speak or even move. Her limbs had felt heavy, as though held down by some invisible force. When the woman thrust the child into her arms, all she could do was silently accept the tiny bundle and watch helplessly as the woman went away.

"Do you suppose she was a ghost?" he asked.

"Whoever heard of a ghost in broad daylight?" his wife countered. "No, I'm positive she was flesh and blood—I took a long hard look at her. Are you sure you're not just trying to wriggle out of this, dear?"

Gorota had had as much as he could take.

"Watch your tongue!" he scolded. "This has got nothing to do with me. I've never seen that blasted woman or her child in my life. If you won't even believe your own husband then you can go ahead and leave me," he declared pompously. "I'll give you the divorce papers right now if you want!"

He got up and stormed out of the room, but his anger did not subside.

"Starting tonight I'm sleeping by myself!" he called out from the hallway. He went to the eight-mat guest room, pulled a futon from the closet, and laid it out on the floor. Then he flopped down on it with his arms and legs splayed out to either side.

He stared up at the ceiling and listened to the scurrying of tiny feet, which, being an old house, could be heard all day long. *That damn woman—all she does is nag, nag, nag. One of these days I'm going to let her have it.* His thoughts continued in this vein until, exhausted, his eyelids closed and he fell fast asleep.

Late that night, a horrible scream brought the manservant and Gorota's wife running pale-faced to his room. They found the master of the house sitting up in bed, trembling violently from head to toe.

"What is it?" they asked in alarm.

In reply all he said was that he'd had a bad dream. Though he couldn't recall what the dream was about, it must have been very frightening indeed to have so deeply affected a man who was widely reputed to be the best swordsman in the fief.

The nightmares continued night after night. Each night Gorota awoke screaming at exactly the same hour and sat bolt upright. Each time his wife asked him what the dream had been about, and each time his answer was the same—he couldn't remember.

Meanwhile, as long as they were stuck with the child—and it with them—Gorota's wife, who had neither wanted nor been blessed with children of her own, ordered the maid to nurse it. But it was not long before she was suckling it at her own breast.

To forestall any embarrassing rumors, Gorota reported the matter to the clan authorities. He was told that so long as he and his wife were willing to look after the child, there would be no objection.

Gorota's wife decided to name the boy Mitsumasa. Though she tried as much as possible to keep him away from prying eyes, people inevitably started asking questions. If anything, Gorota's wife seemed to relish seeing the look on their faces when they heard her answer.

Her one cause for concern, despite the boy's plump proportions, was his meager appetite. Her anxiety eventually prompted her to hire a wet nurse, but there was no improvement in his eating habits. She finally stopped worrying when she saw that his cheeks remained as round and chubby as two ripe apples.

One evening, about six months after Mitsumasa's arrival, Gotoro called his wife into his room.

To her astonishment, he flatly declared, "That child isn't human."

As expected, Gorota's wife shot him a look that seemed to say, *It's you who isn't human.* Then she demanded proof.

"First of all," he began, "the boy doesn't eat anything—unless he's been eating all the mice in our attic. Haven't you noticed how quiet it's become up there lately? Another thing is these nightmares I keep having. Once I woke up and saw two little eyes down at my feet staring at me through the darkness. They vanished just as you and the servant came running into the room… He must have crawled out through the sliding doors when you opened them. Didn't you notice? No child in the world can move that fast. My nightmares began when Mitsumasa came to the house—what more proof do you need?"

Gorota's wife's first instinct was to vigorously defend Mitsumasa against all these allegations, but she stopped herself when she saw the deadly serious look on her husband's face.

"Well, assuming you're right, what do you intend to do?" she asked.

"We can't keep him—he's not of this world. Maybe you haven't noticed but you've become terribly emaciated these past six months. You must get rid of him. If you won't, I will have to kill him."

"What!" she exclaimed, arching her elegant eyebrows. Just then the manservant rushed into the room and announced that "that woman" had returned.

Gorota's wife went to the front door. It was indeed the same lady who had appeared with the baby swaddled in her arms six months earlier.

Quite unlike before, her manner was extremely humble. She apologized, saying she'd made a terrible mistake and had brought the child to the wrong house. It was not Gorota who was the father but another high-ranking samurai who happened to have the same last name.

"I'm terribly sorry," she said, bowing deeply.

She took Mitsumasa and left. It was about one in the afternoon and the sun was high in the sky.

Goroto returned around six in the evening.

"What happened?" his wife asked him, seeming in somewhat better spirits than before.

"I saw her go into the house and come out again empty-handed. I followed her for a while, but she was faster than me and didn't once pause to rest. In the end, I lost sight of her."

"So... she *was* a ghost then?"

"I suppose so."

"That means the husband of that other house slept with..."

"I don't know. Maybe she just keeps trying until she finds a family that will take him in and look after him as though he were their own son. Like the cuckoo..."

His wife's eyes grew wide. Then a strange look came into them and she stared at Gorota.

"Oh, my goodness! Do you think *everyone* is like me—they'd just go ahead and accept the child?"

Gorota shook his head.

What disturbed him more than his wife's behavior was the thought that no man, himself included, when put in that position, could immediately say with absolute certainty, "He's not mine—take him away."

Of course, he kept his thoughts to himself.

Two Peas in a Pod

"JINGO-SENSEI—you in there?" called the voice as the rickety wooden door, which seemed might fly off its runners if one pushed just a bit too hard, was carefully slid aside.

The voice's owner was a regular visitor to the house.

"Can't you see I am?"

Jingo Yukihisa was kneeling on the well-worn tatami inside the dimly lit room, holding a wide stiff-bristled brush coated with glue. His hand stopped in midair before he answered.

It was the height of summer. A sultriness hung about the room, which was a riot of strange-looking flowers: oil-paper umbrellas that the occupant of the house had just finished gluing together, about ten in all.

In addition, the mere sight of Jingo—at nearly six and a half feet, a hairy giant of a man unsuited to the heat of summer—was enough to make anyone feel hot.

"You're just in time to lend me a hand—I'll give you one umbrella for every two hundred we make."

"Cut it out," said the man as he sat down on the step inside the dirt floor of the entranceway. Frowning, he waved his hand in front of his nose to dispel the odor of glue that pervaded the room.

"You can say 'sayonara' to this dead-end job for a while," he continued. "I've got a gig that's worth ten *ryo* for one night's—not even that—one *hour's* work."

"Ten *ryo*!"

Jingo's hand, which had resumed its task of applying glue to the wooden ribs of an umbrella, stopped again in midair. He gave the man a long hard look—one might even say a glare. He didn't believe him. Perhaps it was just his suspicious nature.

"Saisuke," he said at last.

"Yes?"

"Are you pulling my leg?"

"C'mon, Jingo-sensei—why would I do that? I owe you my life, don't I? I may be a good-for-nothing street thug, but I never forget a debt."

Jingo's row house was about two blocks north of the Kuo Shrine. A monthly fair was held on the day sacred to the god Taishaku, to whom the shrine was dedicated. These were controlled by a local gangster and self-styled 'defender of the weak and down-trodden' named Heigoro. Saisuke was one of Heigoro's minions. In his mid-thirties, he had a tough-looking face that oozed charm when he smiled. Once, when Saisuke had taken him to his local watering hole, Jingo himself had witnessed how the barmaids squealed with delight and blushed from ear to ear the minute Saisuke stepped through the door.

As one might expect, this had led to trouble. About two years ago, before Jingo knew Saisuke, another street thug took a fancy to one of the girls in the bar who'd been monopolizing Saisuke's attentions. Heated words were exchanged.

"Let's step outside and settle this, shall we…"

In a nearby alley, steel flashed as daggers were drawn. Saisuke "would've taken him for sure" in a fair one-on-one fight, but not even he could hold his own against *five* attackers. Having sustained several wounds, he had both his arms pinned back and was thinking to himself, *I'm a goner now*, when all of a sudden he heard his savior Jingo's voice.

Thereafter at every opportunity Saisuke would drop by his adopted "sensei's" dingy little back-street row house in Matsushiromachi with various offerings—rice, sake, offers of work, even money—until finally Jingo told him to knock it off. So now he just came round with offers of work. He couldn't help it that most of the time it was work as a bouncer at some gambling parlor or as a bodyguard to a rich merchant. In Saisuke's line of business that just come with the territory.

Just once, Saisuke showed up at Jingo's house with a seemingly respectable offer—a position as assistant instructor at the Keishin Itto dojo in Uedamachi. Jingo turned it down. It turned out the master of the dojo really wanted a ringer—a hired sword to take over when an outside opponent showed up seeking to challenge the master to a duel.

"I'm useless when it comes to *that*," Jingo said, waving him off.

His words surprised Saisuke. "C'mon now," he protested. "You were awesome that night you saved my neck, Jingo-sensei. You had those guys turning' on their heels before you even drew your sword."

"It was dumb luck. I didn't do anything—when you began thrashing about they just started falling over themselves and bumping into one other. Then other people came to see what the commotion was about…"

Thinking back on it, Saisuke had to admit it had happened just as Jingo had described, so he didn't push the matter. Still, tucked away in the back of his mind was the vivid memory of his tormentors scattering like cherry blossoms before the wind. *That wasn't dumb luck if you ask me*, he thought. But how could he explain Jingo's casual dismissal of so good a job offer, one truly worthy of a samurai? He couldn't help wondering if Jingo's massive build—he looked to be about twice Saisuke's size—and thick black beard were all an elaborate charade intended to conceal some inner weakness.

Since then, Saisuke had not brought Jingo any more job offers of that nature—until now.

"Get this, Jingo-sensei—the patron says he's willin' to go as high as twenty *ryo*."

"T-t-twenty!" Dumbstruck, Jingo stared at Saisuke's pointy-chinned face. A look of skepticism crept into his eyes. "How do I know you're not lying?"

"Look into my eyes."

"They're bloodshot."

Saisuke frowned, but the frown soon turned into a wry smile.

"Once I tell you what it's about, will you agree to do it?"

"Twenty *ryo*, right?"

Saisuke's smile grew bigger.

"I'll see what I can negotiate. Leave everything to me."

The job went off without a hitch.

"I *saw* that pretty daughter of yours and her lover boy going into a disreputable teahouse. I even know his name," sneered the man who was trying to extort money from one of the wealthiest lumber merchants in the fief. He was a scrawny two-bit thug, unremarkable in every respect save for the sinister glint in his eye.

When Jingo stepped out of his place of concealment to confront the blackmailer, the man took one look at this heavily bearded manifestation of one of the Buddha's guardian deities and blanched. Then he seemed to pluck up his courage, nimbly reaching into the breast of his kimono and pulling out a dagger.

"You got a death wish?" Jingo intoned ominously, nudging his sword from its sheath.

The man froze.

"You come around here one more time and your head will be looking for its shoulders. And don't even think of trying to run because I'll hunt you to the ends of the Earth. The master of the Kigoeya here will pay all my expenses, you see."

Afterward Jingo withdrew, having ascertained that the face of the Kigoeya's owner had assumed its usual color and confidence.

"You were great!" beamed Saisuke, stopping by Jingo's humble abode the next evening.

Jingo sat gazing for a while at the gleaming pile of twenty gold coins in front of him.

"I'm much obliged to you," he said, bowing his head.

"Whoa—c'mon now. No samurai should kowtow to the likes of me. You earned this money yourself, Jingo-sensei, fair and square."

"No, some of it is yours. Take what you like," he said before hurriedly adding, "Well, half of it anyway."

Saisuke leaned back and roared with laughter.

"That's what I like about you, Jingo-sensei! Don't worry—I got my share already from the owner of the Kigoeya. Go on—keep it all."

Saisuke looked on kindly as Jingo sheepishly wrapped the coins back up in the paper in which Saisuke had brought them.

When he was done, Saisuke made a gesture of tipping an imaginary glass to his lips.

"How 'bout it?" he asked. "Of course, drinks're on me."

"If you insist," said Jingo.

Bars lined the street in Saramachi, about a fifteen-minutes' walk from Jingo's row house. Though most of the bars' patrons were commoners, on any given night quite a few ronin could be seen frequenting the quarter, and some of the establishments even counted clan samurai among their regular customers.

Having helped Jingo polish off nearly ten flasks of sake, Saisuke paid the bill and stood up.

"Gotta get goin'—mustn't keep *you-know-who* waitin'," he said, holding up his little finger.

"Thanks for the drink," offered Jingo.

They parted ways outside the bar, and Jingo set off at a leisurely pace in the same direction from which they'd come.

If he'd been drunk, the cool breeze undoubtedly would have felt refreshing on his flushed skin, but in fact Jingo had sobered up long before leaving the bar.

He'd been casually casting his eyes about the room when he chanced to meet the man's stare. His drunkenness evaporated immediately. Furthermore, he knew he'd remain sober no matter how much he drank. Though he quickly looked away, he could still feel the man's eyes on him.

Upon leaving the bar the eyes had followed him.

They were following him now.

It was a moonlit night and he could see his way clearly. *If it were darker*, thought Jingo gloomily, *perhaps he'd give up and go away*.

He came to an area of town with vacant lots on either side of the road. He was about halfway home.

I don't want him to follow me home. Maybe this would be a good place to—

Just then he heard a voice behind him.

"All right—you can stop there."

Jingo's heart suddenly felt lighter. He turned his head to see a mountain of a man nearly six feet tall. Without a doubt it was the same man he'd caught staring at him in the bar.

Just as I thought.

At the same time he was puzzled.

The man was clearly a samurai of some considerable rank and cut a dashing figure in a fine kimono jacket and hakama. He appeared to be in his mid-thirties, that is, about four or five years older than Jingo. One look at his face was enough to know he was spoiling for a fight, and he looked confident he could win.

"What do you want?" asked Jingo, turning around to face the man.

"I've come about the Kigoeya," the other samurai replied in a low voice.

Had the would-be blackmailer hired him to exact revenge? Unlikely—this man was a different breed of samurai than Jingo. He had class. It was inconceivable someone like him could have any truck with a common criminal.

It crossed Jingo's mind the man might have been hired by the owner of the Kigoeya to shut him up, but he quickly dismissed the thought. A rich merchant like that must be fairly accustomed to blackmail and extortion. He could hardly go around bumping people off every time someone tried to shake him down.

"Maybe," Jingo muttered, "he's decided he paid too much—"

"—My name," continued the man at precisely the same moment, "is Asami Tosuke. I happen to be an acquaintance of the master of the Kigoeya. Today when I went to see him he told me what happened last night. He described how without even drawing your sword you struck terror in a hardened criminal and—"

Jingo raised his hand and cut the man off. He had the feeling a terrible misunderstanding had occurred.

"I'm afraid you've been misinformed. It was just this ugly mug of mine that scared him away. I'm hopeless when it comes to using *this*," he said, placing his left hand on the hilt of his sword and giving it a gentle shake as he stroked his cheek with his right. In the darkness, the man-mountain did not move.

"To hear the master of the Kigoeya describe it, you were a fearsome god. I scarcely credit that your face alone could have provoked such effusive praise; your inner strength must have revealed itself, wittingly or not."

"No, really—"

"I'd like to see what you are capable of. If you'll forgive my presumption… Now, draw!"

With these words, Asami Tosuke gave the hilt of his sword a nudge and whipped it from its sheath. The blade breathed in the moonlight.

"But why—?" Jingo stopped, realizing that any attempt at restraint was useless. His opponent had already assumed the *hasso* position, with the hilt of his sword over his right shoulder and the blade pointing straight up. His murderous intent was clear.

Presumption indeed! Sure, Jingo had done a rich merchant a favor in getting rid of a pesky blackmailer and received a pile of cash for a few minutes' work. But that was nothing to be ashamed of. Now along comes some guy who follows him out of a bar wanting to challenge him to a duel—all on the basis of an exaggerated account of his supposed martial prowess!

If Jingo drew his sword it meant a fight. Judging from Asami's determination, it seemed unlikely he'd back off once he'd sized Jingo up. It wouldn't end until one of them was dead. Jingo chaffed at the outrageousness of it, but he chaffed even more at the thought that he was probably going to die.

"On your guard!" With a sharp cry, Asami began to advance toward him.

A beautiful sound echoed through the darkness. Jingo blocked the strike. Asami hopped deftly away without pressing the engagement. Jingo did not pursue. On the contrary, he abruptly turned his back on his opponent and fled.

Out of the void of uncertainty that receded behind him emanated a cry of "Wait!" Paying it no heed, Jingo kept running. His entire body broke into a clammy sweat and his teeth clattered noisily in his mouth.

They did not stop until he was nearly home.

He groped around for a lantern. When at last it was lit he felt safe. He struggled to get his breathing under control. *My first real fight in years and it had to be against* that *monster!* He'd known he was in trouble the moment he saw Asami's stance. Behind the older man's arrogant presumption was an astonishing mastery of swordsmanship. It was nothing short of a miracle that Jingo had managed to block his first blow. *I don't buy that story of his... He's a madman.* That was why Jingo had turned tail and run. Flight was the best strategy against such an adversary.

Once he'd caught his breath Jingo felt the urge to have a drink. *If ever I needed a drink it was now.* However, he didn't have the energy to go out again.

Some more time passed

"Guess there's nothing left to do but turn in."

He flopped down on top of his thin, sweat-stained futon.

Fortunately, the drink he wanted found him.

There was a knock at the door.

Jingo shuddered.

Without answering, he drew his sword close.

"Excuse me," a voice called out.

It was the voice of Asami Tosuke. Before Jingo had made up his mind how to respond the wooden door slid open and a shaft of moonlight fell onto the earthen floor, the greater part of which was consumed by a large shadow.

"The master of the Kigoeya told me where you lived. I've come to apologize for my behavior. Please accept this token of my sincerity."

In the beam of moonlight Jingo saw the shadow of an outstretched arm holding aloft a large flask of sake, the contents of which sloshed merrily about as it swayed back and forth.

THE NEXT NIGHT Jingo went to visit a house in Teramachi, about an hour's walk from where he lived. The hour was already late. In the light of the lantern he'd borrowed from a tavern keeper some time back and not returned, an imposing wooden gate surrounded by black walls rose out of the darkness. He ducked through the small door set into the gate. The garden was elegantly laid out. It was the sort of place where one might expect to hear the strains of someone practicing a popular ballad.

In the moonlight he could make out a shadowy figure standing at the entrance of the house, which was plunged in darkness.

Holding out his lantern as he approached he quickly saw that it was Asami. He bowed silently. Asami returned the gesture and slid open the front door.

By the time Jingo crossed the threshold into the earth-floored vestibule, Asami had already stepped up into the corridor and lit a candle that had been left there.

"Did anyone see you?" he asked.

"No."

"Good—follow me."

Jingo had already extinguished his lantern. The light of the candle flickered on Asami's face, making him look like a ghost.

The two men walked along the corridor and went into a room. It was surprisingly large and tidy, judging from which there must be at least two servants in the house. It would appear Jingo's hunch—that this was the house of Asami's mistress—had been right. But where was she? And where was the person he was supposed to kill? Was he to wait there for them to come?

With these and other thoughts racing through his mind, Jingo kneeled down on the cushion in front of the tokonoma proffered to him by Asami. He removed his two swords and placed them on the floor to his left, for despite Asami's presence there was no telling if he might not be attacked at any moment; thus it would be suicide to place his swords to his right as proper etiquette required. He must assume he had walked into the enemy's lair.

Telling him to wait there for a moment, Asami exited the room, leaving Jingo alone with just a lantern for company. He couldn't imagine what might be about to happen. All he could do was wait. Stirrings of regret began to gnaw at his insides.

It was because of what had happened the previous night—because of the hour he had spent with Asami—that Jingo now found himself in this position.

Tonight and last night were connected…

Entering the house and stepping into Jingo's room, Asami seemed a different person from the one Jingo had seen outside in the street a little while earlier: he was calm and relaxed.

"My, you *are* good!" he said to Jingo with a laugh as carefree as a spring day.

Jingo eyed him warily.

"Come now," he continued, "no need to be modest. The way you blocked my sword is proof enough. Admit it—you didn't draw on me because you were forced to, did you?"

The stranger had seen right through Jingo. The surprise of this realization hit him like a slap in the face. The truth was that he had felt a bloodlust stir within his breast when he drew his sword.

"The thought of losing didn't even occur to you," continued Asami. "When we crossed swords a chill went down my spine. *What speed!* I thought. That's the Jikishin Kage style, right? Well, whatever it is, you've obviously mastered it."

Jingo said nothing.

"You didn't run because you were afraid of getting hurt. No, you were thinking, *I might hurt* him. That's why you ran—isn't that so?"

Asami had already poured himself several cups of sake by this point. Another teacup sat in front of Jingo. His uninvited guest had grabbed them from the cupboard by the front door as he stepped into the house. He didn't seem the least bit drunk.

What Asami said was true. Jingo had not been afraid of his opponent—it was *himself* he was afraid of. The physical trembling he'd experienced was not fear but excitement. Deep down his soul had rejoiced at the thrill of battle.

There was no longer any point pretending. Jingo reached out for the teacup that lay untouched before him.

Smiling, Asami picked up the sake flask and filled Jingo's cup, then waited as Jingo drained it dry. "My intuition is still as sharp as ever," he said, nodding. "When I heard the master of the Kigoeya's story, I just *knew*. You didn't disappoint me; you *are* as good as I thought…"

As he uttered the words, *I've got a favor to ask you,* Jingo detected a spark in Asami's eyes for the first time.

When Jingo flatly refused Asami bowed deeply and repeated his request more insistently. "Think of it as an act of kindness," he said. "Here—this is for your trouble."

He reached a hand into the breast of his kimono and brought it out again, then placed his clenched fist down on the tattered tatami. He drew it away to reveal a small, round bundle of purple cloth.

Jingo removed the cloth. Inside was something wrapped in white paper.

"Twenty-five *ryo*; your reward for an act of kindness…"

Jingo felt his resistance begin to crumble. *Easy now*, he admonished himself. But the fact was that the twenty *ryo* he'd received from the master of the Kigoeya would be gone in no time. Barring some unforeseen act of providence, it was unlikely he'd ever get his hands on so much money ever again. Imagining a never-ending succession of days spent gluing umbrellas, guarding rich merchants, and performing manual labor, Jingo heaved a deep sigh.

"And?" prompted a distant voice. Jingo realized it was his own.

"I'll give you the address of a house," said Asami. "I want you to go there tomorrow night, at one hour past midnight. There you will kill someone. Don't worry—I promise that you won't be inconvenienced in the least. I'll take care of everything. Of course, absolute secrecy is required—that's why I'm asking you, an outsider. I'll explain everything tomorrow when you come to the house. I know I'm asking a lot, but please say you'll accept. You can take the money now."

Asami paused and stared at Jingo, as though willing the spark in his own eyes to enter Jingo's. "There's one more thing I must say. The person I want you to kill is a skilled swordsman—my equal or perhaps even slightly better. You must understand that before you accept."

With these words, Jingo stopped resisting. Asami had frankly admitted that the man he wanted Jingo to kill was a very formidable opponent. If Jingo were to gamble on his life at least he would know what the odds were, and he could even take his winnings before placing the bet.

"Why can't you tell me the details *now*?" asked Jingo.

"In case you should happen to tell someone."

"Why don't you just do the job yourself?"

"I told you: he's better than me. That's why."

"And what will you do if I take the money and run?"

"Nothing—what could I do? It would just mean I was a poor judge of character."

Jingo steeled himself.

"Okay, I'll do it. But keep your money for now. I'll only accept it when the job is finished."

"Well… okay," said Asami, somewhat taken aback. "But at least accept half of it now."

For the first time, Jingo felt something akin to friendship toward his strange guest.

Jingo heard the floorboards in the corridor creak.

The sound came to a halt on the other side of the sliding doors. There was a pause—presumably while the person knelt down—and then he heard a woman ask permission to enter the room. Her voice did not sound all that young—he guessed she was about twenty-five. Its hollow ring disturbed him somewhat.

As she entered, Jingo's eyes grew wide.

She wore only a thin undergarment clasped around her waist with a narrow cord that cut into her ample flesh.

Bowing to him, she moved to the right-hand side of the sliding doors and sat on the floor. Her hair was tied up in a bun and fastened in front with a hairpin. Jingo's eyes moved down her body and came to rest on her plump, sensual bosom. There was an unmistakable brazenness about her.

Just then another woman entered the room.

The second woman was dressed in the same manner and appeared to be not much older than the first, but her hair was swept up in the matronly samurai style of a married woman, and her countenance and bearing bespoke refinement. Not only was her comportment more formal than the younger woman's, but her face bore a stiff expression—though not, it seemed to Jingo, out of shyness or hostility but rather tension, such as one might feel prior to some sort of test or competition.

The second woman went and sat to the left of the sliding doors.

Jingo could not imagine what was going on.

The first, more sensual of the two, must be the mistress of the house's owner, he mused. Was the other then Asami's wife? Surely Asami did not intend for him to kill one or both of these two women. Was his intended victim going to appear, and Asami as well, and if so what then?

The women sat facing him without moving a muscle, as though they, unlike him, were fully cognizant of what was going on. Their silent presence was suffocating.

He hadn't been told he mustn't speak, he considered. Should he say something? He was just about to open his mouth to ask a question when the first woman bowed deeply and said, "The master has explained everything." Head still lowered, she introduced herself as Oshigi, a singing instructor. Then she sat up again. "The master has done me the honor of asking me to keep madam here company this evening."

Here voice contained a note of—no, not irony—but contempt. Jingo turned his gaze to the woman seated beside her.

"My name is Sanae—I am Asami's wife," she said, betraying no emotion. She bowed to him silently.

Sanae… Jingo turned the name over repeatedly in his mind.

"My husband," she continued, "has instructed me to explain to you why he has asked you here tonight. May I proceed?"

"Of course." Jingo nodded.

Compared to Oshigi, Asami's wife was relatively slender and had clean, neat features, and her voice was clear and crisp.

"My husband was born with a strange, evil obsession; a curse you might say: anything that he loves he feels compelled to destroy."

Jingo said nothing.

"No doubt you find this hard to believe. But consider how many people there are in this world. It should not be surprising that among all these millions there should be a few who are less man than monster."

Was she really talking about Asami? Jingo thought of their first meeting in the street, when Asami had suddenly drawn his sword; of Asami sitting in his house, a carefree smile on his face, pouring himself cup after cup of sake.

"When my husband was seven years old, his father was cut down by an unknown assailant in the street. His mother was unharmed. My husband apparently did not get along at all with his mother. He also had a younger brother and sister, but when he was thirteen, his sister died in the same manner."

"And Asami and his brother—?"

"—fought like cats and dogs."

"And?"

A horrible expression rose to Sanae's face. Her voice shriveled to a whisper, like someone standing at death's door.

"You are to kill my husband before he kills one of us."

Sanae lowered her eyes. Jingo was at a loss for words.

Just then:

"The master certainly *is* a strange one," quipped Oshigi, her voice echoing across the room.

Sanae glared at her.

Oshigi put her hand over her mouth as though to say, *Whoops!*

"Forgive me," she apologized. "It's not my place to speak like that. It's just that… Well, the master *means* well, but even *I've* had my doubts about him."

"Meaning?" prompted Jingo.

"Well, as madam knows, when the master set me up in this house he bought me a dog, saying it wasn't safe for a woman to live alone. The dog was inordinately fond of him, and he of it—so much so I almost wondered if it wasn't the reincarnation of the child he'd lost long ago… Anyway, about four days ago I returned to the house to find the master in the garden, a big smile on his face, stroking the dog's head. They both seemed so happy and content I actually felt jealous. But what do you think happened next? All of sudden, his face became contorted, like a demon's, and without warning he stood up, drew his sword, and lopped off the dog's head, just like that. The poor creature barely had time to let out a yelp."

Jingo remained silent.

"I just stood there frozen, too shocked to utter a word. For a moment I thought, *Maybe this person isn't really the master*—but I knew in my heart it was. *He must've gone mad*, I thought; *maybe I'm next*. When he turned and looked in my direction, blood dripping from his sword, I thought, *Good gracious!* and nearly fainted dead away. But he did nothing… Thinking back on it, that's what made it a hundred times more eerie. The master just nonchalantly wiped his sword with his handkerchief and, smiling at me, said, 'I trust you are well, Oshigi?' He had the same look on his face as when patting the poor creature's head, which now lay pitifully on the ground.

'How could you *do* such a cruel thing?' I asked. That's when he confessed: 'It's my nature,' he said. 'Anything I love—anything beautiful—I feel compelled to kill. Once, as a child, I killed another dog, our family pet. I also killed the neighbor's cat. I don't know why, I just... They were so *adorable*, I couldn't help myself. Forgive me, Oshigi. Please forgive me!' 'I forgive you,' I replied. Then a chill ran down my spine. He wasn't talking about the *dog*... He was talking about *me*!"

"You said this happened four days ago," said Jingo. "Didn't you think of running away?"

"No," Oshigi replied in a small voice. She wore a contemptuous smile. But her eyes were on Sanae. "After all, *any* woman would be honored to spill her blood for the man she loved—wouldn't she?"

So that's the way it is, thought Jingo. He couldn't help but feel sorry for Asami's beautiful wife. With two women of such different temperaments and breeding thrown together, how could one expect anything but discord between them?

Oshigi's insinuation was so blatant as to be openly hostile. Jingo detected a slight tremor pass through Sanae's child-like cheeks, but that was all. Despite her slight advantage in age, the cloistered samurai lady was no match for the worldly ballad singer. All Sanae could do was bear her humiliation with dignity. If she could have cut her tormentor down it might have brought her some satisfaction, but as it was, her only solace seemed to be in remaining silent and not allowing herself to be provoked.

But why had Asami brought the two women together in the first place? If he loved Oshigi, then surely it was *she* whom he should kill. Just then a horrible thought began to take shape within Jingo's breast.

Before it could fully take shape, the doors to the room opened.

ASAMI ENTERED, smiling quietly. If they had been anywhere else Jingo would have returned his smile. Instead he reached for his sword and jumped to his feet.

"Stop, Asami."

"Out of my way," the older man said quietly.

His tone was friendly, but Jingo felt something cool trickle down his back. He nudged the hilt of his sword out of its sheath.

"This is why you brought me here, isn't it?"

In reply, Asami reached for the hilt of his sword. Jingo took one step forward, drew his sword, and executed a torso-sweeping strike, just missing Asami. *That was too easy*, he thought. The memory of Asami's jovial face the night before flashed through his mind.

Asami leapt backward into the sliding doors, knocking them off their runners as he crashed through them into the hallway. *That was calculated*, thought Jingo. He braced his front leg against the tatami in preparation for his next strike. By this time Asami had drawn his sword. Jingo's advantage had slipped away.

Asami advanced slowly towards him. As his foot made contact with the door on the ground at his feet, Jingo stomped hard on the tatami, momentarily upsetting Asami's footing and putting him ever so slightly off balance—this was perhaps Jingo's last chance for victory. But as he brought the tip of his blade down, Asami deftly pulled away.

He read me like a book! marveled Jingo. He had just begun to raise his sword when he felt a burning sensation shoot through his left shoulder and a cry of pain escaped his lips. Blocking out the pain, he changed his foot position. Now, with only one good arm, he was at a hopelessly disadvantage against Asami's next attack.

The distance between the two men widened.

Asami held his sword out in front of him at waist level, the tip pointed straight at Jingo's eyes. His face broke into a smile.

"Well done," he said. "That bastard chose his assassin well… Oh, wait—was *I* the one who hired you to kill me?"

Jingo frowned. What in the world was going on? Was the man an imposter? He scrutinized his opponent carefully—no, it was Asami all right.

"Yes," he answered at last.

"That damn coward! Still, what choice did I have? It's not as though I can kill *myself*."

"Are you *really* Asami?"

"What do *you* think?" "No matter," he laughed mockingly, "I'll be dead soon enough. Wait for me in hell."

Here he comes, thought Jingo. Concentrating, he put his left hand on his sword hilt. Asami seemed like a giant.

"Tosuke, dear—"

Jingo finally noticed Sanae standing beside him.

"If you want to kill someone, kill me."

Before either of them could stop her, Sanae stepped between Jingo and her husband. The next thing Jingo knew she had stripped off the single undergarment she was wearing to reveal an expanse of voluptuous white flesh beyond his wildest dreams.

"Out of the way!" barked Asami.

"No, kill *me* instead. Right here and now."

"Don't be ridiculous, madam."

The voice and figure of Oshigi approached Jingo from behind and moved past him. Now she too was completely naked. Jingo caught a whiff of something fragrant: the scent of womanly flesh.

"If the master is going to kill anyone," continued Oshigi, "it's *me*. Go ahead, my love—cut down this woman whom you have treated with such tenderness."

"Out of the way!" Asami repeated. "If you don't move, I'll cut you *both* down!"

"Go ahead, Tosuke, dear—kill me."

"No, my love. Kill *me*."

Jingo could not believe what he was hearing. Both women were in complete earnestness; each wanted Asami to kill *her*. Jingo found their sincerity touching to the point of pathos.

"No, I'll kill you both. I have nothing more to say; your wishes shall never be granted."

A ripple of alarm passed through the two women.

Asami broke into a broad smile. Sensing his opportunity, Jingo pushed the women aside and delivered a one-handed thrust, catching Asami completely off-guard. The tip of his sword went clean through the right side of Asami's chest, sending him flying backward. The gleaming blade reemerged. Asami spun around and set off running down the corridor toward the front door.

"Tosuke, dear!"

"My love!"

It was not the women's grief-stricken cries that prevented Jingo from chasing after him but the profuse amount of blood that had soaked his left arm right down to the end of his sleeve. He listened as the front door slid open and Asami's footsteps receded. Then he sank to one knee. He half expected one of the women to reach out a hand and help him to his feet.

Instead the figures walked past him toward the sliding doors on the other side of the room. They were slid open and first one woman and then the other disappeared into the next room.

When the doors had closed again Jingo rose and returned to the room. He felt his shoulder and stuck his fingers into the wound. It was about two fingerbreadths in size and fairly deep. Earlier, upon entering, he had noticed a bottle of distilled spirits and a bundle of white cloths in a corner of the room, no doubt left there by Asami for just such a purpose. The cloths had been cut into suitably long strips. Jingo wiped away the blood and poured the alcohol over the wound.

A low groan echoed through the dim light.

The wound was deep but did not seem especially serious. In the morning he'd go see a doctor.

Wait!—he panicked—*how will I pay?* Then he remembered the money.

At least the pain was a guarantee of one thing.

This isn't a dream—that's for sure.

Jingo bound his shoulder with several strips of cloth to stanch the bleeding. As soon as he'd finished dressing the wound the door slid open, as if on cue.

"You okay?" asked Asami.

"Come back for more, have you?"

An unpleasant desire for revenge welled up inside Jingo. He knew that underlying it was the pain of defeat. Deep in his heart he wished Asami were dead.

"So, couldn't kill me, could you?" Grimacing, Asami lowered his gaze for a few moments. When he looked up at Jingo again, there was a gentleness in his eyes. "Please don't ask me anything. This fulfills our agreement. Remember—what happened here tonight is not to leave this room. From this moment forward, you and I are complete strangers to one another. Understand?"

Jingo had promised to do as Asami said, except when it came to protecting his own life, and he intended to honor that promise; that was some consolation anyway.

The next day Saisuke paid one of his regular visits. Noticing Jingo's bandaged shoulder, he began asking him questions. But the samurai refused to give a straight answer.

Jingo had a premonition something bad was about to happen. He began to be tormented by nightmares of Asami wielding a bloody sword; he would awake screaming to find himself alone in the darkness of his room.

One night he entered a place both of this world and not of it at the same time. Though he somehow managed to escape, he was haunted afterward by the sensation of a long dark hand clamped on his shoulder. He knew that unless he cut off this hand he would never again be able to lead a normal life.

Oddly enough, Jingo did not seek solace in drinking or womanizing as other men might have. Instead he threw himself into making umbrellas. This newfound fervor for his adopted trade excited comment among the neighborhood housewives, who began whispering among themselves whenever they saw him.

One day, about a month later, one of them finally summoned up the courage to come over to his house to ask him if anything was the matter. The rumors, taking a bizarre shape, even reached the ears of the rent collector, much to Jingo's astonishment. "I hear"—he said, a smile plastered on his gargoyle face—"you are to be wed soon."

Around the time that the warm zephyrs of summer turned to chill autumn breezes, Saisuke came to Jingo with an offer of work. He said it was right up his alley. Jingo, who had at last begun to feel the dark cloud hanging over him lifting, accepted immediately. Unfortunately, both men were dead drunk at the time.

The next day Saisuke came by Jingo's house again.

"C'mon," he said, "let's go."

"Where to?"

"The Iizuka Dojo in Kamoncho needs a ringer," Saisuke announced calmly. Jingo's eyes grew wide.

A ringer—as the reader will recall—meant someone to fight on behalf of the dojo when the master or assistant instructor was absent or sick, or simply lacked confidence.

"A ringer? You *know* how I feel about that, Saisuke," Jingo replied, trying to back out.

Saisuke was undeterred. "But I just stopped by there on my way over; I promised I'd bring someone. Mind you, I've no direct connection to the place myself; it was his young lordship—he's in training there—who came personally to ask me to find someone. I can't go back there now and say it fell through. Anyway, don't you remember, Jingo-sensei?—'Leave everything to me,' you said last night, thumpin' your chest. Please, you've got to do it. The duel is set for two this afternoon—that's in less than an hour."

"But Saisuke, you *know* that when it comes to using a sword I'm—"

"What about your shoulder then? That was a pretty nasty wound if you ask me."

"What?"

"Listen, maybe I haven't got any formal sword training, but I'd venture to say I've been in more fights than you and I know this much: the fact you're still alive means the other guy looks even *worse* or else he's dead. Either way, sparrin' with wooden swords must be child's play to someone like you. That's why I thought of you for this job. Please, Jingo-sensei—I'm countin' on you."

Arriving at the dojo, Saisuke and Jingo were met by two samurai: one evidently the assistant instructor, the other the "young lordship" Saisuke had mentioned. The two introduced themselves as Nakazono Uemon and Koda Happei, respectively. Instead of showing Jingo through to a reception room, they dispensed with the usual formalities and took him straight to the dojo's changing room. This put him at ease.

While Jingo changed into his training costume, Assistant Instructor Nakazono departed, on his way out the door telling young Koda to look after things for him.

Their opponent that day—explained Koda to Jingo—was an itinerant performer by the name of Makiwa Bannai who had developed his own style of swordsmanship, which he called "Lightning-and-Fire." Two days ago he had shown up unannounced at the dojo and defeated the trainer on duty and several of the more senior pupils who happened to be there. Nakazone had been out at the time.

Bannai had also challenged the master of the dojo, Iizuka Shoichiro, to a duel. Bannai's technique was an eclectic blend of subtle movements and brute strength, and Iizuka, who was over sixty, no doubt realized he was no match for his challenger's aggressive attacking style.

"Some other day," Iizuka had replied vaguely, intending to put him off. Undeterred, Bannai had insisted on a date. Not wanting to be seen by his students as trying to wiggle out of it, Iizuka had been forced to accept.

When Assistant Instructor Nakazono returned the next day and heard about the humiliation the dojo had suffered, he was incensed. He ranted and raved about avenging their honor.

Iizuka had remained calm. "You're no match for him—we need a ringer."

Nakazono confided this to his three favorite pupils. One of them had been young Koda.

Koda's eyes, as he looked at Jingo, betrayed a mix of hope and concern. Jingo's appearance—the unkempt beard and ragged clothes—were at odds with what the young samurai had been led to expect by his savvy underworld contact, a veteran of many street brawls. Koda undoubtedly felt personally responsible for Jingo there. Though Jingo's prodigious size and strength usually inspired confidence, the well-bred young man seemed to adhere to a different set of standards.

"Will you be okay?" he asked nervously.

"Can't say," answered Jingo.

Koda looked even more worried.

As it turned out, the fight was over almost before it started.

Though Makiwa Bannai had the flair and determination of the professional performer, Jingo quickly ascertained a number of chinks in his armor.

After exchanging one or two blows, for example, he noticed that when Bannai withdrew his sword after a strike he had a habit of pausing for a few fractions of a second to readjust his stance.

It was obviously unconscious, and the pause was so brief that even a very skilled opponent might not have noticed, but against Jingo it was a fatal weakness.

After their third exchange of blows, Jingo waited; the instant Bannai withdrew his sword, Jingo lunged forward and struck at his throat. It was a beautifully executed and unimpeachable strike—not strong enough to kill but not weak enough to leave him any ideas about pulling such a stunt again.

Bannai's body sailed across the dojo, crashed into the wainscoting on the other side of the room, and lay perfectly still.

Afterward, Jingo was shown through to an inner room where he received his remuneration, though he declined Nakazono's offer of food and drink. He found such formalities tedious, and besides, he could tell from Nakazono's excessive courtesy that the assistant instructor considered his services, and his presence, no longer necessary. Koda, meanwhile, was staring at Jingo with awe. Jingo's own attention, however, was riveted just over Koda's shoulder, on a woman who had come into the room carrying a tray of tea and cakes.

Her beautiful countenance—averted demurely downward to avoid his gaze—reminded him a delicate flower. She seemed a different person entirely from the voluptuous beauty whose naked flesh he'd glimpsed at the house of Asami's mistress a few months before.

"My name is Sanae," she said, politely introducing herself as though for the first time. "I am Iizuka-sensei's granddaughter."

"Sanae…" murmured Jingo quietly to himself.

NAKAZONO AND KODA were unable to hide their astonishment when Sanae announced that she wished to speak to Jingo alone for a few moments. But prompted by a stern look that belied her delicate beauty they grudgingly withdrew.

"I didn't think I'd ever see you again," said Sanae as soon as their footsteps had died away, getting right down to business. It appeared she had no intention of pretending that nothing had happened that night. Jingo liked her style. *But*, he wondered, *what is she doing here?*

She seemed to read his thoughts.

"This is the house," she said, "where I was raised."

Sanae explained that her parents had both died when she was young and, since neither of her two elder brothers had any interest in sword fighting, her grandfather planned to hand the dojo over to one of his students.

"I just returned today," she continued. "It's been ages since I was last home. It never occurred to me you might—"

"Indeed," said Jingo, bowing his head. He felt as though the memory of that bizarre night, which had begun to fade from his memory, was unfurling its wings and enfolding the two of them in its dark embrace. He tried to resist, knowing at the same time it was useless.

"And your wound?" she asked him in dead earnestness, just as he was about to announced that he must be leaving. The look of concern on her face was impossible to ignore.

"A mere scratch," he replied, "I've already made a full recovery. It's as though it never happened."

Sanae closed her eyes and breathed a deep sigh of relief. "Thank goodness," she murmured.

She ought never to have been there that night, he thought, *it didn't concern her*—that much he was acutely aware of.

Resignation urged him forward.

"And your husband—?"

Sanae glanced down at the floor before looking at Jingo. *Do you really want to know?* her fervent expression asked. Jingo nodded.

"I went straight home that night," she explained. "My husband had left a palanquin waiting nearby."

"Then he hadn't intended to kill you after all?"

"He had—it was meant for *him* not for me."

"But in the end your husband killed neither you nor his mistress?"

"Correct."

She said Asami had explained that his love hadn't been strong enough.

"Then why did he ask me there that night?"

"Things didn't go according to plan, it seems. He'd intended to do it, but when he reached for his sword his feelings failed him—apparently it happens sometimes."

So instead he'd threatened to kill them both.
"Then the two of you are still waiting?"
"Yes."
Jingo looked into her eyes. She quickly lowered her gaze.
So she would wait patiently for her husband to kill her—was *that* the proof of his love she sought? If so, Jingo could only feel sadness for her. Her husband had a mistress who was confident he loved *her* more than his wife. But perhaps Sanae felt that, too, was only natural.
Jingo told himself that now was a good time to make his exit.
"Well, take care of yourself," he said, rising to his feet.
Just then he heard her voice.
"If he kills her, I won't be able to go on living." Her words tumbled out, as though she had something in her mouth that she was chewing on as she spoke.
Jingo tried to convince himself that day was far off.

Sanae and Koda saw Jingo off at the front door.
Jingo bid them farewell and, as etiquette dictated, walked to the front gate without looking back. Then he passed through, still without turning, and set off down the street.
Sanae's parting words—*I won't be able to go on living*—rang in is ears for some time.
As he came to the next corner, Saisuke suddenly appeared from the gap between the walls on his left.
"I know you're good, Jingo-sensei," he said, "but all the same, winnin' 's a matter of luck, ain't it? To be honest I was gettin' a bit worried 'bout you…"
"You're too kind."
"C'mon, cut it out," chided Saisuke. "Don't look so serious all the time!"
He invited Jingo to join him for a drink, and the two men set off for a bar in Teramachi.
Saisuke was in high spirits. He'd already heard the result of Jingo's duel from Koda's attendant, who'd been at the dojo.
"I was right about you all along, Jingo-sensei, wasn't I? Listen, I can get plenty more work like that for you if you want it, so if

anyone comes round askin' you to be a bouncer at some gamblin' joint, don't do it, you hear?"

"Okay, okay," replied Jingo feebly. It'd been a long time since he'd sparred and his nerves and muscles were frazzled—he needed to unwind. He could feel the alcohol going straight to his head. But he still couldn't get drunk.

As he felt the alcohol spread through the pit of his stomach with each gulp, Sanae's words kept coming back to him:

I won't be able to go on living.

A forest of white sake flasks grew up around him, to no avail.

"You all right, Jingo-sensei?" Saisuke asked solicitously.

Just then a samurai seated at a table near the doorway stood up and came over.

"You'll forgive the intrusion," he said by way of greeting. He appeared to be in his late twenties. "I hesitated to interrupt your fun—that and the sensitive nature of what I wanted to discuss—but I thought that if I didn't I might not get another chance. So that's why I came over. Anyway, I—"

The young samurai paused and glanced at Saisuke.

"Go ahead, take your time," said Saisuke, rising and looking around the room for another place to sit. "I'll be over there."

"Thank you."

"Don't mention it." Saisuke flashed his white teeth and went and sat at table some distance away.

"Shall we go to a private room?" Without further prompting, Jingo rose. "My name is Iizuka Sohei," he continued in the same courteous tone, once they were seated behind closed doors. "My grandfather is the master of the dojo you visited a little while ago. I am Sanae's elder brother."

There's no escape, is there? thought Jingo with a deep inward sigh.

To Jingo's surprise, Sohei was already cognizant of Asami's bizarre proclivities. What's more, while Jingo had been sparring with Bannai, Sanae had told her brother all about what had happened 'that night.' Though Sohei was the younger of Sanae's two elder brothers—and therefore still lived at home with their grandfather—he'd been very close to his sister ever since they were children.

Even after her marriage, Sanae, on her rare visits home, would confess things to Sohei—the truth about her husband included—that she dared not tell any of her other siblings.

"To be honest," Sohei told Jingo, "I could scarcely credit it at first. But I know my sister never lies. 'Don't go back to him,' I told her, 'I'll speak to Grandfather about it.' But she said, 'Please don't breathe a word of this to Grandpa or Kihei'—that's our elder brother—'When I married I gave myself body and soul to my husband, for better or worse.'"

"She's a brave woman."

"I for one cannot agree," said Sohei, suddenly becoming impassioned. "What Sanae says is wrong. If Asami loved no one but her, then even I would bow to the inevitable and accept her sacrifice. But he has a mistress—and has for more than five years, from what I hear. The thought of him weighing my sister against that *whore* like some piece of merchandise and saying, 'I'll kill the one I love more; the other shall just have to grin and bear it'—Why, it's sheer lunacy! My sister may be willing to put up with it, but I won't have it I tell you! It's simply unacceptable!"

Overcome with emotion, Sohei broke off and rested his clenched fists on his knees, which trembled violently. The veins stood out on his temples so much that Jingo feared they might burst. This young man and his sister obviously enjoyed a stronger bond than any married woman ought. Wasn't that in itself the opening for a whole new tragedy?

"Excuse me for asking," said Jingo, once Sohei's excitement had subsided, "but what do you intend to *do* about it?"

"What would *you* do?"

"There's nothing one can do," said Jingo. "It's a private matter between husband and wife."

"How can you say that having fought on behalf of my sister?"

"You've got it all wrong," countered Jingo. "Asami hired me to fight him. To be perfectly blunt, I did it for the money. It's obvious he despises his nature and is ashamed of his behavior. Why don't we let the two of them work it out on their own?"

"Asami kills that which he loves. If he lets my sister live, that means he doesn't love her. As a wife, to outlive his mistress would be an insult worse than death. I've no doubt she'd choose to take her own life."

I won't be able to go on living.

Sohei stared off into space. "I intend to kill him," he murmured.

"Don't be a fool."

"No, that was rash of me," said Sohei in a suddenly lighthearted tone, as though his fiery determination of a moment earlier were a distant memory. He reached for a flask of sake. "Forget I said it."

The final blow to Jingo's fatalism came five days after his encounter with Sanae's brother at the bar when one evening Asami himself dropped by his house.

Hearing a knock on the storm door, Jingo assumed it must be Saisuke. To his surprise, he heard Asami announce himself.

"What do you want?" asked Jingo.

"Hide me—I'm being pursued."

Asami had apparently been passing through the neighborhood when he'd remembered Jingo lived nearby. Giving in to the inevitable, Jingo opened the door.

Asami entered smiling and looking completely unconcerned. Once inside, however, he shut the door quickly, though not before peering out to see if his unnamed pursuer was there. Jingo took this as a sign the stated reason for this unexpected intrusion was not a fabrication.

"Now *who* exactly is chasing you?" asked Jingo, once they were seated in the tatami room.

"I don't know," replied Asami. "He must have been following the light of my lantern... But say, Sanae told me you trounced some interloper at her grandfather's dojo. I guess you've improved—or should I say you've just come into your own?"

Jingo did not answer.

"C'mon, don't give me that look. I know you're capable of more than what I saw that night. How about it—want a rematch?"

"Asami, there's something"—Jingo peered into Asami's face, which reflected the flickering lamplight like a mirror—"I want to ask you."

"What is it?"

"Do you have a doppelganger?"

This time it was Asami's turn to remain silent.

"You see, I just realized something," Jingo continued. "When you came to my house before, you sat in exactly the same place, with the lamp exactly as it is now. But the Asami then was different from the Asami now."

Asami looked at Jingo with narrowed eyes.

Jingo recalled how the seeds of doubt had been planted that night at the house of Asami's mistress. The shoulder strike that had wounded him clearly belonged to an altogether different style of swordsmanship than the blow he'd blocked during their very first duel. Then there was something else: the matter of Asami's clothes. When he'd met Jingo at the door that night he'd been wearing a gray kimono jacket and hakama, but when he returned to the room later his clothes had had a bluish tinge. After the fight, he'd reappeared wearing the same gray outfit as before. He didn't seem wounded in the least. Jingo had convinced himself that he must have only grazed his opponent, but thinking back on it later...

At first Jingo had concluded Asami must have a twin. But in that case there'd have been no need for the deceit of asking Jingo to kill him. Even assuming there *were* some plausible reason, why hadn't Sanae said anything to Jingo at her grandfather's dojo about her husband having a twin?

Which left only one—very bizarre—conclusion:

"You know what *I* think? I think there are *two* Asami Tosukes," he said, "and they detest one another. I can imagine you'd never be able to relax with a doppelganger hanging around all the time—your strengths and weakness laid bare, constantly on display. And if your other self had a compulsion to *slaughter* the ones you loved... well, you'd *have to* kill him, wouldn't you, though it'd be like killing yourself. Yes, of course... What else *could* you have said but 'I want you to kill me'? Even if you'd told me the truth, I wouldn't have believed you."

"You've got it all wrong," said Asami, grabbing the sword on the floor beside him.

Jingo reached for his too. Asami rose but made no move to draw his blade.

"There's only one Asami Tosuke," he continued. "Since you say it was my sword that led you to this conclusion, then let me use my sword to disabuse you of it."

JINGO FOLLOWED Asami outside. There was a bright half moon.

Despite Jingo's initial fears, Asami showed not the least sign of wanting to commence the duel. Instead he walked to the end of the street and set off calmly in the direction of a nearby shrine.

When they reached the stone steps leading to the shine, Jingo noticed that Asami had put away his lantern; it must have been one of those collapsible types.

"Wait here a moment," commanded Asami. He looked up and down the street. Nothing stirred except the wind. Suddenly, at the top of his lungs, he shouted, "Asami Tosuke is here!"

Jingo winced as Asami's voice shook the air and echoed through the night. The houses all around remained dark; the entire neighborhood seemed fast asleep.

Jingo began to think his companion had gone mad as Asami continued looking around and calling out in all directions. Then he suddenly uttered a sharp "Ah-hah!" and stood still, facing west. In the moonlight, Jingo saw a man walking toward them along the narrow path.

Seeing them, the man kept up his pace until he finally stopped a little more than ten feet away from Asami. He was breathing hard. It would appear he had been searching for Asami for some time. It was Iizuka Sohei.

Jingo sighed. "Don't do it, Sohei," he said. But one look at the young's man rigid expression told Jingo it was useless. His resignation began to turn to anger. So this was why Asami had dragged him out of his house in the middle of the night—to show him *this*.

"I've been following him for two days," said Sohei. "It's useless interfering. This is a grudge match between me and him." Sohei's tone was cold and impersonal, as though relaying a message to a complete stranger. "If I die," he went on, "don't go to any trouble on my account—just leave my body where I fall."

"Well, at least I'm glad to see you're prepared." Asami had just removed his kimono jacket.

Sohei followed suit. Underneath his jacket the sleeves of his kimono were already tied back with a sash.

Two blades glinted in the moonlight.

Both men assumed the middle position with their swords out in front, pointed at their opponent's eyes. Sohei made the first move, raising his sword over his head and bringing it down in a magnificent stroke. There was a satisfying *clang!* of metal as Asami easily blocked it and stepped back. While Asami's stance remained rock solid, Sohei began to wobble: the apparent effortlessness of Asami's blocking maneuver belied a skillful application of force designed to off-balance his opponent.

Asami waited for Sohei to recover his balance. This infuriated the younger samurai, who turned white with rage.

Then with a piercing screech Sohei charged Asami. No sooner did they meet than Sohie's battle cry became a shriek. He took five or six more steps forward, then dropped his sword and fell face down in an ungainly heap. The ground trembled ever so slightly.

Jingo rushed to the young man's and felt his pulse; he was dead. Jingo's anger swelled up like a balloon until it was ready to explode.

Asami wiped the blood from his sword and returned it to its sheath. "Serves him right for lifting his sword against his own kith and kin," he said, "even if I am just his brother-*in-law*." There was laughter in his voice.

Oddly enough, the image that popped into Jingo's head at that moment—blocking out the sight of the young man's grotesquely twisted body at his feet—was Sanae's pale, ethereal beauty.

I won't be able to go on living.

"Not so fast," said Jingo, his right hand resting on his sword hilt. "Don't sheathe your blade just yet." Jingo, a fire burning in his belly, nudged the hilt of his sword from its sheath. "The Asami *I* know didn't strike that blow. I don't know if you're a shape-shifter in Asami's guise or what, but I'd draw if I were you. It's time to meet your maker."

"A shape shifter, huh?" Asami looked calmly at Jingo. He seemed not the least phased by Jingo's murderous glare and made no move to draw his sword. "Assuming," Asami went on, "that this bizarre explanation you've concocted is correct, then how can you—how can *anyone*—claim to be able to distinguish the *real* Asami from the *false* Asami?"

Jingo said nothing. Asami continued:

"Tell me, how did you conclude *I* was the false Asami in the first place? Wasn't it simply because you met the *other* me first? Or was it because the *me* you crossed swords that night is the same *me* who just cut down Iizuka? Now, is that a sound basis for distinguishing truth from fiction?"

Jingo felt his strength drain from his body. Even supposing what the Asami standing before him said were true, it didn't alter the fact that it was Asami *himself* Jingo was angry with.

"—but regardless, the fact is *I'm* the one you're angry with," continued Asami, as though reading Jingo's mind. "Which means, let's see now... Why don't we settle this at a later date? I imagine *this*"—he indicated Sohei's lifeless body—"will take a while for me and my in-laws to sort out. I'll come to your house once all the fuss has died down. All right?" Jingo nodded, though he himself was unsure why. "Please, allow me," added Asami, hoisting Sohei's corpse onto his shoulder. "I wouldn't want to offend your delicate sensibilities." With that, he disappeared into the night.

For some time Jingo remained rooted to the spot. He felt as though he was staring into a dark abyss opened up by the monstrous Asami, his demure wife, and his sensuous mistress.

Finally, hearing voices in the direction from which Sohei had come, Jingo finally set off for home, taking the abyss with him.

Jingo came to hear a great deal about the goings-on at the houses of Asami and his late brother-in-law. His informant was the well-connected Saisuke, who claimed to be related to one of the maids in the Iizuka household.

"It seems Sohei's family suspects Asami of being involved in their son's death," the mobster informed him. "Word has it that he's always been a bit odd, which is why his servants don't stick around long. I hear his wife's a comely, good-natured sort, but a bit on the gloomy side on account of her husband's strange proclivities—like one of those artificial flowers encased in glass, people say."

"Let me ask you about those 'proclivities'—"

"Yes?" The serious tone of Jingo's voice made Saisuke sit up straight.

"I don't suppose you've heard it rumored that Asami's got an identical twin?"

Saisuke waved a dismissive hand in the air.

"Never," he replied. "But now you mention it, people *do* say he's got extreme mood swings. Just the other day, I hear, he was walkin' around with a smile on his face, saying kind things to everyone right down to the old footman; the next day, veins were popping out on his temples and he was threatenin' to thrash the scullery maid—like there were two people in the house with the same face."

About ten days after his conversation with Saisuke, Jingo received a visit from a member of Asami's household, an old manservant by the name of Heisaku. He informed Jingo that his mistress wanted to meet him the following day at a teahouse in Akemiyacho. Jingo agreed. His heart grew heavy at the memory of Sanae's brother being cut down before his very eyes while trying to defend her honor.

Sengoku—the place Sanae had chosen for their rendezvous—was widely considered the most reputable of Akemiyacho's half dozen or so teahouses. Unlike other establishments, such as *Red Silk* and *Mount Penglai*, which offered their waitresses' sexual services to customers on the side, *Sengoku* counted many high-ranking clan samurai among its clientele.

Arriving at the teahouse, Jingo was shown through to a secluded private room looking out onto an immaculately tended Kyoto-style garden. Seated gazing out of the window, lending the scene outside even more quiet refinement, was the woman who had summoned him there.

As Sanae turned her white countenance toward him, Jingo found himself incapable of speech. Managing a curt bow, he kneeled on the cushion across the small table from her.

A serving woman brought tea. Jingo emptied his cup his in one gulp.

Sanae was the first to speak. "My brother Sohei is dead."

Jingo put down his cup.

"My brother's attendant," continued Sanae, "was present the day you came to my grandfather's dojo—perhaps you spoke to him?"

"No," answered Jingo quickly. Before coming, he'd intended to tell her everything, holding nothing back. But the moment he laid eyes on her he'd changed his mind. He knew Sanae already suspected that her husband had murdered her brother. Confirming it would only make the poor woman's suffering that much worse.

"I never met your brother either," said Jingo. "I hadn't heard about his death—I'm sorry."

"Oh, I see." Sanaei's shoulders drooped. He hadn't noticed before now how narrow they were.

He felt there was more she wanted to tell him, but for his part Jingo could think of nothing to say.

It's over, he thought. What had he ever seen in this beauty who belonged to another man? From the beginning, he'd had nothing to say to her.

He rose. "I'm sorry to have disappointed you."

Sanae remained silent. He'd just crushed any hope she had left.

As he put his hand on the door to open it, he glanced over his shoulder one more time. He saw a woman staring down at the table, not moving a muscle. He understood her, but she understood nothing about him.

Without another word, Jingo slid the door aside and stepped out into the corridor.

Asami's words continued to haunt Jingo like a curse.

He felt the urge to get drunk but he ignored it and headed home instead.

As he approached his house, Jingo saw a crowd of people outside. Catching sight of him, one woman came running over. It was the wife of the plasterer who lived three doors down from him on the right.

To his astonishment, she offered him her congratulations.

"So you're to receive an official commission at last!" she exclaimed. "A *very* important looking samurai arrived a while ago to see you."

In the dark drawing room, Asami Tosuke bowed silently to Jingo. "I'd like you to come to Oshigi's house again."

Jingo flatly refused. "Excuse me, but *which* Asami are you?"

Asami's face twisted into a rueful smile. "The Asami who asked you to save the lives of two women— that one."

"But are you the real Asami or the false one?"

"Beats me. I thought *I* was the real one, but *he* seems to think otherwise."

"Have you spoken to him?"

"I can't. When he's around I black out," explained Asami, "and it seems no one can see me. I only found out there was *another* me once when I heard my family talking about something he'd done. They all thought he was *me*."

Asami maintained there'd been two of him from the time he was born. Everyone—from his nursemaid to his old manservant—had always thought they were one and the same. Only the two Asami Tosukes knew differently. He'd lived with the secret his entire life.

"Sometimes," continued Asami, "we'd have an especially perceptive servant who seemed to guess the truth—I remember getting some strange looks. Perhaps my parents suspected and just never said anything."

"But did you know he intends to kill your wife?" inquired Jingo, getting to the heart of the matter.

Asami nodded, his face turning suddenly grave. "It seems *I*— meaning *he*—told Sanae my love for her was stronger than ever before."

Which meant, Jingo knew, a tragedy was about to play out at Oshigi's house. If her husband killed her, Sanae would die contented; if not, she'd take her own life. But the slaughter would not end with her death.

"What will happen to you," asked Jingo, "if I kill the *other* you?"

"I don't know. If I *am* the real me, then I'd like to think I'll remain here among the living. But perhaps that's wishful thinking. I'll tell you this much, though, I'm not afraid of death. On the contrary, it intrigues me."

An intense anger welled up in Jingo's breast. Something about Asami's answer rubbed him the wrong way, but he didn't know exactly what.

"It seems," said Jingo, "it'd be best for everyone if I killed you *both*."

Asami grunted and began stand up. "So," he said, "you accept?"

"First I wish to ask one more thing."

"Be my guest."

"Either the other Asami will deem your wife sufficiently worthy of his affection and kill her, or she will take her own life. How do *you* feel about that? Will you tell her it's not your doing? Have you ever thought of running away from here with her?"

"That's not my prerogative."

Jingo shuddered. "You don't mean—!"

"Yes," said Asami, as though uttering a curse, "*I* wasn't the one who married her."

Jingo was speechless.

"At some point," Asami explained, "Sanae realized she had two husbands. But she said nothing to me. She knows what type of man she married, and that made her love *me* all the more. One night, in bed, she broke down in tears: 'Why couldn't I have married *you?*' she asked. That's when I realized I had to do everything I could to protect her… Tell me, Jingo—is Sanae my wife or does she belong to another?"

"A woman—a woman belongs to the man who loves her. That's as it should be. But—" A thought had begun to form in Jingo's mind. "Okay. I'll do it."

"I'm much obliged. I wouldn't have asked you if I didn't consider Sanae to be my wife. But as long as *he* is alive, I'm helpless to act."

"When will he appear?"

"I don't know. If I knew *that*, none of this awful—" Asami broke off in mid-sentence. Finally, he said, "Tomorrow night; same time, same place." Then he left.

The hubbub in the street outside had died away.

Jingo felt his spirits rise. He wasn't alone after all. Something burned in his breast: a desire to fight. Just now, Jingo had felt sorry for Asami. That sense of pity was what had aroused this desire.

I shall prevail.

He didn't know where his actions would lead or what fate lay in store for him—or for Asami or Sanae for that matter—but he knew it would be a fitting end to this long dark episode.

EVERYTHING WAS AS BEFORE. The same moonlit night, the same sequence of events:

Entering by the unlocked front gate, Jingo found his host waiting at the front door; Asami showed him through to an inner room and withdrew, leaving him alone; Jingo waited, kneeling on the tatami; after a while, two women entered.

Without even looking, Jingo knew it was Oshigi and Sanae. Moreover, it was obvious nothing that had occurred during the intervening months had succeeded in altering either Oshigi's or Sanae's mental state. The realization cast a pall over his mood.

Even in the room's dim light Oshigi radiated confidence. Sanae stared quietly down at the floor. *Merciful lord*, prayed Jingo, *let her husband appear soon.*

The time ticked away. Oshigi, apparently growing bored, repeatedly attempted to engage Jingo in conversation and made insinuating remarks to Sanae. Both ignored her. They had been waiting an hour longer than on Jingo's previous visit when finally he heard footsteps and sensed someone's presence on the other side of the door.

As it slid open, Jingo rose to his feet. "Miss Oshigi," he asked, "do you love Asami?"

"Indeed I do."

Oshigi's flushed alluringly from her face down to her chest.

"And you, madam?" Jingo asked Sanae.

Just then Asami entered the room, holding a sheathed sword in his left hand. He looked at Jingo and grinned.

"Ah, you again—I hired you, did I?"

"Please," implored Oshigi, opening the front of her thin undergarment, "kill *me!*"

"Oh, fear not—this time I shall, my beloved."

Seeing Asami's right hand reach for the hilt of his sword, Jingo took a gliding step across the floor and, in one smooth motion, drew his blade and struck. Asami blocked it with his sheathed sword without flinching and circled to his right.

"How about it, madam?" asked Jingo, still waiting for an answer to his question. He stared straight at the tip of Asami's sword, holding his own blade pointed down and to his right. "Do you love your husband?" There was only one way to save Sanae. When no answer came, he continued, "Well, it doesn't matter if you do or not—I'm not going to allow him to kill either of you."

With a short intake of breath Asami lunged. Jingo knew the shallow strike was a feint. He easily deflected his opponent's blade and waited for his next attack. To his relief, this time he felt calm and his breathing remained normal.

"By the way," said Asami, "does Sanae know you were next to me the night I killed Sohei?"

Sanae's shock was palpable—Jingo's heart skipped a beat. Sensing he'd been rattled, Asami attacked again.

Jingo managed to block the first blow, but the second one caught him on the side of the shoulder and bit into his flesh.

A thought flashed through Jingo's mind:

If you flinch you're finished.

Sensing victory in his grasp, Asami raised his sword over his head and prepared to strike. Jingo followed his blade with his eyes and lunged at Asami.

For a split second, a smile rose to Asami's lips and Jingo's face registered astonishment. But it should have been the other way around—Jingo should have been the one smiling.

A voice went off inside his head: *It can't be! What's going on?* His thrust was steady and true, with plenty of force behind it. It caught Asami just above the solar plexus, passed clean through his chest, and emerged out his back. As the sword entered his body the air came rushing out of his lungs, and Jingo's forward momentum sent Asami crashing against the wall.

Jingo twisted his blade as hard as he could and began to withdraw it. As he did, Asami pitched forward, as though grasping at the sword. As soon as the tip emerged, he sank to the ground.

For a few moments there was complete silence. Jingo took one or two breaths. Then a clamor of women's voices erupted.

"My love!"

"Tosuke, dear!!"

Oshigi rushed over and picked up Asami's sword with both hands from where he had dropped it. "You bastard!" she cried. "My love, I shall avenge your death!"

With his upper body, Jingo gently batted away the blow she leveled at him. Then, grasping her elbow with his left hand, he pinned her arm behind her so she couldn't move. She continued to shout defiantly.

"Stop!" groaned a voice down at their feet.

"My love!"

Asami placed his right hand under his chin and raised his head. His eyes looked past the two figures standing before him, searching for some other shape.

Sanae was standing as still as a statue in front of the sliding doors, staring down at her husband and the dark stain slowly spreading from under his body across the floor. She had not moved since Oshigi had rushed to pick up the sword.

"Tosuke, dear—"

"My love, which of us—?"

There were tears in Oshigi's voice. As Jingo relaxed his grip, she stumbled forward and sank to the floor beside her lover.

"I... can't say... who I love more..." murmured Asami in a hoarse whisper, which was rapidly losing its strength even as he spoke. "Jingo... *you* understand, don't you? I..." Asami's pupils suddenly clouded over, his head slumped forward, and his limbs went limp. Then his whole body seemed to implode—Jingo had never before seen anything like it.

Just before he died, Asami called out a name. As though in reply, the two women gasped in unison—quietly, but to Jingo it sounded like a peal of thunder.

The draft seeping into the house through the gaps between the doors and windows bore the harsh chill of winter.

Jingo continued gluing oilpaper to the frames of the umbrellas, even though the fading light filtering into the room told him that outside dusk was gathering.

As his thoughts turned to how Sanae had been keeping herself these past few days, he was gripped by a terrible fretfulness.

At least, he thought, her husband must be doting on her lovingly. That night she'd watched as the other Asami Tosuke, cut down by Jingo's sword, had faded away like a dream and vanished into thin air, releasing Sanae from the menace she'd been under. When Oshigi screamed bloody murder and threatened to go to the authorities, Sanae responded by lopping off the hussy's right ear, then shut her up with a promise of fifty *ryo*.

Jingo had left after receiving his fee—twenty-five *ryo*—from the real Asami, who'd reappeared soon afterward. Jingo didn't so much as look at Sanae or speak to her, nor had he since.

There were a number of things he would have liked to ask her, but he'd resolved not to think about her. It no longer mattered. Soon he would even forget her face.

"Tosuke" was the name Asami had uttered the instant before his life left his body. When all was said and done, were human beings only capable of loving themselves? Perhaps in deliberately exposing himself to Jingo's sword, Asami had achieved a kind of true love.

There was a tap on the door. The lightness of it struck fear in Jingo's heart.

Before he could answer, the door opened and a samurai entered. His sleeves were tied back ready for battle.

Jingo knew his face. "So, Nakazawa, you've come." There was a note of nostalgia in his voice.

"Yes. Oi and Suda too." The man's voice was like a wintry sea. "The clan does not rest in tracking down a deserter, much less one who murdered his wife in cold blood. For what it's worth, Takeuchi committed suicide."

When Jingo had discovered his wife's affair, he'd cut her down without so much as demanding an explanation. It was at that moment he'd realized how much he loved her.

No doubt his pursuers had tracked him down through the money he'd secretly sent back home to his parents.

Jingo calmly picked up a sword and went outside.

His neighbors, concern written on their faces, had come out of their houses to watch from a safe distance. It irked Jingo that theirs were the last faces he'd see before he died, but given what he'd done it had probably been inevitable.

Oi and Suda were waiting outside with another samurai whose face Jingo didn't recognize. The four men surrounded him and began walking toward the temple where Asami had struck down

Sanae's brother. It seemed he was fated to meet his end in the same place.

Inside the temple precincts, four more men were waiting.

"Let's hurry up and get this over with—it'll be dark soon."

At the sound of Nakazawa's voice, eight swords were unsheathed.

Jingo, drawing his as well, tried without success to picture his wife Sanae's face. He wasn't even sure *which* Sanae he was trying to remember.

As the circle of figures closed in around him, the rays of the setting sun glinted on eight swords.

The Sparring Partner

AH, DETECTIVE. Come in. You're here about my husband again, I presume. You must've had a strenuous journey in this deep snow. Fancy a city person like you, who's lived in Edo all his life, braving the Oshu Road and trekking all the way up north to Mutsu at this time of year! But then again, you hail from these parts, don't you?

You know, even all these years later I still don't know what to make of it... Oh? Is that so? I'm terribly sorry to hear that. To look at you one would never guess you're suffering from a chronic illness like that...

Yes, I understand. I must say I'm amazed that you've been good enough to take an interest in my husband's case for so long. His commanding officers back when he served at his lordship's residence in Edo—Chief Steward Osone, Captain Oribe and Captain Nakamine—have all passed on. Those who are still alive have long since retired from his lordship's service, so I suppose it can't do much harm now to talk about it now. Seeing as you haven't got much time left to live, I'll tell you everything just as I remember it—my parting gift to you, so to speak.

Just as you suspected back then, there was something very peculiar about that incident that took my husband's life. Dare I say it, but supernatural forces were behind that swordfight...

Now, hold on a minute. First listen to what I have to say. How old are you by the way?... In your fifties? My, still young! You don't have a single fleck of gray on your temples. I suppose that's got something to do with why you haven't forgotten what happened.

As I recall, you were just as gung-ho the first time you came to speak to me twenty years ago as you are now.

Of course, you'd good reason to be then. There's my husband, only his second day in Edo, and during a visit to Ueno Hill to see the great Kan'ei Temple he attacks another samurai he's never laid eyes on in his life, and both of them wind up dead.

That first time you came to question me it was the height of summer and terribly hot as I recall... Indeed, it was. Don't you remember how profusely you were sweating?

You visited me a number of times after that; with each visit I could plainly see frustration etched more deeply on your face. No doubt that was because no matter how hard you tried, you found not a shred of evidence linking my husband to that fellow Yamagiwa... Come now, don't give me that stern look. Back then if I'd told you what I'm about to tell you now, you wouldn't have believed a word of it. Well, for that matter, neither would any of the clan officials in charge of investigating the case.

My husband had gone to Ueno that day with two of his colleagues who also had just arrived in Edo. As they were walking amongst the throng of people visiting the temple that day he spotted Yamagiwa, and, without a word to his colleagues, he suddenly charged, sword draw. But Yamagiwa was ready—he drew his sword at the same time and the two began fighting like sworn enemies. My husband's colleagues and the astonished bystanders who witnessed the fight all agreed it seemed perfectly normal—as though Yamagiwa and my husband had arranged in advance to meet in that spot, on that day, at that time. Yamagiwa was the first to fall, but my husband died soon after from his wounds.

I'm sorry to belabor you with all these facts, of which you're undoubtedly aware, but when one gets to be in one's sixties like me one can't tell a story without remembering all the details first.

Well, you know the rest. My husband's body was taken to the Edo Magistrate's Office before being transferred to his lordship's residence. That's when the task of finding out what really happened was placed in your capable hands.

After a six-month investigation, Inspector Mizuno reached the conclusion that my husband and Yamagiwa must have met on the way to Edo and had a falling out that left a lingering resentment which festered and finally exploded with such tragic consequences when they ran into each other by chance in Ueno.

This explanation, as you said to me at the time, is simply preposterous. It's true they both arrived in Edo around the same time, but Yamagiwa and his retinue had come from way down south in Hizen Province, whereas obviously we'd come from up north—how on earth could they have run into each other?

But, as you know, I held my tongue and said nothing. The Inspector's word was final and everyone accepted it—what other recourse was there? I imagine Yamagiwa's family reached the same conclusion.

Now, take a look outside in the garden. See that large camphor tree? That's where my husband used to practice his swordsmanship. He'd always boast about how he'd been born in this house and had practiced under that tree for as long as he could remember—first with a stick, then a bamboo rod, and finally a wooden sword. Even after we got married he never missed a day. He'd be out there wielding his wooden sword come rain or snow—even when his face was flushed with fever from a bad cold.

His hard work must have paid off, for not a single man at the clan dojo, nor the private dojo in town where he went in his spare time, could hold a candle to him. People said that when my husband's name was mentioned, even the most cocksure swordsman would shuffle his feet and admit that *that* was one man he couldn't beat.

I've no doubt this was part of the reason my husband threw himself into his training with greater fervor than ever. He'd be up at the crack of dawn practicing until it was time for him to go to work, then be back at it upon returning from the castle in the afternoon, and again after dinner until late into the night. Sometimes his face took on a look of such ferocious intensity that it scared me half to death, and I fretted I'd made a terrible mistake in marrying such a man.

Then, late one night, just after my husband had finished practicing and come into the house panting and exhausted, I asked him why it wasn't enough for him to practice at the dojo.

"No sensei can teach me anything" was his answer.

I was tempted to reply, "Then I don't see how you can expect to get any better," but I kept my thoughts to myself. Then, as though he'd read my mind, he suddenly grinned and said, "You're right. What I need is a worthy sparring partner. Since I don't know of any, I better start looking."

Well, that's what he said, but it seemed he couldn't find anyone, for he continued to practice alone in the garden as usual. I didn't notice something had changed until about a year before my husband was ordered to go to Edo with his lordship.

One day, while I was doing some chores around the house, I heard my husband practicing in the garden, and every now and then he'd shout out commands such as "Come!" and "We're not finished!" as though he was sparring with someone. Since I hadn't seen him bringing anyone to the house, I went and peeked outside, but sure enough he was alone. However, I didn't think much of it at the time, for when he practiced it was his habit to pretend he was sparring with a real opponent, and so I just assumed he'd gotten unusually carried away.

"So, dear," I asked him, half-teasingly, sometime later, "have you found a worthy sparring partner?"

To my astonishment, he nodded vigorously and replied, "Indeed. A *very* worthy sparring partner—my equal in every way. Out of ten bouts I win five and he wins five. Out of five, we each take two and one ends in a draw. It's given me a new lease on life."

I can still remember, as though it were yesterday, the chill that ran down my spine as I looked into his eyes and saw the pure excitement of battle that is the hallmark of a true samurai facing down a worthy opponent.

But that excitement did not remain pure for long.

As the days wore on, my husband developed a hatred of his invisible sparring partner.

People say a worthy adversary is the best adversary. They say if your opponent gives you a good fight you'll see into one another's souls. Those are all lies; no, the greater one's confidence in one's own ability, the greater one's hatred of anyone who shakes it.

One morning at breakfast my husband suddenly turned and stared out into the garden with bloodshot eyes. "That bastard has mastered a new technique," he said, his voice dripping with hatred. "I'm helpless against it."

I sat there, amazed and dumbstruck. Ignoring me, he went on, "But just you wait. I've almost perfected a counter-technique. Dishonor by the sword must be cleansed by the sword."

But no such opponent existed. I would often peek into the garden while my husband was practicing, but he was always alone. Nor when we were bathing did I ever find so much as a single bruise on him. And yet my husband's invisible sparring partner did not submit to his will as easily as he'd imagined, but only seemed to get stronger to keep pace with my husband's own progress.

"I'll never best him with a wooden sword," he announced one day, trembling with anger and despair. "Now, a real sword—that's how I'll prove my mettle one of these days!"

I resolved to get my husband to a doctor before that day arrived. But apart from his obsession with sword fighting, there was absolutely nothing physically wrong with him. Before I could think of a plan, the order came for my husband to accompany his lordship to Edo, ultimately leading to his death.

Maybe *now* you understand. I know it might not make sense, but maybe you can understand…

Don't you see? At Ueno my husband finally *met* his sparring partner—the worthy opponent he'd created in his mind. At that moment he knew exactly what he had to do because he'd been preparing for that duel for months…

What's that? You still don't see why he chose Yamagiwa?

Yes, I understand what you're saying. Yamagiwa Daigaku was a wealthy and high-ranking samurai, not some figment of my husband's imagination. That's true, but—

Ah, *now* you understand, do you? I can tell by the look on your face. You were the one who told me in the first place: Yamagiwa— just like my husband—was far and away the best swordsman in his clan; that he spent all his waking moments, when he wasn't at work, honing his technique.

Now can anyone doubt that Yamagiwa's *own* sparring partner was my husband?

The Uninvited Guest

DUSK WAS GATHERING and a cool breeze announced the arrival of autumn as surely as the mackerel sky overhead.

Osato found Mizumori Daisuke out behind the inn.

Entering the kitchen carrying the dinner trays, the sixteen-year-old maid had been greeted by the cooks, looking pale, who mumbled something and gestured to the door leading out to the back garden. She felt a chill run down her spine.

"What's he doing down *here*?" Osato wondered aloud. Had the rice balls she'd served him for lunch not been enough? Had he nipped down to the kitchen for something to nibble on? True, he'd turned up on the inn's doorstep half starved, but he was *still* a samurai—he always ate his meals with the utmost restraint and decorum, leaving a good quarter of the tray untouched. Osato was sure he'd sooner die of hunger than stoop to anything so undignified.

What the cooks said confirmed this:

"Our samurai came down a few moments ago," said one, "and Mizumori-*sama* followed him into the garden."

"He must have run into him upstairs," chimed in another. "Well, let's hope it's nothing."

"Just what we need," added a third, "another samurai like *that* around!"

Shivering from more than just the autumn breeze, Osato stepped through the back door from the earthen-floored kitchen into the garden. Once outside she caught her breath, stifling the urge to cry out.

Immediately to her right she caught sight of Daisuke's broad back and shoulders. Osato was reminded of an enormous slab of stone upended in the ground—a massive immovable object that had metamorphosed into Mizumori Daisuke.

Too intimidated to speak, Osato followed his gaze.

There before them was the *thing* that struck terror in Osato's heart.

In front of it stood the samurai, sword drawn, perfectly still, waiting it seemed for dusk to fall. He was stripped to the waist to reveal a mass of sinew; it reminded Osato of her late father and elder brother, both strapping farmers. His entire body bristled with strength—from his naked torso to the powerful legs outlined against his threadbare hakama, right down to the tips of his straw sandals.

"Incredible..." A sleepy-sounding sigh of admiration escaped Daisuke's lips.

Just then the samurai began to move...

After some time the samurai stopped.

"Amazing!" gasped Daisuke a second time.

As the samurai sheathed his sword darkness, as though held at bay until now, suddenly slipped down, painting his silhouette a deeper shade of night.

Only as a burst of air escaped Osato's lips did she realize she'd been holding her breath almost from the moment she stepped outside, and she felt slightly light-headed from the lack of oxygen. *Now what was* that *all about?* she thought vaguely.

Redirecting her gaze to Daisuke, out of the corner of her eye she saw the other samurai turn in their direction. By the time she'd focused on him, he'd already taken a step toward them; he had a big stride. His sword dangled from his right hand. *He's coming!*

"Mizumori-*sama*!" she cried.

Daisuke didn't move. Osato grasped his right arm.

"Oh, Osato." Until that moment Daisuke hadn't even been aware Osato was there.

"Let's go, Mizumori-*sama*," she pleaded. "You don't want to get mixed up with him." Circling in front of Daisuke, Osato grabbed his other arm and pushed him back toward the kitchen.

"What do you think you're *doing*?" he barked.

Osato paid no attention. Behind her she knew the samurai was closing in on them. They mustn't get within reach of his sword.

Daisuke—perhaps sensing something amiss—offered little resistance as Osato slowly guided him through the door into kitchen and across the earthen floor. The cooks scattered in alarm. A few screamed.

A step away from the stone for removing one's sandals to enter the main part of the house, Daisuke suddenly froze.

A shriller scream, almost a chorus, arose inside the kitchen.

A dark figure stood in the doorway. In between its outline and the frame of the doorway Osato could see the blue night sky.

"Don't look at the samurai behind the inn"—that's the rule and I've gone and broken it...

Just then Osato felt her hands being pulled forward. But before she could tighten her grip on whatever it was that she was holding, it slowly slipped away from her.

"No, Mizumori-*sama*, don't!"

It was too late—Daisuke had already begun to address the dark figure in the doorway.

"I don't know who you are," he said calmly, "but in all my life I've never had the privilege of witnessing such extraordinary technique. Allow me to introduce myself—my name is Mizumori Daisuke. I am on a quest to perfect my skill as a swordsman. It would give me great honor to sit down with you and while the night away discussing life, politics, and the Way of the Sword."

Everyone present stared at the two samurai and held their collective breath.

The smell of cooked rice, grilled fish, and miso soup assaulted Osato's nose; she thought, *If anyone speaks we're all done for.*

Fortunately, she was wrong.

"Out of the question," came the reply.

At the sound of the samurai's voice a subdued shriek arose from the cooks. Then the dark figure turned and stalked off into the night. No one had died.

Reassured that she was still alive by the pounding of her heart, Osato sensed that Daisuke was staring unblinkingly into the blue darkness which now completely filled the doorway.

"Osato?" came a voice from above her head. The top of Osato's head came up just below Daisuke's shoulder.

"Yes?"

"Will dinner be ready soon? I'd like to eat something."

The only other guests that night were three merchants. Osato had finished clearing away the dinner trays and was laying out the futons in the main room when Daisuke came over and whispered, "I like to speak to you—alone."

"In the Bamboo Grove," she replied without missing a beat, for she'd been expecting his request. Of course it would have to be later, after everyone was asleep.

Having finished all her work, Osato was returning to the maids' room thinking she'd have a quick wash with the leftover bathwater when she was accosted by Hikobei just outside the door.

"Osato," called the innkeeper, "come here a moment."

Looking uncharacteristically bedraggled, Hikobei led the girl to a corner of the deserted corridor.

"When," he asked with undisguised disgust, "is that sponger leaving?" The innkeeper looked in the direction of the main room. Though not a complete miser, Hikobei *was* a skinflint, a fact clearly evident from the look on his face at that moment. Osato knew he had every reason to be annoyed, but still she couldn't help feeling hurt.

"It's been five days," he went on, "since you found him outside the inn. Now, any *self-respecting* samurai would have hightailed it out of here in the middle of the night long ago. But not *him*—he just sits around shamelessly eating our food without paying a single *mon*!"

"Please, sir," implored Osato.

Looking at her in surprise, Hikobei's expression softened.

"Well, of course, he can stay here as long as he likes, seeing as you've offered to pay for his food and lodgings out of your own wages. But look here, Osato—are you *sure* you know what you're doing? Your family back home depend on the money you bring home, don't they?"

Osato looked down at the floor.

"That's true, sir," she said, raising her head, "but I'll work twice as hard as usual—please let him stay just a little longer."

Hikobei sighed. For once he looked the indulgent employer.

"That's fine. *I'm* not the one who's losing out here. I'm just worried about you and your family, that's all. But as long as you're fine with the arrangement, you can look after him to your heart's content. Just don't go all gaga over him just 'cause he's a samurai."

"I'm not!" protested Osato indignantly.

Jeez, Hikobei's face clearly seemed to say, *show a bit of concern and she bites my head off!*

"Well, suit yourself. But remember, starting tomorrow I'm holding you to your promise to work twice as hard. Come, now. Your family must be worried about you. I'm just concerned, can't you see that?"

She followed Hikobei with her eyes as he walked away. His slender figure made him look as though a gust of wind might knock him over. She imagined herself sticking her tongue out at her employer.

No one around those parts could ever have accused Hikobei of caring about his employees—even the neighborhood dogs would have laughed at the suggestion. The mere idea of doing a good deed for someone would have outraged the famously stingy old codger.

The Taniya was one of four wayside inns which stood cheek-by-jowl in a small post town on the highway that ran along the southern edge of the Suzuka Mountains—one of several such post towns that dotted the highway like so many lumps on a weather-beaten old bone.

The inn's clientele consisted principally of traveling salesmen who came to peddle their wares in the nearby farming villages; they slept shoulder-to-shoulder in the inn's one large main room. But like its competitors the Taniya also had one or two private rooms for the use of the rare samurai or rich merchant who might happen along in need of a place to stay.

The "Bamboo Grove" was one of these private rooms. Osato had told Daisuke to meet her there because it was the one place in the small inn where they could talk without being seen or overheard.

Osato had a good guess what it was Daisuke wanted to talk to her about. As usual with bad premonitions, it turned out she was right.

"Who *is* he?"

Seated in the dark room, with only a bit of moonlight filtering in from the corridor through the shoji, Daisuke got straight to the point; then, without waiting for Osato to answer, he continued:

"To be honest, when I saw him coming at me with his sword drawn I froze. You see, I passed him in the corridor and followed him down to the garden because I immediately sensed something special about him. Boy, did you see his technique! I can safely say that in the annals of history there hasn't been a swordsman to compare with him. He's reached a level I could never hope to attain. The world's a big place, Osato. What's a person like *that* doing in a dusty little post town like this?"

Daisuke's eyes flashed and flecks of saliva clung to the corners of his mouth.

Osato no longer knew what to make of this young samurai, who was not much older than herself. What kind of man was he?

Five days ago she'd found him lying unconscious by the side of the road in front of the Taniya, hunger written in his sunken eyes and hollow cheeks. As she helped him sit up he'd mumbled, "Need…food…"

Osato carried him upstairs to the main room with the help of one of the houseboys. Then she informed Hikobei. Though not at all pleased by the news, the innkeeper grudgingly allowed her to give the young man something to eat, starting with rice broth to settle his stomach, and later stopped in to check on him once he seemed to have recovered his senses. The samurai introduced himself to Hikobei and explained he was on a quest to hone his swordsmanship; he'd traveled the length and breadth of Japan. About ten days earlier, while staying at some other inn, all his money had been stolen. Since then he'd tried unsuccessfully to sell his services, subsisting all the while on nothing but water, but ultimately he succumbed to hunger and fatigue, collapsing in front of the Taniya.

"I fully expected to be left there on the side of the road for dead. I'm grateful to you for putting a roof over my head and taking so much trouble over me. In a day or two my strength will return.

Would you let me stay until then? In return I'll chop wood, fetch water, and do anything I can to earn my keep."

Given his situation, Daisuke's request must have seemed quite reasonable to him, but Hikobei considered it a presumptuous imposition.

"Sir," broke in Osato, observing the growing look of displeasure on her employer's face, "think how embarrassing it must be for this gentleman—a samurai of all people—to have collapsed from hunger in front of our inn. Fate must have brought him to us. With your permission, I'd like to look after him until he is better. You may deduct the cost of his lodgings from my wages. I promise not to put you or the Taniya to any trouble."

HIKOBEI WAS even more astonished by Osato's unexpected request than Daisuke; he pressed the girl to find out if she was sure she knew what she was doing.

Osato's father, a farmer, had fallen ill and died just over a year ago, and her frail mother had since become bedridden. Apart from an elder brother who'd died young, Osato had three siblings, a younger brother and two younger sisters, who were now in charge of looking after the family farm.

In reply, Osato explained that Daisuke reminded her of her late brother.

"Well, if you feel *that* strongly about it…"

For the moment Hikobei relented, seeing the girl was determined to have her way. But later, as soon as she emerged from the main room, he called her into his office and gave her a good lecture.

"You've been with us for a year now, Osato, and are no doubt good at sizing up our guests. So I can't understand why you're wasting your time on that penniless wastrel. He *claims* he's a samurai, but what sort of samurai collapses from hunger and lives off the charity of others? When I suggested he send word back home and have money sent to him, he told me he's abandoned his clan. Now, I'm just telling you this for your own good. You can look after him for one more day, but make sure you send him packing tomorrow."

As the Taniya's proprietor, what Hikobei said was perfectly reasonable. Having an emaciated, bedridden samurai hanging about the main room all the time was off-putting to the other guests, plus once the other inns in town got wind of it they'd use it to badmouth the Taniya and steer customers their own way. To the notoriously stingy innkeeper, it was simply an intolerable situation.

"Please," begged Osato, biting her lip and bowing her head again and again, "just grant me this one favor!"

When Osato first arrived at the Taniya, Hikobei had sized her up immediately as both well brought-up and good-natured. She was obedient, normally very quiet, and a hard worker, plus she had a cheerfulness that endeared her to others. Just as the innkeeper had predicted (and with a bit of scheming on his part) within a month of her arrival Osato had become someone whom her fellow maids and the other employees looked up to. Hikobei's calculations had gone badly array in just one respect, however, and it soon gave him cause for regret—namely, Osato possessed an iron will, and once she'd made up her mind that she wanted something, wild horses couldn't move her.

Of course, Hikobei was her employer and master. With anyone else he'd have barked, "Get out!"—end of story. But not Osato. Deep down Hikobei was basically a decent sort. Seeing how hard Osato worked and how, under her leadership, his shiftless band of malcontents were transformed into model employees, he realized his hands were tied.

Now, yet again, Hikobei found himself giving in to Osato's iron will.

"Alright—fine," he said, grimacing as he twisted the hem of his work apron tightly around his finger. "Do as you please."

For the next four days Osato looked after her young samurai so diligently that at first even her devoted coworkers began to doubt her sanity. To make matters worse, Daisuke, having gone so long without food, was suffering from malnutrition. But by the third day the skeptical glances cast at her from all sides had turned to looks of sympathy and admiration.

"I take my hat off to her," said one of the maids. "I could never look after 'im the way she does. That samurai is one lucky fellah, that's all I can say. So don't any of you go givin' her any funny looks, you hear?"

If Daisuke had cast aside his initial gratitude and turned haughty and arrogant like the samurai that he was, the situation could well have turned ugly. But the young man never forgot the promise he made to Osato and Hikobei that first day.

Whenever Osato brought up a tray of food to where he lay in a dim corner of the main room, he always bowed his head and muttered some simple words of thanks, though never in a servile way. The other maids and traveling salesmen who shared the room with him kept a respectful distance at first, but he struck up friendly conversations with them and laughed and smiled a lot.

"It's no wonder dear Osato dotes on him as she does," they all agreed. "But at this rate he'll never become a real warrior."

It was that same Daisuke who now, in a sudden display of martial spirit, had sent Osato's emotions into a tailspin.

"That samurai—what's his name and where does he come from?" he asked her again. "While I was bedridden I saw him pass by in the corridor several times. Has he been staying here long?"

"I... don't know," said Osato evasively, turning her head and looking away.

That's not like her.

"Don't worry," he said, scooting toward her on his knees, "I promise I won't cause any trouble—neither to you nor the Taniya. If you say 'don't do such-and-such' I won't do it. If you say 'don't ask such-and-such' I won't ask it. But look, it's clear there's something different about him besides his extraordinary swordsmanship. Judging from the kitchen maids' reaction, I'm guessing this isn't the first time he's stayed here. What I don't understand is why you all seem to be afraid of him. What's he done to you?"

Far from eliciting any answers, Daisuke's zealous interrogation only caused Osato to clam up more tightly. He decided to try a different tack.

"Actually, on my way here I saw him going into the Lotus Room. I suppose he was returning from the garden. So I went and knocked on his door." At this Osato sat bolt upright and turned to face him, wide-eyed and speechless. Daisuke gazed back at her in amusement. Then his face became serious again. "I called out to him several times," he went on, "but got no response. At first I thought he must be asleep, but I was sure I heard him moving around. Finally I decided to go ahead and open the door."

"Oh, no..." groaned Osato quietly.

But the door had not opened.

"I wonder what was holding it shut?" continued Daiuske. "No matter how hard I pushed it, it wouldn't budge. I pushed up and down, left and right—it didn't give so much as a fraction of an inch. I wonder if that's somehow part of his sword technique... Anyway, I kept at it for a while, but then I was overcome by a queer feeling, and I stopped. But I'm not giving up, Osato. Sooner or later I'll sit down and talk to him face-to-face, mark my words. Then I'll ask him to teach me what he knows."

Daisuke had become so engrossed in his story that he had forgotten his purpose in telling it—but it worked nonetheless.

"Stop, please!"

In the moonlight, Osato prostrated herself before him on the tatami.

"Why?"

"I... can't say."

"Then you leave me no choice," said Daisuke, looking down at the girl, who trembled either from sadness or in fear. "I've found my sensei. You can't expect me to walk away and pretend he doesn't exist without telling me why."

Daisuke's unwavering and passionate desire to become a great swordsman had turned him into a haughty, arrogant, and cruel human being. Osato resigned herself to the inevitable.

"That samurai," she said, looking up at Daisuke, "is no ordinary man. In fact, he's not a man at all. The first time I saw him was last autumn, just over a year ago. It was only my second day working at the Taniya."

Hikobei had called for Osato to bring the wooden bucket used for washing guests' feet. When she reached the front door, Osato saw a middle-aged samurai dressed in a sleeveless jacket and pantaloons, covered from head to toe in dust as though from a long journey. Osato recalled how, as she washed his feet, she felt a strange and sudden gust of cold wind, as though summoned by the denizens of the Taniya in silent protest at the arrival of this uninvited and unwanted guest.

For the next five days, the new guest ensconced himself in the Lotus Room. Oshige, one of the old-timers, was given the task of taking his meals to him. Osato would see Oshige going in or out of the room with a tray, a horrible look on her face. Just the memory of it sent shivers down Osato's spine.

Osato finally summoned up the courage to ask one of the other maids about the mysterious visitor.

"I've worked here for fifteen years," replied the woman in a hushed voice, "and Oshige for twenty-one; for twenty years she's been looking after that gentleman every year when he comes to stay."

Twenty years! Had the samurai really been visiting the Taniya for so long? asked Osato, her eyes growing wide in innocent disbelief.

"My dear," said the older maid, casting her a contemptuous look, such as one might give an ignorant child, "he's been coming here *much* longer than that. He's been coming for over forty years—long before the Taniya was even built. None of us knows his name or where he comes from. One of the maids asked the head clerk that very question once, and he well near bit the poor dear's head off. So what can we do? Since none of us knows his name, we all just address him as 'Samurai-*sama*.' Oshige and I both had it from the former head housekeeper, who passed away long, long ago, that the Taniya has been around for thirty-odd years. Before that an inn called the Kanekoya stood on this spot, and for the first ten years he used to stay there."

Gesturing as she spoke, the maid's sleeve slipped back to reveal an arm covered with goose bumps, as though she'd become frightened by her own narrative. Osato couldn't help giggling.

How could the samurai, who looked to be in his early thirties, have been coming to the post town for forty years? The idea was absurd. Picturing a toddler striding through the front door, a sword on either hip, Osato burst into renewed laughter.

Though Osato expected to be scolded for her impertinence, the woman only frowned, and in a calm and measured tone continued,

"To be honest, I find it hard to believe myself. But I've seen him come and go for fifteen years—always at this time of year—and in all that time he hasn't changed one bit. He's looked the same thirty-something from that day to this."

Osato felt she now understood the horrible look Oshige wore whenever she visited the Lotus Room.

"At first I didn't believe it either," Osato told Daisuke. "But last year when he came, twice something eerie happened." Despite having resolved to reveal everything, Osato's voice still trembled almost uncontrollably. She coughed twice.

"Something eerie, huh?" repeated Daisuke pensively. The moonlight from the hallway suddenly grew dim.

A shadow passed noiselessly along the corridor on the other side of the shoji—the shadow of a person holding a sword in his right hand. Osato followed the shadow of the sword with her eyes.

"Look!" she whispered. "He also goes out late at night…"

Daisuke had been struck by the same thought.

Despite lying awake until dawn before falling into a fitful sleep, the next day Daisuke's eyes were clear and his mind sharp. He had a fire in the belly.

Come evening the longtime guest whose name no one knew, having remained sequestered in his room all day, appeared in the kitchen carrying his long sword in one hand and went out through the back door. The kitchen maids tried to pretend he wasn't there but with limited success.

From the main room Daisuke saw him as he passed along the corridor. Then he got up and followed him downstairs. Mindful of the previous day's events, Daisuke kept his distance and tread softly, expecting the older man to be on his guard. But the Taniya's mysterious guest gave no indication whatsoever that such was the case, though not in a way that suggested he had simply forgotten the whole thing. Rather, it left Daisuke with the distinct impression that everything which had transpired between the previous evening and the early hours of that morning had been a dream, and he was filled with a fathomless emptiness and fear. When a man does not show himself during the day and emerges only as the dark blue of twilight has colored the sky, one begins to think he must not be of this world.

Once outside Daisuke expected to see the samurai unsheathe his sword and begin practicing, as he had the previous evening. But instead he headed straight for the *thing* that stood in the middle of the garden, opened the door, and disappeared inside. *I bet no one but he can open that door*, thought Daisuke, listening to the sound of the hinges creaking as it shut.

The *thing* in the middle of the garden, which had struck terror in Osato's heart, was a sort of shed, about the size of a small dojo; it was made entirely of wooden boards and had a shingle roof. Though sturdy looking, it appeared extremely old. The roof and outer walls had been burnished black to protect them from the elements.

According to the story Osato had been told, the shed had stood there since before the samurai had started coming to the inn. Apparently it dated to the time of the Kanekoya, but whether it had been built expressly for his use or for some other purpose was unclear. Even after the Kanekoya went out of business and was torn down, the shed was left standing.

And so every year for the past forty years, when the autumn winds arrived in Suzuka, the lone samurai had appeared. He stayed in his room all day, taking his meals alone and never exchanging a word with anyone at the inn. In the evening he came down to the garden and went into the shed cum dojo. When he at last emerged, he returned straight to his room and ate a late dinner. In the middle of the night he returned once again to the outbuilding.

Osato told Daisuke that Hikobei had instructed the staff of the Taniya not to pay the samurai any heed.

"So whatever he does," she said, "just leave him alone. Anyway, he won't do anything. He hardly ever shows himself to anyone except for a brief moment before he disappears into that black building. Nobody knows what he does in there."

Even if one cared to find out, Daisuke conceded, it would not be simple—for the shed did not have a single window.

THE ATMOSPHERE in the back garden was tense. Everywhere—from the kitchen to the upstairs rooms—the Taniya's staff was holding its collective breath.

It was not actually much of a garden. At the bottom of the garden just the traces of a hedge and a bamboo thicket could be seen. There was no pond, no rocks—just an expanse of black dirt.

Perfect for a practice ground, mused Daisuke. It was then that he was struck by a strange realization. In all that expanse of dirt there was not a single weed or blade of grass to be seen. Someone must be tending diligently to the garden.

That the inn's strange guest had not aged for forty years was surely something of which Hikobei—not to mention the previous proprietor and, yes, even the proprietor of the Kanekoya—must surely have been aware. So why didn't he turn him away? Why did he give him a room, provide him meals, allow him to use the garden, and even go so far as to order the staff to stay out of his way? And surely it was Hikobei who had instructed his employees to weed the garden once the samurai's short stay was over and he'd gone back to wherever he came from.

Daisuke stood outside the back door listening attentively. Though he could hear sounds and movements all around him, only a deathly silence emanated from the black building itself.

He took a few steps forward. He wondered what Osato was doing.

At the twelfth or thirteenth step, a faint echo from inside the building made Daisuke's heart skip a beat. He felt something warm in the pit of his stomach and a tingling sensation all over his body, as though he had walked into a swarm of insects.

It had been the unmistakable sound of steel clashing against steel.

Daisuke quickened his pace.

A slab of stone had been placed in front of the door of the small black building, as though as a place for someone to stand while removing his shoes. On it, facing away from the door, sat the samurai's straw sandals.

Daisuke began to walk around the perimeter of the dojo. The natural sense of decorum and restraint bred into him from an early age prevented him from trying the door. *Don't touch without asking!*

he'd always been told. And in this particular instance, he couldn't bring himself to go to the door and ask permission to enter.

Imagining the other samurai inside, using his god-like skill against an unseen opponent—sparring not with bamboo or wooden swords but *real* ones—Daisuke ached with envy and his excitement knew no bounds. He clenched his fists so tightly his fingers dug into his palms. *But of course he'd use a real sword! Skill like that isn't learned in the dojo but in the heat of battle, with the fear of steel cutting through flesh and bone driving one insane.*

Then he began to pray: *Let me watch. Even if I'll never be able to attain that level of skill, I'd give my life just to watch. Isn't that why I embarked on this journey?*

At last he overcame his natural restraint.

He ran to the door and raised his fist.

Just then, from behind him, someone grabbed his wrist.

Astounded, Daisuke turned his head.

"Don't!" growled a voice, only inches from his face. It was Hikobei. "No one is allowed to enter this building. It's not of this world."

"Let go of me!"

The two men struggled. By now Daisuke had regained his full strength. Since boyhood he'd been trained in martial arts, aspiring to be a swordsman. Even so, Hikobei managed to hold his own. Desperation gave the wizened old innkeeper the strength of a hardened warrior.

"There's no one else inside," Hikobei growled again. "I've been keeping watch over this building for thirty years, and no one but that samurai has ever stepped in or out of it. And yet from the night he arrives to the day he leaves, he goes inside and spars."

Daisuke felt the strength leave his body—that had been the *first* eerie thing Osato had mentioned. The sudden loss of strength left him feeling dizzy. If Hikobei hadn't been there to support him Daisuke probably would have fainted on the spot.

"But who is he sparring with?" he finally managed to ask.

"Come," replied the innkeeper.

Daisuke offered no resistance as Hikobei took him by the arm and led him back into the house.

Hikobei showed Daisuke to an inner room where they sat down on opposite sides of a large desk. Unlocking a small strongbox on the floor beside him, Hikobei reached in and took out five gold coins.

"Here, take these and leave this inn at once."

If Hikobei had imagined this would settle everything he was wrong. At this point Daisuke was not about to pocket the money and walk away. He knew what he'd seen, what he'd heard. Instead he began interrogating Hikobei about the black shed, the mysterious samurai, and the other person inside.

By way of reply, Hikobei threatened to call the local officials and have Daisuke thrown out, then denied he'd ever said anything about the shed or its occupants.

But Daisuke would not back down. He cross-examined Hikobei again, but this time was met only with stony silence. This was repeated several times with growing intensity, and although it had become quite dark in the room, the maids were too afraid to come in and light the lamps.

Suddenly, from the front door, a young woman's scream was heard, followed by a scuffling of feet outside in the corridor.

Hikobei stood up and poked his head through the curtain hanging in the doorway.

"What's going on?" he demanded

In response the head clerk came scurrying along the corridor and whispered something in Hikobei's ear.

"Well, hurry up and get rid of them!" the innkeeper barked. "We can't have anyone dying on our doorstep—call the officials at once!"

When Hikobei returned to the room Daisuke inquired about the cause of the commotion. The innkeeper explained that a couple of travelers had fled into the Taniya to escape some local gangsters. It seemed the husband had run up a large gambling debt and the gangsters wanted to take his wife as collateral. It was by no means an uncommon story. Gangsters would set up shop on the edge of the small post town and bribe local officials to turn a blind eye to their illicit activities. Was it any surprise travelers fell into their clutches like flies into a spider's web?

"The guy probably thought he'd just make a little bit of extra traveling money," said the innkeeper. "No—people like that gamble because they enjoy it. If he was foolish enough to lose all his possessions *and* his wife, then he was obviously in way over his head. Some people just go around asking for trouble. Mizumori-*sama*, you'd better stay put for a while."

Hikobei might have saved his breath, for Daisuke had absolutely no intention of getting involved. A samurai's first instinct when coming upon the scene of some disturbance was to walk quickly past. This was to avoid bringing trouble upon one's lord.

Even so, Daisuke's curiosity couldn't help being aroused by the goings-on around him. As he listened distractedly to Hikobei's story he caught snatches of rough voices raised in anger. Were the man and his wife being dragged away by the gangsters, having being mercilessly refused sanctuary at the inn? Or had the local officials turned up in a halfhearted pretense of doing their job?

Suddenly there was the sound of feet thudding along the corridor, as though someone was being chased by a wild animal, and the next moment the head clerk stuck his head through the curtain.

"Boss!" he cried. "Th-that samurai… he's going to fight Sengoro's gang!"

Apparently, the hapless gambler had gone and pulled out a cheap sword, such as travelers often carried for their protection in those days. In response, the gangsters drew their own weapons.

Then the nameless samurai had appeared out of nowhere and stepped in between the two sides. "If you've got something to say," he told the gangsters, "say it to me."

As Daisuke rushed out of the room he heard the head clerk say behind him, "They're outside right now—"

"Bring me sandals!" he shouted, reaching the entrance hall. It was taboo for a samurai to set foot on the ground in his bare feet.

Dressed in their traveling clothes, the fugitives cowered in a corner.

Osato ran up carrying a pair of straw sandals that the inn always kept on hand.

Outside a man cried out in surprise. Someone must have drawn his sword—was it the samurai or the gangsters?

Osato placed the sandals on the step just inside the front door. Slipping his feet into them, Daisuke stepped down onto the earthen floor, left foot first. As soon as he touched the ground, a second cry arose from the same direction as the first—this time it was a cry of agony.

"Dammit," shouted Daisuke, "I'm too late!" He lifted aside the doorway curtain and stepped out into the street.

The figures were closer than he'd imagined. To his right, about fifty paces away, two dark masses, darker than the darkness of the night, lay on the ground.

Then he saw the other gangster—a cruel-looking figure, standing, legs wide apart, holding a sword. Daisuke could hear his breathing—*hee, hee, hee*—almost like someone crying. His hands trembled violently and light glinted on his blade. Daisuke realized the moon was out.

Directly in front of the gangster stood the samurai, so close that the tips of their swords were nearly touching. His blade was tilted upward, pointing directly at his opponent's eyes.

"Strike!" a voice cried. Daisuke realized it was his own voice.

The gangster raised his sword high over his head and brought it down with all his might. As he reached the bottom of his swing he toppled forward onto his face. The motion seemed so natural that Daisuke expected him to get right back up, but he just lay on the ground motionless. The samurai sheathed his sword.

Without a word to Daisuke, who stood rooted to the spot, the samurai went back inside the inn.

"They drew first and attacked me," he said to the Hikobei and the others, who were gathered inside the dirt entryway, "so I disposed of them. You may inform the local officials."

Without another word he went straight to his room, not even turning to look at the young couple groveling on the dirt floor and thanking him profusely.

At the door of the Lotus Room, Daisuke caught up with him.

The samurai had his hand on the shoji and was about to open it.

"Wait!" said Daisuke. He half expected the other man to ignore him, but instead the samurai turned his head slightly toward him while keeping his hand on the shoji. Without a thought to appearances, Daisuke prostrated himself on the wooden floor.

After stating his name, he said, "I've been traveling the country, hoping to make my living by the sword. Here I've at last found my sensei. Please accept me as your apprentice."

When he was done speaking Daisuke waited silently.

"Did you see my technique?" the samurai asked. His tone was surprisingly gentle.

"Yes."

"Then I should think a more appropriate response would be to run the other way, not ask me to be your sensei—no mortal can learn to fight like that."

"That's *precisely* why I want you to initiate me into your art. The greatest thing an apprentice can aspire to is to master that which is beyond other men."

Removing his hand from the shoji, the samurai at last turned to face Daisuke. "Men must master the ways of men," he said. "Do you understand?"

"I understand. But I have glimpsed something beyond—I can no longer be satisfied with the ways of men."

As soon as he'd spoken, Daisuke gulped. The samurai's face suddenly turned black—as black as lacquer. It took Daisuke a few moments to realize that this illusion was the result of his facial muscles contorting themselves into a fearsome expression.

"Haven't you realized what I am?"

"No."

"It is because of *what* I am that I am able to do what you have seen. Do you understand what I am saying?"

Daisuke did not answer.

"He who does what no man can do is *other* than a man."

Daisuke had the feeling a gaping hole had opened from his chest to his stomach.

"It means you cannot have the soul of a man. You cannot know love, hate, pity, empathy, or anger. Even if a thief is about to kill a little girl before your very eyes, you must turn away without a second thought."

"But..." protested Daisuke, "but didn't you just save that couple?"

"That is so. And one day I will be punished for it. Mizumori, don't attempt to speak to me ever again. Got it?"

Before Daisuke could answer, the samurai slid aside the shoji and disappeared into the room, leaving Daisuke kneeling in the darkness of the corridor. He felt its weight more than the moonlight.

It was some while later that Osato came to tell him the local officials had arrived.

As a witness to the incident, Daisuke was asked to come to the guard station to provide testimony. Also present were Hikobei, the head clerk, the young couple, and one Suzuki Sengoro, leader of the gang that had attacked them. During the proceedings, Daisuke was made keenly aware of the strange influence the samurai wielded over the people of the post town.

The official began by questioning the brutish-looking gang leader.

"I'm truly sorry, sir," said Sengoro, the very picture of docility and contrition. "Everything is my fault. My men only got what they deserved for pulling their swords on Samurai-*sama*. I seek nothing from this nice young couple and will make a full apology to the good people of the Taniya for scaring them out of their wits."

To Daisuke's astonishment, the examining official stopped writing and put down his brush.

"In light of Sengoro's testimony," he said, "I declare this case closed."

After everyone else had left, Daisuke, thinking he might have been able to use the official to uncover the samurai's true identity, grilled him about why he hadn't ordered a full investigation.

"Okay, then," the official only replied. "How about I start by investigating *you*?"

That shut Daisuke up.

His thoughts in disarray, Daisuke left the guard station. He now had no hope of finding out what he longed to know.

As he walked through the gloom, he was full of despair.

ON THE SIXTH DAY the samurai left.

Only this incontestable fact enabled the people of the Taniya to regain their sanity, for they had been living in dread.

A tense calm had presided over the samurai's fifth and final day, everyone fearful lest some fool should cast a stone and break it.

Then evening came.

Breakfast and lunch had passed uneventfully. Of the Taniya's two resident samurai, one remained in his private room not making a sound, as though it had swallowed him up. The other, the occupant of the main room, had gone out immediately after breakfast. By evening he still had not returned.

In due course, one of the two samurai went into the small shed behind the inn and emerged about four hours later.

After that, only silence. The darkness of the night deepened and the peaks of the Suzuka Mountains glowed in the moonlight.

In the middle of the night, the samurai came down to the garden. It was to be his last training session.

He stopped in front of the black dojo. Daisuke lay prostrate in front of the door.

"I thought I told you not to come near me again," he intoned.

At the sound of his voice, Daisuke lifted his head.

"Today I visited a vacant lot on the edge of town," he said, his face and voice communicating an earnest intensity. "I was told that there, at dawn tomorrow, you will fight a duel; that you have done so for forty years, if not far longer. I was told it was almost like some sort of sacred ritual."

This had been the *second* eerie thing Osato had mentioned.

"I was told all this," continued Daisuke, "by the gangster, Sengoro, whose men you killed last night. His father and grandfather told *him* they had both witnessed these duels for as long as they could remember. You've never lost. Is *that* the reason you have such superhuman skill—why you have been coming here for so long?

"Your opponent—*opponents*—come, like you, to that vacant lot from some unknown place. After you have destroyed them the local officials dispose of their bodies. Who are they and where do they come from? If *you* are defeated by one of them, will someone like you come and take your place, visiting the inn every year and fighting an endless succession of new opponents, never growing older, until he in turn is defeated?"

"Out of my way!" growled the samurai.

"No," replied Daisuke. "First tell me why it is you come here and cheat time the way you do—no, that doesn't matter. I'm not interested in who you are or where you come from, or even why you do what you do. I don't want to know. I'm just interested in one thing: the skill that prevents you from aging. It is *that* desire which, like darkness, is slowly consuming me from within. I don't care what fate awaits me, just teach me one of your techniques—that's all I ask. Please try to understand how I feel as someone who aspires to the Way of the Sword."

As he pressed his forehead to the ground, Daisuke had the feeling that *he* was more obsessed with the samurai's futile annual ritual than the samurai himself.

"I do not listen to people's requests," the samurai said in reply. "But as I said before, I shall be punished for what I did."

"Who shall punish you?"

"My sensei."

"Sensei? *You* have a sensei!"

"I am merely flesh and blood—my skill is not superhuman. Everything I learned, I learned from my sensei."

"Where is he, this sensei of yours?"

The samurai looked straight ahead—at the black building behind Daisuke. Now he understood.

"He is in there. He does me the favor of practicing with me every year so I do not lose my fighting edge."

Daisuke turned his head, but he couldn't detect any presence inside the dark dojo.

"If you wish to learn my technique, you must learn it from my sensei. Provided you are qualified. We shall leave it for him to decide."

Daisuke stood up, turned to face the dojo and bowed his head. He believed every word the samurai said. His heart burned with a pure and single-minded passion.

How much time had passed? In the darkness Daisuke heard the creak of the hinges and looked up.

The door was slowly opening.

"My sensei has agreed."

The samurai's voice echoed into the distance.

Darkness filled the rectangular frame of the doorway. Daisuke stood up, walked to the stone slab and removed his straw sandals. Then he entered. He had already forgotten all about the other samurai.

Beneath his feet the floor felt very cold. It was wood. That was all he knew.

Just then, with a *creak*, the moonlight behind him grew dim as the door began to close.

He reflexively rushed toward it. Then he stopped. A wooden sword clattered to the floor at his feet.

The sensei had agreed.

As he stood frozen, behind him the door closed completely. The world went black.

But Daisuke was not afraid. He groped around on the floor for the sword and picked it up. Then he waited. He was alone in the pitch dark with his burning passion.

The samurai stopped outside his room.

Osato was kneeling upright on the floor of the hallway, one shoulder almost pressed against the shoji, staring at him.

"What are you doing?"

Osato pressed her palms on the floor and let her head droop. She had become strangely accustomed to the gesture.

"Please accept Mizumori-*sama* as your disciple."

Her voice was soft, like the buzzing of a mosquito, but it communicated a strong determination.

In the moonlight, the nape of her neck peeked out palely from the collar of her simple kimono.

"I do not listen to people's requests," he replied. "But I have fallen—I am now a man. I shall listen to what you have to say."

He slid aside the shoji and entered the room.

As Osato followed him inside, the door slid shut of its own accord.

The next day, several events occurred in the tiny post town.

First the middle-aged samurai who had visited the Taniya for five days each autumn for the past forty-odd years was found dead in a vacant lot on the edge of town, having committed *seppuku*. In death his face remained unchanged, causing those aware of his terrifying secret to mutter (apparently disappointed at the lack of any unearthly transfiguration), "Was he human after all?"

Next the young samurai who'd being staying at the Taniya around the same time disappeared, taking with him only his long and short swords and leaving his other possessions behind. Someone suggested he must have become embarrassed about sponging off one of the maids, and everyone seconded this conclusion. Only the innkeeper, Hikobei, and Osato herself, it seemed, were of a different mind.

Strangely, since then several people claim to have seen the young samurai.

One local resident, who was peering through a crack in the storm shutters of his house at dawn, testified to seeing this same young samurai cut down an opponent in the vacant lot outside town—the continuation of the annual duel that had taken place every year for as long as anyone could remember and for who knew what purpose. However, the local official who took the testimony neither mentioned it to anyone nor filed a report. For that matter, no written record exists of the dawn duels that had taken place for forty years. In accordance with the usual practice, the official disposed of the body of the unidentified fallen samurai.

The following autumn Osato was at home during the time when the samurai usually would have come to the Taniya. She passed the five days in the grips of a deep emotion.

The next morning when she awoke, a light rain was falling. Undeterred, her brother and sisters went out to work in the fields, leaving Osato all but alone in the house.

Though the events of the previous year now seemed like a distant dream, she couldn't help feeling a sense of nostalgia as she thought of the young samurai who had set her heart aflutter for a short time before disappearing without so much as a word.

She'd lost track of time when suddenly she heard a knock on the storm door. As she stepped down into the dirt entryway, thinking her brother and sisters must have returned, the stick used to secure the door fell away and the door slid open. There, framed in the gaping doorway, blocking out the light and rain, stood a tall figure.

It was Daisuke.

She stood frozen for a moment before crying out his name and running toward him. It was then she realized that the person looking at her was not the Daisuke she knew.

His face was the same but he was a different person.

Sensing her fate, Osato sank to the ground.

"I have come from the post town," he informed her. "I killed my adversary."

"Then you... have you—?"

Her teeth were chattering.

"Yes, I have taken over from him." His face was so dark that he looked altogether different than before. "A year ago, in the dojo behind the inn, I acquired the skill I had been seeking. I cannot say who I fight or why. But if we do not fight, or if I should not prevail, a crisis of unprecedented scale will befall this land. I must prevent that from happening at all costs."

"But why... Why have you come here?"

In reply, the young samurai gazed past her into the house with a look that made her blood run cold. From inside came the sound of the other person in the house crying—the child Osato had given birth to two months ago.

"That child is his, is it not? I am very sorry, but I must take its life. Stand aside if you value yours."

The young samurai reached for his sword with his left hand and nudged the blade out of its scabbard.

"But why!" screamed Osato, throwing herself in front of him. She didn't understand. Her year at the Taniya had belonged to a strange other world. She'd come to understand that people could live even under such conditions. But that strange other world still existed, and now it had tracked her and her child down.

"Why? Why him?" she gasped, backing away as he advanced silently into the house.

It is said that when Osato's sister returned to the house in the afternoon and discovered the body, her scream could be heard throughout the village. The child was nowhere to be found.

Like many of the mysteries connected with that little Suzuka post town, no one knows where the young samurai had been until then, or what he had been doing, or why he came for Osato's child—the child of the middle-aged samurai whom one might call Daisuke's predecessor.

Incidentally, according to the diary of one of the local residents, the annual duels that took place in the vacant lot on the edge of town came to an end in the fifth year of the Ka'ei era—that is, in 1852. The outcome is not known. That is the one and only written record of them that exists.

The following year, 1853, Commodore Perry's fleet of Black Ships appeared off the coast of Uraga and demanded thenceforth that American whaling vessels be allowed to call on Japanese ports to receive wood for fuel, water, and provisions. But the Americans' real intentions and the consequences thereof is a question better left to historians.